Mildred's anguished cry echoed around the circular ruins

Ryan's heart seemed to seize in his chest. He ducked behind the wall and turned.

The Armorer stood as if rooted in place. Ryan could clearly see the spot where a small portion of his leather jacket had been pushed aside a fraction of an inch by the heavy-caliber slug that had blown right through the small man's chest, front to back.

Time froze. A thin streamer of blood hung in the air behind J.B.'s back, fractionating into red droplets as it distanced itself from him.

With a roaring in his ears and an abyss of emptiness opening in his gut, Ryan watched his oldest living friend, the man who'd had his back since he was a young pup, spin and topple into the dust.

**Other titles in the
Deathlands saga:**

JAMES AXLER

DEATH LANDS®

Playfair's Axiom

A GOLD EAGLE BOOK FROM

W❂RLDWIDE®

TORONTO • NEW YORK • LONDON
AMSTERDAM • PARIS • SYDNEY • HAMBURG
STOCKHOLM • ATHENS • TOKYO • MILAN
MADRID • WARSAW • BUDAPEST • AUCKLAND

For the St. Louis Science Fiction Society
for years of friendship. Your lovely hometown
deserves better than it gets herein.

Recycling programs
for this product may
not exist in your area.

First edition March 2011

ISBN-13: 978-0-373-62607-6

PLAYFAIR'S AXIOM

Printed in U.S.A.

We do not so much need the help of our friends
as the confidence of their help in need.
—Epicurus
3rd century BCE

THE DEATHLANDS SAGA

This world is their legacy, a world born in the violent nuclear spasm of 2001 that was the bitter outcome of a struggle for global dominance.

There is no real escape from this shockscape where life always hangs in the balance, vulnerable to newly demonic nature, barbarism, lawlessness.

But they are the warrior survivalists, and they endure—in the way of the lion, the hawk and the tiger, true to nature's heart despite its ruination.

Ryan Cawdor: The privileged son of an East Coast baron. Acquainted with betrayal from a tender age, he is a master of the hard realities.

Krysty Wroth: Harmony ville's own Titian-haired beauty, a woman with the strength of tempered steel. Her premonitions and Gaia powers have been fostered by her Mother Sonja.

J. B. Dix, the Armorer: Weapons master and Ryan's close ally, he, too, honed his skills traversing the Deathlands with the legendary Trader.

Doctor Theophilus Tanner: Torn from his family and a gentler life in 1896, Doc has been thrown into a future he couldn't have imagined.

Dr. Mildred Wyeth: Her father was killed by the Ku Klux Klan, but her fate is not much lighter. Restored from predark cryogenic suspension, she brings twentieth-century healing skills to a nightmare.

Jak Lauren: A true child of the wastelands, reared on adversity, loss and danger, the albino teenager is a fierce fighter and loyal friend.

Dean Cawdor: Ryan's young son by Sharona accepts the only world he knows, and yet he is the seedling bearing the promise of tomorrow.

In a world where all was lost, they are humanity's last hope....

Chapter One

"We followed!" Jak Lauren stated.

The long-haired albino teen had his pallid lips pressed so close to Ryan Cawdor's ear that he could smell his funk, even though after days of harsh exertion in close unwashed company his nostrils had become inured to such. The fact that it was nuke hot and swamp humid close to the Sippi River didn't much help.

"I know." A canny fighter and consummate survivor, veteran of years of trekking across the hellscape of the Deathlands, Ryan reckoned that a low grunt of acknowledgment was less likely to alert their shadowers that they had been spotted than even the slightest nod of his head.

Picking his way over a mound of dust-covered rubble, Ryan swept the ruins with his lone blue eye. It was morning, bright and hot. They were in the midst of what had been a great city's downtown. Now it looked as if it had been picked up about two hundred feet and dropped.

They'd left the gutted bunker an hour before and had seemingly made scarcely any progress at all clambering south through the urban devastation. Around them jumbles of busted-up masonry rose in heaps against the sides of mostly intact buildings, some as high as three or four stories. Behind them rose taller buildings, skyscrapers, some canted precariously, with windows blank of glass like blinded staring eyes. Not all of them had fallen the same way, although it was clear that a nuke-blast some distance to the west had done most of the damage.

To their right rear rose a vast mound, its white surface cracked like a colossal egg. Over everything a single dark skyscraper towered like a nail impaling a pale yellow sky. It dominated the devastated downtown. South of it a solitary flying creature kited on huge wings.

Sweat ran down Ryan's face from the line of his long black curly hair. His mouth felt as if it had a prickly pear lobe lodged inside it. The long ragged scar that ran down the side of his face throbbed.

He ignored his discomfort. Minor pains meant nothing to Ryan Cawdor. A person could never tell from looking at him that he'd been raised in privilege and comparative luxury in the prosperous eastern barony of Front Royal. He was a creature of the Deathlands; and like the Deathlands everything had been stripped away from his six-two frame but the hard and the tough. He was the ultimate adapter. The ultimate survivor.

Perching on a tilted chunk of concrete with rebar protruding like twisted fangs, he halted to let his small party pass. Jak, taking a quick swig of water from a worn canteen, headed back out in the lead, skipping over the treacherous footing like rocks in a stream. Ryan used his brief halt to grab some relief from his own tearing thirst, swirling a tiny bit of water from his own canteen around his mouth and swallowing. It went down his throat as if it had knives in it.

At least we know where we are, he thought. J.B.'s sextant had identified the anonymous mass of cracked blocks and twisted steel as St. Louis, by the great river most people now called the Sippi.

He tried not to react to the furtive flickers of movement, visible through gaps in standing walls or past man-high heaps of debris that stank of concrete dust and rotting flesh. He waited until their rear guard, a short man with wire-rimmed spectacles and a fedora he used to cover the steady retreat of his hairline, came up to him.

"So you saw our little shadows," John Barrymore Dix said as he approached. He carried his heavy 12-gauge Smith & Wesson M-4000 shotgun easily in front of his hips. There was a lot more strength in his wiry little frame than there looked to be.

Of course, that could be said for all of them. The truth was, no one looked tough enough to live through what they had.

"Jak's got them," Ryan said quietly.

"What do you reckon they want?"

Ryan's mouth tensed up. "Hard call," he said. "Can't read much 'cause they haven't hit us yet. May just be looking for the best spot to make their move."

J.B. showed him a quick thin smile. "Chill or enslave, doesn't matter much, does it?"

"Sure doesn't," Ryan said, lengthening his step to move up through the rest of the group.

He made no move for the P-226 blaster holstered on his right hip, or the big-bladed panga scabbarded on his left, or even the scoped, long-barreled bolt-action Steyr sniper rifle strapped on his back alongside his bulky backpack. He didn't want to alert their shadows that he was onto them. He trusted his cougar-keen senses and rattlesnake reflexes to get a weapon into play in plenty of time when things went south.

Ignoring the increasing sense of unease crawling up his spine, Ryan drew alongside an apparently elderly man who walked with the aid of a gleaming ebony cane. The man resembled a bag of bones held together by a worn frock coat.

"Doc," Ryan said conversationally, "how's it swingin'?"

"As well as ever, my youthful friend." Although he looked a hard-traveled sixty with his pale blue eyes sunk deep in a well-seamed face framed by long straggly silver-hair, Dr. Theophilus Algernon Tanner was chronologically in his thirties, a couple of years younger than Ryan.

Then again he looked pretty hale and hearty for a man who was well north of two hundred years old. Born in 1868, he had been trawled out of his own time by a late-twentieth-century secret experiment, then heartlessly dumped in a desolate future by the hard-hearted white-coats who had decided he was too difficult to handle.

"I take it you're aware of our furtive friends?" Doc said, covering the question with a cough and a raised hand.

"Yeah," Ryan grunted. He touched the old man briefly on the shoulder. He wouldn't insult Doc or any of his people by telling him to be ready.

They were always ready. If they weren't, they wouldn't be alive. Ryan was utterly devoted to keeping his companions together and breathing, but they still had to do their parts...none of which was easy.

He moved up, falling into step alongside Mildred, a brown-skinned woman a head shorter than he was, with dark hair swinging and tinkling gently in skinny beaded plaits. She wore baggy cargo trousers, a green T-shirt and an overall sheen of sweat. Despite perpetual trudging on perpetual short rations, her figure remained on the stocky side. She carried a ZKR target pistol in a holster hung from her web belt.

"Got company," Ryan said softly.

Her eyes got wide. "Really?"

"Easy," he said. "Don't let on we know—"

Jak darted to his left. His right arm struck like a snake. It came out holding the scruff of a flailing tangle of long matted hair and naked limbs turned almost uniform gray with concrete dust stuck to a long accretion of grease and grime. The figure wore a foul-looking loincloth and squalled like an angry bobcat.

Ryan saw sun flash on the blade of a hunting knife in Jak's chalk-white hand and heard a clash of metal on something hard. The captive had stabbed Jak with a knife whose filth-crusted blade had been ground down to little more than a sliver. It had struck one of the random bits of glass Jak had sewn to his camou jacket.

Jak's knife hand worked in a blur of speed, stabbing his wildly writhing captive twice in barely a second. Then he tossed the scrawny figure away.

A second creature, larger than the first but still stick-skinny and smeared with grease, launched itself at the albino teen's unprotected back.

A boom crashed out from behind Ryan's left shoulder. The noise was like a thumb gouging his eardrum, and the blast wave slapped the side of his head. It was J.B.'s big scattergun going off.

Even with the shot's aftermath ringing in his ears Ryan heard a soggy, chunking sound as the charge of double-00 buck slammed home. Blood sprayed black in the sunlight. The figure fell short of its target, kicking the grit with bare heels and groaning.

Another sound of impact and a surprised grunt came from behind Ryan. More shots rang out from his right. Drawing his own handblaster, he looked that way.

A big-busted, slim-waisted woman with long slender legs knelt on a pile of busted brick and concrete, firing a snub-nosed hammerless revolver with two hands. Brilliant red hair was curled into a tight cap at her nape. When he'd glanced that way a few moments before it had hung past her shoulders.

J.B. was also on one knee, looking down at his fallen glasses. Nearby, his fedora lay upturned on a round-edge chunk of concrete. Behind him a nearly naked man with hair and beard fringing his face like a brown dandelion was spinning down in reaction to being hit by Krysty Wroth's .38-caliber slugs. Apparently he'd just hit J.B. from behind with a thrown chunk of pavement.

Another figure reared up from behind a waist-high broken section of wall at the top of a slope of rubble. Ryan snapped a shot at him from his 9 mm Sig Sauer. The man's head jerked as the bullet smashed the outside of his right cheekbone.

But he shook himself, shedding blood like a wet dog, then resettled his grip on the improvised spear he was about to hurl. Ryan shot him again. He went down out of sight with blood spurting in a red tubelike arc from his throat.

Ryan sprinted back the few paces to where J.B. was still on all fours shaking his head. He held the SIG out ready at arm's length. Behind him he heard the boom of Doc's big black-powder blaster, then the louder crash of the short-barreled shotgun mounted beneath the huge LeMat's barrel. Somebody screamed.

It didn't sound like anybody Ryan knew.

"Got move!" Jak shouted. "Rad suckers everywhere!"

"You all right?" Ryan shouted.

"Oh, yeah," the Armorer muttered. "Just fine."

"Then grab it and go!"

Ryan jammed J.B.'s hat onto his head. The man fumbled his glasses onto his face, then seized his fallen shotgun. He may have been dazed, but he had the presence of mind to jack a fresh shell into the chamber as Ryan hauled him to the feet by the collar of the bombardier jacket he never surrendered, even to the sweltering heat.

The sun-baked rubble mounds and wall stumps on all sides seemed to be lined with gibbering oddly shaped people.

A rock glanced off Ryan's shoulder. On a concrete shelf at the base of a yellow brick wall he saw one of the skulkers bent over as if it had just thrown something. *She,* judging by the pendulous dugs that dangled in front of knobbly knees in her follow-through.

On the run Ryan shot at her twice. She screeched and fell onto her back. He couldn't tell where he hit her, but she stopped moving at once.

"J.B., rearguard," he shouted. "Mildred, you cover left."

Krysty already covered the right, hastily opening the cylinder of her Smith & Wesson and reloading.

Having emptied both the fat cylinder of his big handblaster and the shotgun barrel, Doc had reholstered the antique weapon and drawn his sword from his silver lionhead walking stick. As Ryan glanced his way, sprinting past, he saw Doc fend off a thrown sharpened stick with the sword, then deftly stab an attacker lunging at Krysty's blind side.

"We gotta keep moving!" Ryan ran for the front to support Jak. The best way to deal with an ambush, he knew, was assault into it and do your best to blast through. Since they were already surrounded, straight ahead looked like as good a way to go as any.

Jak's .357 Magnum Colt Python boomed twice from where he stood on a low brick mound in a gap between walls. The painfully loud reports echoed throughout the area. Ryan accelerated his run as Jak smashed an attacker across the face with the ribbed six-inch barrel, hot from the friction of high-velocity 125-grain hollowpoint rounds. The wiry attacker sat down hard on a canted concrete block.

Jak shot him in the face. A saucer-size chunk of skull blew out of the back of his head, to the accompaniment of a bloody spray of gore.

Evidently they were moving through the ruins of some largely fallen building. Since leaving the mat-trans gateway, they had struggled across fields of rubble so random and comprehensive it was largely impossible to tell what had been street and what had been structure before the big nuke. They headed south simply because from Mildred's recollection of late-twentieth-century St. Louis the densest concentration of big buildings had stood north of where they were. Where, indeed, a few surviving buildings still loomed or leaned against gathering clouds that began to move rapidly and take on an ominous orange tint.

Once they got clear of the rubble they could at least move faster and with less chance of turning an ankle in some hidden pocket of debris. They might even stand a chance of finding shelter against the likely coming of corrosive rains.

If they got clear. These scrubby, stinking ambushers didn't seem inclined to let them do so.

Attackers sprang at Jak from either side even as he spun to face a third, whipping out a hunting knife. Ryan snapped a shot first at the right-hand assailant, then the one to his left. The right-hand ambusher went down. The one on the left, though, only went briefly to a bare bony knee. Then she stood up and with a screech attacked again, something slim and glittering jutting from the bottom of the fist she held over her head.

And the slide of Ryan's SIG had locked back. Its high-capacity magazine was empty. He'd had to fire too many shots to keep attackers' heads down. And now he had no time for a combat reload. Nor could he risk fumbling a magazine full of precious 9 mm cartridges away by trying to reload on the run.

Instead he whipped the panga free of its sheath with his left hand. He screamed like an eagle to attract the ambushers' attention away from the slim white-haired teen.

The woman he'd shot looked his way, then she lunged for him. He saw that she held a simple sliver of broken glass with some kind of hide wrapped around one end to keep it from slicing her hand. It was primitive even by the standards of postdark improvised weapons, and liable to break on any kind of contact with a target. But it could kill you just as dead as a megaton nuke warhead.

Or just wound you badly enough to slow you down, which in an ambush like this was the same thing.

They both swung at the same time. Despite her wound, the woman had triple-crazy speed. But Ryan's backhand cut was panther-fast and as precise as a needle. The panga hit the inside of the woman's knife arm just beneath her wrist. Backed by the weapon's considerable mass, the edge, which Ryan kept honed to razor keenness, parted tendon and bone almost as easily as skin. The hand spun away on a geyser of red, still clutching the crude glass shank.

Odds were she was out of this fight. Out of this life, if she didn't get her arm bound before her adrenaline-frenzied heart pumped her lifeblood out the stump. Ryan hacked her across her twisted screaming face on the forearm return anyway. He couldn't leave his own knife-arm swinging in the breeze. And he had learned as a mere stripling when he was running with trader's crew that it never hurt to make sure.

Jak straightened from the body of the ambusher he'd just gutted with his big-bellied Bowie. "Clear," he shouted as Ryan came up beside him. "Move!"

"Go!" Ryan said. He tracked his good eye left and right and saw no more figures emerging from the rubble. As Jak sprinted forward, the bits of sharp glass and metal he'd sewn to his camo jacket flashed in the sunlight.

Krysty came through the gap. Flashing an "I'm okay" smile at Ryan, she knelt to cover to the right. A moment later Mildred appeared, all but towing the scarecrow figure of Doc like a sturdy little tugboat. She let go and took up position to cover left.

Ryan reloaded the SIG handblaster, stuffing the empty magazine in a back pocket of his jeans. The mags were nearly as precious as cartridges. Without them a semiauto blaster was a single-shot weapon as slow and clumsy to reload as a crossbow.

With a parting boom of his shotgun J.B. passed through the gap as Ryan momentarily transferred the SIG to his left hand so he could properly sheath the panga with his right.

"Don't hang around gawking, boy!" the Armorer shouted as he jacked the slide and turned to run. "This ain't a vacation resort!"

Laughing a silent wolf's laugh, Ryan took his SIG in his right hand and followed his companions at a slogging run.

Chapter Two

"One thing you gotta say for a ruined city," J. B. Dix said. He had his hat lifted to mop his forehead with a dirty blue handkerchief. No sooner had he made a pass than more sweat sluiced down his sallow skin. "'Specially here hard by a big river. It sure does hold the heat in."

"Wow," Mildred said. Her words came out between heaving breaths. "Looks like Busch Stadium mostly survived."

Without much interest Ryan looked at the stubby cylinder the freezie physician had pointed out. Several hundred yards to the west, it looked to be made up of tall, open arches supported by columns, and ramps that ran up behind them. He had unslung his longblaster and hunkered down, cradling it, hoping that if the hairy naked crazies chose to keep pursuing he'd get some shots into them at long range.

"Went to a game there once," the stocky physician said. "Cards versus Cubs."

She smiled with fleeting nostalgia. "*That* was a rivalry."

"We don't want to get too close to that thing," J.B. said. "Who knows what's nesting in there now?"

"Speaking of nesting," Krysty said, "there seem to be a lot of flying things starting to swarm around the top of that really tall building."

Jak turned his ruby eyes that way. It was easy to see

which one she meant. It was easily the tallest standing as far as the eye could see. And Ryan saw twenty or more flyers orbiting high up.

"Screamwings," he said.

"Never saw them big as that one before," Ryan said. The giant flyer now orbited the tall 'scraper with the lesser ones surrounding it.

The albino youth just shrugged.

"Yeah," Ryan said after a moment. "Don't mean much, right? Always coming across something new."

"Doesn't mean much." Krysty smiled as she corrected him.

"That's what sucks about the modern world," Mildred said, tipping a canteen to shake the last droplets of water into her mouth. "Well, part of a long, long list."

They huddled in a bowl-shaped depression in yellowish-gray rubble about forty feet wide and high enough at the sides to shield them from view from street level. Despite being in excellent shape from the never-ending trudge across the devastation wrought by the big nuke, all six were winded by their run. Except Jak; little seemed to bother him.

With little to weigh them down but grubby skins and a few crude weapons, their ambushers had chased them fast and hard. But they hadn't chased them far.

"They gave up pretty quick," Ryan said, squinting around at their surroundings, taking in the huge matched stumps of gleaming metal Mildred told him had once joined in an arch hundreds of feet above; the nearby huge building that once had to have been fronted entirely in glass was now a strange open-faced steel skeleton; the strip of dense east-west woods they had crossed to get here; the flooded waterfront district just east of them with warehouses sticking up out of green-brown water; the intact section of highway overpass to the south.

"We inflicted grievous hurt on them," Doc said. He was laboriously reloading his huge old handblaster, tamping down a bullet into a chamber over a fresh charge of gunpowder with a special rammer built into the LeMat. He was recovering with surprising quickness, given that he looked like Death got up for a last walk around. Times like these proved his claim that he was nowhere as old as he looked, biologically. "It must have been quite discouraging."

"There's that," Krysty said. "But mebbe they were afraid of what was in the woods. Or this side of them."

Ryan grunted. "Give us some good news for a change, why don't you?"

Her smile was like the sun coming out from behind storm clouds. "We're alive, lover. And we've got each other. It's worked so far."

He felt his mouth struggling to smile. He still had to say, "Always works. Till it don't."

"'Doesn't,'" she corrected him.

She had a temper on her, this redheaded beauty. But her mutie hair, sentient and prehensile, lay still across her shoulders. She just smiled more at him and wouldn't be drawn.

"Nothing here but misery," J.B. stated simply. "Why don't we go back?"

"Back where?" Ryan asked.

"To the redoubt."

"Not remember?" Jak said. "Nothing there, either. No ammo, no water, no self-heats."

Mildred mopped her forehead with the hem of her shirt. "Never thought I'd see a day when meals refused by Ethiopians tasted like ambrosia."

"I mean, try the luck of the jump," J.B. said.

"If we find a place with steak bushes and beer springs," Ryan said, "it'll be guarded by ten thousand coldhearts, sure as a dead man cools."

J.B. gestured around at the jumbled edges and angles and dust-softened mounds of the urban deathscape. "Don't know if you noticed, Ryan, but every square inch of this place is guarded by muties as crazy as nuked yellowjackets, and it ain't nothing but hammered dogshit."

"Boys," Krysty said softly but firmly, "step back. Fighting among ourselves won't fill our bottles or our bellies. Makes us more likely to fill cannie bellies instead."

"At times like this," Doc said with a grand sweep of his arm, "I find it helps to seek the consolations of philosophy."

Everyone looked at him. He sat blinking vaguely.

"Why are you all staring at me?" he asked.

"Well," J.B. said, "out with it."

"Out with what?"

"The consultations of philosophy or whatever you were talking about."

Doc blinked in amiable puzzlement. "What?"

For his part Ryan was taking note of how unusually talkative the Armorer was. Normally J.B. said just a little more than an old hickory stump, although when he spoke it was usually to the point and dead-on accurate.

"What's eating on you, J.B.?" he asked. "You don't normally say so much in a whole month."

J.B. slapped his thigh. "Everything, Ryan. I just got bad feelings creeping up on me from every side."

Mildred frowned. "You wouldn't think there'd be many people here. The place is a mess, even for taking a nuke west of here."

"Plenty to scavenge in the area," Ryan said.

"Those people who jumped us didn't look like they'd bothered much with that. They barely had loincloths."

"I surmise they were cannibals," Doc said, sighting along the barrel of his blaster to make sure the bore was clear before snapping the weapon closed. "When we parted company with them, the other side of these woods, I thought I saw them begin tearing at their fallen kin."

"Yeah," Ryan said. "Chasing us probably worked up a double-big appetite."

"Muties," Jak said.

"No," Mildred said, shaking her head. "I don't think so."

"Not see? No chins, plus fingers."

"Typical symptoms of inbreeding, lad," Doc said.

"Yeah," Ryan agreed. He'd seen it not far from his birthplace of Front Royal.

"They have to have something to eat besides each other," Mildred said.

"They probably prey on scavvies," Krysty said. "Cities usually draw those like flies to jam. Especially as the rads die down."

"But what do *they* eat?"

"Game," Jak said. "Plenty here."

"In a city?"

He shrugged. "Always." Then he nodded his pale, pointed chin back the way they had come.

"Forest."

It was indeed. It wasn't wide but it was significant. A lush and densely undergrown stand of trees ran in a broad strip from near the river toward the nuke strike a couple miles west.

"Evidently this vicinity receives a great deal of rainfall of the nontainted variety," Doc said.

"Well, that's another reason to be on the move," Ryan

said, looking at the clotting clouds rushing and swirling overhead. They had gone the color of mustard, with alarming orange highlights. "Looks like some of the 'burn the hide off you' kind is on the way. We need to get under cover triple fast."

"Trouble," Jak said, turning suddenly.

A bullet cracked off the top of the heap of rubble where Jak had lain, and his eyes skinned toward the woods for sign of pursuit. The shot-sound that followed a heartbeat later seemed to have come from the northwest, although the way everything echoed around these ruins made it hard to tell. Ryan turned to scramble up to the top of the heaped stone and concrete dust and flopped down behind his Steyr.

Having only one eye was something the black-haired man had adjusted to years ago. Sometimes it was a drawback, but there was nothing he could do about it. Now he had to hold his good eye away from the scope initially to look for targets.

And targets there were. If the gunshot hadn't been a major clue, the way this new set of attackers was dressed showed they were a whole different breed compared to the crazy group that had jumped them. They wore real clothing, no dirtier and in no worse repair than what Ryan and friends themselves wore. Camo in various patterns was a consistent theme, as were predark cartridge blasters: rifles, shotguns, handguns.

Scavvies, Ryan thought. Well-equipped ones, too. He cursed under his breath. At least half a dozen of them, advancing quickly but cautiously through rubble just north of the stadium. Like it or not there were others: he glimpsed them through big gaps in the walls of the building.

The most dangerous attacker Ryan could see carried

a remade M-16, with the nontapered A-2 foregrip. He swung the Steyr to cover the scavvie, then put his good eye behind the eyepiece of the SSG-70. His skill was such that, though the coldheart wasn't dead-centered in the view-field, he was just a twitch away.

Drawing a breath as he centered the single post reticule on the man's chest, Ryan exhaled half as he gently squeezed the trigger. The 7.62 mm cartridge lit off, kicking his shoulder with the steel buttplate. Ryan reflexively worked the bolt, reloading for a follow-up shot.

The M-16 man was in the process of folding onto his face. Ryan thought he saw a trace of pink mist hanging in the air behind him. It rapidly vanished. The scavvie's buddies dropped, seeking immediate cover.

Muzzle-flashes winked at Ryan, pale in cloud-filtered daylight. These new attackers were no cowards. They also weren't stupe enough to just keep walking up on someone who had them in the sights of a big-bore longblaster from good cover.

Instead of pulling off another shot, Ryan slid back down the brief slope. He felt the hard hot chunks of rock and debris roll against the hard muscles of his gut. His right hip throbbed where a hard corner had caught him when he went to his belly. He barely noticed. It was just pain. And for Ryan Cawdor, pain was just a reminder he wasn't yet chilled.

The gray-white concrete dust that rose up to invade his nose and mouth and turn the inside of his eyelid into sandpaper as it scraped across the vulnerable cornea was a greater problem. He blinked furiously as he rose to a crouch and ran south after his companions.

They stumbled through a nightmare of urban devastation. The concrete dust, which seemed to dry quickly despite frequent rains in the valley of the great river, sucked down their boots, and concealed pockets and loosened blocks that could snap an ankle like a dry twig. So they couldn't run very fast. And no matter how desperate their need they had to pay attention to where they put their feet, slowing them even further.

At the edge of a relatively clear stretch of street Ryan stopped, spun and knelt to cover their backtrail with his longblaster. A bearded head appeared above a heap of gray rubble. Ryan lowered his head behind the scope, carefully maintaining a distance between his eye and the lip of the telescope eyepiece that protected the lens. Otherwise the sharp recoil of a 7.62 mm NATO cartridge lighting off would die-stamp the eyepiece housing right into socket, giving him a nasty half-raccoon mask of purple bruise or even cutting a ring in his flesh.

His target hadn't learned the real danger in pursuing armed prey. Unfortunately for him. Ryan held the reticule centered on his forehead, and he could see the sweat etching rivulets in the black grime that covered the man's face, see his lips working inside his rat's-nest beard as he cursed the effort of climbing up the low but treacherous slope. He was carrying a rusty double-barreled shotgun in one hand and using the other to climb with.

At the top of the heap he paused. For the first time he raised his eyes to scope the longer distance before him.

That pause was what Ryan waited for, knowing it would come. It wasn't that a head was a hard target; the target was barely fifty yards off, an easy shot for a marksman like Ryan over open sights. What made it a challenge was the way the target tended to move around.

As the grubby hair-fringed face came up, Ryan was releasing half of a held-in breath. The trigger cracked; the rifle bucked and roared. Ryan jacked the bolt as the weapon rode up and then settled back down.

The scavvie lay slumped with his face in the dust. The back of his head was a steaming mess.

Though his ears rang from the shot, Ryan heard the man's buddies curse in guttural fury. One stuck a remade M-16 up over the top of a low stub of yellow-brick wall and triggered a random burst.

Even though Ryan had pulled his eye back from the scope so he could cover a field of vision wider than the tiny little circle the glass gave him, he couldn't see where the shots hit. He didn't even hear the secondary cracks when the needlelike .223 bullets passed.

He turned and sprinted across a mostly level stretch, covered in what looked like a mix of river silt and concrete dust. To his right, a building appeared to have fallen mostly west. He raced for the far more promising cover of the ruin in front of him. At one time it had been a circular tower. Now all that remained was a chest-high ring of white masonry.

Ryan vaulted the remnants of a broken wall. Mildred and J.B. knelt inside the rubble, covering the one-eyed man's dash for cover. J.B. had his shotgun shouldered, while Mildred had her blocky ZKR 551 target pistol in a two-handed Weaver grip, left hand folded over right, elbow bent down to provide stabilizing tension against the almost-straight gun arm. Ahead Ryan could see Jak cautiously scoping the remains of a low-curved structure, at least half-intact, that led from the first ruin circle toward a much broader tower a hundred yards south. Krysty and Doc knelt to cover the albino teen.

"Got it," Ryan shouted.

He turned and hunkered down behind the wall, placing the Steyr's forestock into a sort of notch in the solid masonry of the broken wall. As Ryan searched the ruins behind for targets he wondered why the scavvies were pressing them so hard. The scavvies kept dogging the companions despite losses, and were willing to burn way too much ammo to do it. Even if they were cartridge-flush from trade or finding caches, it didn't make sense to burn so many bullets just for the fugitives' own handful of blasters and the contents of their backpacks, whatever those may hold.

Must be Krysty they really want, he thought grimly. *And Mildred, too.*

Krysty was a beauty with the stopping power of a 12-gauge slug, even by the standards of the glossy mags and vids that survived skyfall. Mildred—Dr. Wyeth—wasn't to Ryan's taste, frankly, a little too stocky. But she was still far better-looking than most women in Deathlands.

What drove them so hard, likely, was pure lust: for the use they'd get out of the women themselves, and then for the jack or barter they'd reap from selling them in what would still be considered prime condition, even if they wound up badly bruised and shy a tooth or two. Selling a pair the likes of Krysty and Mildred would bring them more than two months' good scavenge, if the going rate in St. Lou was comparable to other places Ryan had known.

The one-eyed man heard and felt Krysty and Doc peel away from either side of him. Then there came the crack of a bullet passing fast, followed by thump and a grunt of surprise as much as pain.

And then Mildred's piercing scream.

Chapter Three

"J.B., no!" Mildred cried. The despairing echo chased itself mockingly around the circular ruins.

Ryan's heart seemed to seize in his chest. He ducked behind the wall and turned.

The Armorer stood as if rooted in place. Ryan could clearly see where a few threads of his leather jacket had been pushed out a fraction of an inch behind him by the heavy-caliber bullet that had blown right through the small man's chest, front to back.

Time froze. A thin streamer of blood hung in the air behind J.B.'s back, fractionating into round red droplets as it distanced itself from him. With a roaring silence in his ears and an abyss of emptiness opening in his gut, Ryan watched his oldest living friend, his best friend, the man who'd had his back since he was a pup, spin and topple to lie on his back in the dust with his glasses disks of emptiness, reflecting the troubled yellow sky above.

Mildred scrambled toward the fallen Armorer. Though tears dug gullies through the dust on her cheeks, her professional training and experience had taken over. She was kneeling over J.B., checking his vital signs even before Ryan snapped out of it.

"He's still alive!" she called. "Missed the heart." She shrugged frantically out of the straps of her backpack.

Ryan's attention snapped back into focus. The blood pennon had streamed away east toward the great river.

That meant the shot had come from the west. Bringing the Steyr to his shoulder, Ryan turned his blue eye that way.

Fifty or sixty yards away what looked like a parking structure had pancaked, creating a stratified slab a story or so high. At least half a dozen people in scraps and oddments of salvaged clothing advanced across a broad area overgrown with green weeds to their knees, pausing to shoot then charging on. Four were men. Two looked to be women.

As Ryan watched, one man rocked back to the recoil of what he reckoned to be a battered Springfield M-1A, the semiauto-only civvie version of the old M-14 battle rifle. The same caliber as Ryan's Steyr, it was a weapon well prized in the Deathlands. It was likely, Ryan thought, this was the bastard who shot J.B.

But he wasn't shooting at Ryan. Instead he aimed north toward the rubble of the westward-fallen building that the companions had bypassed. The scavvies who had been chasing them appeared to be taking cover there.

Rival bands? Ryan wondered as he lined up his scope on the center of the rifleman's chest.

He fired. The enemy rifleman jerked as the steel-jacketed slug punched through his ribs and transversed through his heart. Gray dust puffed from his gray, black and white camo blouse, confirming Ryan had hit his mark.

The scavvie collapsed bonelessly. The heavy rifle was dropping from his fingers even before recoil kicked Ryan's field of view up over the man's head. A chill, sure, he thought.

The other five dropped into the weeds, vanishing instantly from sight. From the top of the dumped structure behind them more blasters opened up to cover them, producing the vast grayish smoke clouds characteristic of black-powder blasters.

Ryan ducked out of the line of fire, popping the magazine from the well of his own rifle to stick in a fresh box. It was his next to last, another worry he couldn't allow to distract him now.

Krysty and Mildred knelt, flanking the supine J.B. Krysty was furiously ripping open the plastic wrapping of an ancient package of fuzzy white scavenged Sno Balls that was among the last of their remaining edibles.

"I know you're the expert," Ryan said, with more of a rasp to his voice than usual, "but are you sure what J.B. needs is a quick dose of century-old snack food?"

"Sucking chest wound," Mildred snapped without looking up. "I need to cover the holes before his lung collapses."

Ryan nodded, then turned back to the rubble-parapet.

The two sets of attackers were keeping their heads low now. Ryan positioned himself at the northwest side, where he could keep an eye on both. The heat beat him into the ruins with increasing anger as the sun rolled up the sky, a patch of brightness in the roiling mustard-colored clouds that now stretched horizon to horizon.

They don't have to make a move on us, he thought. *Just wait for us to run out of water. Or for the acid rain to start scouring the flesh from our bones. Whichever comes first.*

With quick glimpses over his shoulder, Ryan kept track of what his friends were doing. Jak lay by the gap at the stone circle's south side with his .357 Magnum Colt Python propped on his pack in front of him, covering the curved structure that led from it. Doc kept watch to the west, cautiously peering up over the low wall for brief periods, then ducking and shifting left or right unpredictably. For all that he acted sometimes like a half-crazed old man, he was cunning as well as intelligent. And he very seldomly lost focus in a combat situation.

Another look out over the wrecked cityscape. No movement.

The river smell was thick here. The humidity felt as if it were climbing right up out of the ground around them. A stench of old corruption and decaying flesh likewise began to rise. It told Ryan that plenty still lived here in this cubicle concrete wasteland. The last decay byproducts of a million or so chills in the big nuke had burned away long since, he knew. Any decomposing organics were recent.

Where there's life there's death, he thought, with a certain bitterly appreciative humor.

From somewhere far off came a rumble of thunder, rolling around among the surviving structures. "Storm's coming on," he said.

He glanced back. The women had J.B.'s jacket and shirt off. He was propped up against Krysty as Mildred wound duct tape tightly around the makeshift patches of plastic wrapper that covered the holes in his chest and back, and the pads of relatively clean spare clothing folded up for bandages. Ryan winced.

"That tape's gonna sting when it comes off," he said. "I don't envy J.B."

"I'll settle for being alive to feel the sting, Ryan," J.B. said weakly. He had a bit of a wheeze to his voice. Ryan glanced back at him, startled. The wiry man gave him a thin smile.

"You hush up, now," Mildred said sternly. "Save your breath. We've gone to a lot a trouble to keep it from leaking out."

Ryan's lips twisted in a brief smile as he looked to the north again. This time he glimpsed a flicker of motion, left to right, behind heaps of rubble on the street's far side. He started to raise his rifle, then halted the motion and regretfully lowered the longblaster.

No target, he thought. He didn't have a single round to waste on shadows.

"The nuke-suckers are starting to get restless," he said. "Make a move soon, mebbe."

"Okay, I've got it from here, Krysty," Mildred said. "Why don't you take J.B.'s scattergun and help watch our little friends out there."

"Good idea, Mildred." Ryan heard the crunching of footfalls on dust-covered rubble as the redhead took up position between him and Doc.

Time passed. The day got hotter. The clouds grew thicker, more clotted, more orange and threatening. Occasionally one of the other set of besiegers would pop off a shot as if to remind the companions they were still out there. None of Ryan's crew was stupe enough to shoot back.

At a soft-voiced request from Mildred, Doc helped her shift J.B. up close to the short wall on the west side, where there was some shade. Doc had a surprising wiry strength to him. The Armorer had lapsed into unconsciousness again. Mildred poured water on a hankie from her canteen and bathed his face.

"How's it look?" Ryan asked her.

He could feel her shrug. "I've done all I can do. Doesn't seem to be much internal bleeding, thank God. He's tough, but I don't give him even odds of living to nightfall if we can't get him some kind of better care by then."

"Dear lady," Doc said softly, "do I understand you give any of us even odds of living until nightfall?"

"You got me, Doc," Mildred said. She was too depressed and worried even to rise to the bait. Under normal circumstances she and Doc spent plenty of time sniping good-naturedly at each other.

"You know," Doc said, "one would certainly think the base of the elevator shaft and the stumps of the structural members in these collapsed buildings should have survived the blasts. Yet many have become little more than mounds."

"Elevator probably went to a basement level," Mildred said.

"But structural members usually survived at least partially, even near ground zero," Krysty said. "I've seen pillar stumps standing right next to craters."

Ryan bit down on a caustic remark about wasting air on speculation that wouldn't load bullets in a blaster. Under the circumstances idle chatter was far preferable to thinking too deeply about their situation.

"Why don't you take over the scattergun, Mildred?" Krysty asked. "You're more comfortable with it."

The physician shrugged. "Sure." Krysty passed the weapon, then drew her more-familiar Smith & Wesson 640.

As she did, a storm of blasterfire erupted from the north. Bullets struck sprays of concrete powder off the top of the low circular wall and whined mournfully overhead as they tumbled through the thick, hot air. A short burst from an M-16 snapped over Ryan's head like a sail in a brisk wind.

"Get ready for it," he said during a lull in the shooting. "They're nerving themselves to make their move."

"No doubt they sense the immediacy of the impending storm," Doc said. "I can smell the rain and sulfur already."

"Hear that?" Jak called from the south wall.

"Hear what?" Krysty asked.

Ryan was switching his vision back and forth between the scavvies lying up in the weed-grown field to their west and the forted attackers to the north. Though the western bunch weren't firing, he was pretty sure they weren't sharp enough to have backed off and left without him or one of his sharp-eyed friends spotting them. Apparently they were biding their time and awaiting events.

"Whine," Jak said. "Triple high. Like giant mosquitoes, you know?" He winced and shook his head. "Not like."

"I can't hear it," Krysty said.

Mildred and Doc said they heard nothing out of the way, either. Of course with the blasters cracking off from not so far away that was perhaps not so surprising—the wonder being Jak *could*. But he had the sense of hearing of a white-tailed deer.

Ryan heard a loud rattle from his left. He risked sticking his head up to scope it out. Flashes and billows of smoke were coming from the pancaked structure.

"Black-powder blasters," Ryan said. A ball sailed over his head. "Shooting at us."

"They want to help the other bunch crack us," Krysty said. "Then roll in, take them down, get all the swag themselves."

"But why, dear lady, would they act now? Why not let us and our pursuers settle things and then eliminate the victor—in accordance with the ancient Oriental adage that when two tigers fight, one dies, the other is wounded?"

Mildred had turned away to check J.B. His cheeks were pale, his eyes closed, his breathing shallow. Now meeting Doc's eye, she jerked a thumb upward.

"That's why."

Thunder split the sky. Something wet struck the back of Ryan's left hand. It stung like an ant bite.

He looked up. "Shit."

A blue-white crack appeared in the roiling orange and black clouds above, jagged and blinding. It pulsated three times. A sound like a colossal explosion beat down on them, a sound so loud Ryan could feel it.

"Acid gully washer on way," Jak called.

"Tell us something we don't know," Mildred said, hastily moving to shield the wounded Armorer's face with his hat. No other raindrops fell in the vicinity. But none of the companions doubted it was only a question of time.

"Here they come!" Krysty called.

Ryan raised his Steyr again. An acid downpour was no joke; it could bubble unprotected skin in minutes, sizzle muscle away to leave yellow bone in a shockingly short time, depending on the strength and length of the downpour. But the really virulent falls tended not to last long.

Ryan laid the rifle's iron battle sights on a goggled figure who had sprung up from a clump of brush that had grown around an old fire hydrant and was charging forward, holding a beat-up semiautomatic longblaster diagonally across his chest. He squeezed off a quick shot and saw the man jerk as the bullet took him in the left shoulder.

The attacker kept coming. Ryan cursed and dropped his aim. His second shot punched the man in the gut right above his web belt. He fell, rolling and squalling like a catamount.

The Armorer going down had rattled even the hard-core Ryan more than he realized. Until now. He'd just forgotten one of the prime rules of combat: the chest was mostly air, the very fact J.B. owed his survival to—for however long it lasted.

A man well-wired on jolt or just adrenaline overdrive could keep motoring on even with a collapsed lung, and the fact he might die horribly in a matter of minutes wouldn't hold him back from busting your head open with a club before collapsing. The heart, like the head, was a tricky target actually to hit. And even a clean heart shot didn't always drop a man, or big animal, that was already in furious motion. The working of his limbs could keep his blood circulating long enough to inflict a chilling wound on you. The best target for stopping a man was from the ribs down.

"The miscreants to the west of us are advancing as well," Doc reported. He was reserving his own fire until the enemy gave him closer targets. It took a long time to reload his own black-powder revolver.

The M-4000 shotgun bellowed. Ryan heard Mildred grunt as the 12-gauge's heavy recoil punished her shoulder. She was running rifled slugs through the blaster against targets too far away for buckshot to be effective. She knew to snug the steel butt-plate hard against her shoulder. But it was a painful weapon even for a man as big as Ryan or as battle-hardened as the stricken J.B. to shoot in sustained fire.

"Jak!" Ryan called, racking his bolt and slamming it shut on a fresh cartridge, one of his rapidly dwindling store. He wasn't sure whether his last shot had hit the red-bearded scavvie he had targeted or if the man had dived to cover. They were under fifty yards away now. It would seem to be a walkaway for a precision-sniping piece like the Steyr, in the hands of an expert marksman such as Ryan, to take down targets that close at hand. And it would have been—had he been shooting at pebbles on fenceposts.

It wasn't quite so simple when the targets were running, ducking and weaving. And shooting back. The heavy bolt-action rifle was never meant for close-in combat: it was meant to reach out and touch enemies hundreds of yards distant, a slow, measured, precise form of warfare. Nothing at all like close combat, which was crude and dirty and above all *fast*.

Ryan was just wondering if it was time to forget the longblaster and try to get his SIG handblaster into play when a figure loomed up right in front of him with a terrible screech.

Chapter Four

Desperately Ryan rolled back onto his butt, away from the low wall. He flung up the Steyr crosswise just in time to catch the haft of a rusty-headed tomahawk descending toward his face.

Heat stung his left cheek as Krysty shot the scavvie in the face with her short-barreled handblaster. Ryan sensed minute bits of unburned propellant clacking against the patch that covered that eye. Though the short barrel of the little .38 produced a shattering muzzle-blast that close up, he never heard it. His ears already rang from repeated booms from his big 7.62 longblaster.

He threw himself forward and up, rolling to his feet in time to buttstroke another screaming scavvie across the face. He felt a yielding instant and then a crunch as a cheekbone gave way. The scavenger staggered back, dropping a big 1911-style semiauto handblaster to clutch at its stove-in face.

Her face, Ryan realized. It meant no more to him than what species of bug he'd just crunched beneath his boot heel. Running with the Trader, he'd long ago learned the brutal lesson that those who came to chill you had no sex or age. They had to die if you wanted to live.

Quickly Ryan stooped to prop the Steyr against the wall. Even in emergencies you didn't want to go dropping precision optics on the ground. Using the longblaster as a club was bad enough.

As he put down the rifle with his left hand he drew the big fat-bladed panga from its sheath with the right. The wounded woman, screaming like a stuck steam whistle with fury and agony, yanked a blade from her own belt and lunged toward him for payback.

Krysty's S&W 640 boomed again. She either missed the knife-wielding woman or aimed at someone else. Ryan sensed other figures closing in. He slashed the scavvie rushing him slantwise across a trim belly left bare between a stained tank top and filth-crusted baggy camo pants. The wound was a rising, drawing cut that drew a red line across sunburned flesh. It opened like a red-lipped mutie mouth, spilling gray and purple loops of guts. They tripped the woman up and she went down howling.

Jak's .357 Python ripped out three fast characteristic barks, sizzling with high-energy harmonics. "West! They coming!" the teen shouted. "We triple-screwed!"

Ryan yanked out his SIG, then ducked as a scavvie twenty yards to the north dropped to a knee to spray the defenders with full-auto grief from an M-4. As Ryan dropped he pushed Krysty's right hip hard with the heel of his hand. Adrenaline boosted his own wiry strength enough to tumble the woman right over…and save her life as a burst of .223 bullets ripped the air where she'd stood a moment before.

With the ringing in his ears amped double by the fierce muzzle-blast of the short-barreled carbine, it took Ryan a beat to realize that he was hearing wild screaming from the other side of the wall. In two different voices, or rather, kinds of voices. One was human, uttering throat-tearing shrieks of wild fear and intolerable agony.

The other set came from something not even remotely human.

He risked a fast peek over the parapet.

"Screamwings!" Krysty exclaimed from his side. As resilient as a hard rubber ball, she'd bounced right back up and into the fight from her tumble, even though both landing on the sharp-cornered rubble and the punch Ryan had given her would have left deep bruises.

They watched wide-eyed as a chicken-size screamwing sank its talons into the blond dreadlocked sides of a goggled scavvie's head so deeply that blood spurted. The screamwing struck like a snake at his face with its toothed beak. The goggles protected the man's eyes—until the ravening flying mutie ripped them off and tossed them away with a screech of triumph.

And then the man cried out much louder than the mutant bird.

A flock of the winged horrors had descended as if from the churning orange-and-yellow clouds. After unleashing a few stinging droplets, the clouds had held off spewing lethal acid. But this fall of flesh and feathers and claws wasn't much improvement.

For the scavvies, anyway. The monsters seemed attracted by the movement of the attackers charging the ring-shaped ruin. Ryan saw at least a dozen. Some battled as futilely as the blond-dreaded man who was sinking to his knees as the horror clutching his head ate his face. Others ran for all they were worth back the way they had come.

It usually meant they died tired as well as screaming. No matter how inspired they were to run, the screamwings flew faster.

And wheeling above, a black crucifix against the mustard clouds, was a shape that seemed as big as a predark light plane.

Not all the screamwings found prey. Some helped their comrades swarm the scavvies. Others turned their attention toward the defenders in the circular ruin. One uttered a squawk and swooped down from twenty yards up.

A blast of .33-caliber double-00 balls from J.B.'s shotgun caught it square and ripped it apart in midair.

The muties turned and flew away. Even the ones sitting and ripping strips of skin and flesh from fallen quarry, some of which still writhed and hollered, snapped open their wings and took off. They flew not in pursuit of the scavvie survivors, now in full retreat, but northwest, toward the top of the tall, dark tower. The ones chasing the scavvies sheered off to join them, uttering hoarse cries.

"Wow," Mildred said. "I know I busted that one like a blood piñata. But I never knew screamwings to let a little thing like that discourage them so easy before."

"Hey!" Jak called. "Other coldhearts run, too!"

The words hit Ryan like a fist to the gut. So remarkable, not to mention horrific, had the sudden screamwing attack been that it had all but hypnotized him. He'd stone forgotten they were being hit in a flank attack by what was apparently a second set of enemies.

His eye caught Krysty's emerald gaze in passing as they both cranked their heads west. Pink spots glowed on her cheeks. She'd got caught up in their unlikely rescue-by-monster, too. And that kind of thing could get you chilled.

Ryan looked toward the flattened building and the stadium looming beyond to see a scavvie stagger and slap his hand to his neck. A short thick feathered shaft transfixed the man's neck right to left. Ryan knew a crossbow quarrel when he saw one.

The boom of black-powder weapons echoed through the ruins, shot through with the sharp crackle of a full-auto smokeless blaster. Another of the west-side attacker fell. This bunch looked more clean-cut and less grubby than the others. The others turned to race back toward the cover of the collapsed parking structure, some loosing quick shots toward the south, others just beating feet.

"Uh-oh," Ryan heard J.B. croak. "We got company."

Something buzzed between Ryan and Krysty to strike off the stub wall with a crack and a little spray of concrete grit. Both tracked the crossbow quarrel as it fell to the mounded dust and broken masonry.

Then both turned as one to look toward the gap in the south portion of the ring that led to the ruined walkway-curved building. A half-dozen men and women stood or knelt there, leveling crossbows and longblasters at them.

Jak already had his hands hoisted over his head. He was normally as bitter-end a fighter as any of them. But a skinny kid in a T-shirt and shorts had appeared right across the ring-wall from him and held the twin muzzles of a long black-powder scattergun a handspan away from Jak's pale right ear.

Ryan glanced at Krysty, who turned to stand by his side. She shrugged.

"Reckon you got the better of us," he called.

"Reckon we do," said a tall, lanky man with a fair complexion, a sort of narrow carrot head topped by a tangle of ginger hair. He wore loose khaki cargo pants and a green T-shirt, both too new-looking to be anything but salvage recently unwrapped from the original plastic. His voice was soft, and he looked a bit unhealthy to Ryan. But he carried the M-4 as if he knew which end the bullets came out of, and he showed no hesitancy in voice or posture.

Ryan dropped his panga beside him. "Do what you gotta do."

Men armed with crossbows disarmed the companions. Like their leader, they were dressed in crisp predark clothing that mostly fit them. One of the benefits of living in or near a nuked-out city was the ability to reap its bounty.

One of their captors, a burly young man with brown hair, scraped the housing of the Steyr's scope against the concrete wall.

"Careful with that, son," Ryan rasped. "That's delicate precision optics you're dealin' with, there."

"Show some respect, Lonny," the man with the M-4 said long-sufferingly.

"Aw, Tully," Lonny said. "They're just coldhearts."

"They were fighting coldhearts," Tully said. "So do we. That don't make us coldhearts."

"Indeed," Doc said. "So why not leave us our weapons and gear and let us go our merry way? We will not cause you a bit of fuss."

"Remains to be seen. Now if you like keeping your skins on you better get ready to hustle. Acid rain's coming. Smells like a bad one."

As if in response, raindrops pattered off the top of the wall and dug little craters in the gray dust. Ryan felt his facial muscles wince tightly in anticipation of the pain of an acid strike on exposed skin. But the drops that struck the hands held over his head and his cheek were just normal rain. Fat and somewhat greasy, but not corrosive.

Not yet. This was merely a little harmless foreplay.

"What about J.B.?" Mildred demanded. "We've got a wounded man. You don't propose we just leave him here to die?"

"No," Tully said. "But if he can't walk you'll have to carry him. Now get moving, or we'll leave you all to sizzle!"

"But he needs a stretcher!"

"Woman, do we look like we're carrying a stretcher

with us? Pick him up and carry him, or leave him, but get moving *right now*."

"Easy, lover," Krysty murmured. "He's right."

"Yeah." Ryan forced himself to unwind a notch as he unlinked his hands atop his head. When no one shouted or shot at him he hunkered down and grabbed J.B. by the shoulders. "Being ordered around by strangers goes straight up my back."

Krysty moved to Ryan's side to help. He didn't worry about her carrying her share of the load. She was a strong woman. He flashed a narrow-eyed look at Mildred.

"You gonna help or let us drag his feet through the rubble?" he asked.

Tears ran down Mildred's cheeks. "It might kill him, just carrying him like this for any distance!"

"You think the acid won't? Jak, help her get his legs. Hang on, J.B. This is gonna hurt."

"Don't be a stupe," J.B. croaked. "Just leave me." His eyes rolled up in his head and he passed out again.

"Not gonna happen," Ryan said. "Nobody gets left behind."

Shooting a final ruby glare at the captors to either side of him, Jak moved toward the wounded Armorer. Doc moved forward.

"Allow me, lad," Doc said, stooping beside Mildred. He grabbed one of J.B.'s boots and stood with his three companions.

"Now, as I heard it said—let's make tracks!"

Chapter Five

They traveled south. Tully led them out of the ruined building into the street, which was relatively unobstructed there. They made for the shelter of an intact section of overpass. It should protect them from the acid rain, if the wind didn't blow too hard.

The Armorer was a small man and not carrying any excess flesh. He was all bone and wiry muscle. Ryan was surprised by how heavy his friend actually was.

Their captors had shouldered the companions' packs. Ryan guessed that had more to do with preventing them from whipping out any nasty hidden surprises than a desire to lighten the loads of four people carrying their wounded friend.

He felt impacts on the back of his shirt and head. He heard a frying-egg sound and smelled a nasty stench like burning hair as the concentrated acid in the rain dissolved its proteins.

J.B.'s head hung between Ryan and Krysty. He moaned as an acid drop hit his cheek, clinging and burning like napalm.

"Run!" Ryan shouted. He didn't care what their captors had to say about it. If they decided their prisoners were making a break for it and chilled them, it was an easier death than acid.

But the dozen or so locals were concentrating on not getting dissolved themselves. Those who could held bits of clothing over their heads for cover, or yanked their shirts over their heads. The angry welts some of them sported on their backs showed they'd made this particular unpleasant choice before.

The four friends carrying J.B. were already straining. But as the rain began to sting like wasps they accelerated anyway. They were used to walking and even running long distances. But each of them, Ryan realized, had been holding back out of concern for jostling J.B.

Now that was forgotten. As always, the demands of survival overrode everything else. They ran flat out, and the rain hissed in the white-gray dust that lay on the frost-heaved asphalt beneath their feet.

Toughened as they were, their chests were working like bellows when the section of highway a hundred feet over their heads cut off the rain as if flipping a switch.

They staggered a few paces and then laid J.B. beside a thick concrete support pillar as near the middle of the span as possible. Then they collapsed around him, gasping like so many beached Sippi giant catfish.

Around them their captors took up a defensive perimeter. Some splashed water from canteens on their comrades to wash away acid. The rain pattered hard on the blacktop around them and the overhead pass. It raised a stinging stink that made Ryan's eye water.

A couple of blocks north the wounded scavvies who'd been left behind by their bugging-out pals were screaming. It was surprisingly loud at this distance. Or maybe, not so surprising.

Ryan tuned it out. He'd heard people dying in unspeakable agony before. It wasn't as if he liked those bastards melting alive out there.

Mildred was on her knees cradling J.B.'s head on her thigh. She was still a pro; though she stroked his wispy brown hair tenderly she didn't waste breath begging him to speak to her.

"How's he look?" Ryan asked, taking a pull from the canteen at his waist.

She shook her head. "Not good," she said. "But if he's got internal bleeding he's not showing any sign it's gotten worse from being jogged around like a bag of mail."

"Not bubbling out nose or mouth," said Jak, who squatted nearby, panting like the bipedal white wolf he resembled. "Good sign."

The skin went tight at the corners of Mildred's eyes and mouth. Then she forced herself to relax. "Yeah," she said. "Yeah, it is."

"So who are you?" Ryan said as the tall patrol leader approached. It suddenly struck him: what he'd taken for unhealthy pallor was clean skin. These folk were well-scrubbed by usual ville standards, even after however many hours on patrol.

"Aren't you getting things backward?" Tully said. "We got the blasters. Who the hell are *you?*"

Ryan shook his head. "Just folks passing through," he said with unfeigned weariness. "My name's Ryan. The woman here's Krysty. The other's our healer, Mildred. The sawed-off runt she's tending to's named J.B. Old guy's Doc and the teenager's Jak."

"Dr. Theophilus Algernon Tanner, at your service," Doc said. He managed to make his introduction sound grand despite the fact he was sitting on his bony old ass on an ancient weed-cracked highway. He gestured with his ebony walking stick. Ryan was startled to see their captors had allowed him to keep it, apparently presuming he needed it to walk. None of them seemed to have noticed the fact he'd stuck it through his belt to help carry J.B.

So we're not completely disarmed after all, Ryan

thought with a slight smile. *Not as if it does us any damn good.* The fact that only a few of the patrol carried modern blasters didn't fool him. A black-powder blaster would chill a person dead as any machine gun. And so would a crossbow bolt.

"Where'd you come from?" the tall ginger-haired man asked, putting his back to a support pillar and sliding to sit. "'Cross the river?"

Ryan shook his head. "North," he said. It was true, as far as it went. That was the easiest lie—true but for the bits it left out.

Tully raised a brow. "That's a triple-hard road, friend," he said. "Leads right through cannies and coldhearts swarming like angry wasps."

"We noticed," Mildred said.

"Now would you mind telling us who you are?" Ryan said.

"Shouldn't we make 'em stop talking, Tully?" a black kid with a single-shot black-powder longblaster asked. He looked to be no more than twelve and his eyes were saucer-large with excitement.

"Why'd we want to do a thing like that, McCoy?" the leader asked laconically.

"Well. Um." Evidently McCoy hadn't thought that far ahead. But he was game, and resourceful. "Mebbe they'll plot their escape."

"Why, then, you'll just shoot them dead with that big scary blaster of yours, won't you, McCoy?" Tully said. "Speaking of which, you did remember to reload that smokepole, right?"

The youngster puffed himself up. "O' course! What do you think I am?"

"A greenie on your first patrol outside the wire," Tully said. "You put a fresh cap on, too?"

"Well, don't be a— Oh. Um, wait." He fumbled at a pouch at his waist. "Wait one."

Turning his head so the kid wouldn't see him smile, the patrol leader turned back to Ryan. "To answer your question, we come from a ville called Soulard. A mile or so south of here, along the old highway. Peaceful place."

"Why did you kidnap us, then?" Krysty asked.

He smiled. "Looks to me like we rescued you."

"Looks to me like you captured us," Ryan said. "Saving us for the stewpot?"

"What, you think we're fuckin' cannies?" shouted the man who'd mishandled Ryan's longblaster earlier. He wore a T-shirt with even the brief arms torn off to reveal bulky biceps and triceps. Though he looked barely in his twenties, he was a big old slab of beef, with a blunt face fronted by a mashed tuber of a nose and a couple of brown eyes narrowed with angry suspicion. The sides and back of his head were shaved up to a clump of brown hair that stirred in the acid-tangy breeze.

"Ease off, Lonny," the ginger-haired man said coolly. "They got a right to be a bit testy. I would be, in their circumstances."

"But they run with a mutie!" He waved a hamhock of a hand toward Jak. "Look at him, white as clean snow and rat-red eyes!"

"I'm no mutie!" Jak shouted, spittle flying from his pale lips.

"He's an albino," Ryan said. "It's a natural condition, if a rare one. He's no mutie."

"Bullshit," Lonny said. Jak's red eyes flamed. He looked likely to spring for Lonny's throat, despite the huge disparity in size.

"Lonny!" The patrol leader didn't stir, but his voice cracked like a whip. "Back off. We need to talk to these people. Brother Joseph will figure out what to do with them."

Lonny spit in the pale grass that grew in the shade of the overpass. "Brother Joseph."

"Enough, Lonny. We don't need to be airing our dirty laundry in front of strangers, either."

But Jak's hot blood was up. "How we know they not cannies?"

"Lord, lad," Doc murmured. "Let it go."

"Look at them," Mildred said. "Ever see cannies look that healthy?"

Jak frowned. His white teeth made paler dimples in his lower lip. "No," he admitted after a moment.

"Me neither, now that she mentions it," Ryan said. "All right. Truce. We might as well go along with these people, even laying aside they got the drop on us. We already know this ain't a healthy vicinity to wander at random."

"No kidding," McCoy said. "You're triple-lucky you didn't stir up a pocket of serious rad-death emitters. That's worse than getting eaten by cannies, any day! The baron, he—"

"McCoy," Tully said sharply, but nowhere near as sharply as he'd spoken to the beefy Lonny. The black kid shut his mouth and swallowed hard. Tully looked back to Ryan.

"Let's just say you seem a bit too dangerous to allow to wander around freely kicking over hornets' nests. We have to live here."

"What if we tell you we don't mean you any harm or trouble?"

"I'd say evidence suggests otherwise. Least so far as trouble's concerned. And I can tell you plain, you'll have every chance to state your case once we get back safe to our ville. Which is far from certain yet, so less talking, please. None of us wants to draw more hassles."

"People want avoid trouble bad," Jak grumbled, indicating their captors with a nod of his head.

"If we tried a little harder to skip trouble," Krysty said, "*we* might be a whole lot happier."

"Only a droolie looks for more trouble than looks for him," Ryan replied.

"What does that make us?" Mildred asked.

"People a triple load of trouble looks for. Now shut it."

Mildred looked miffed, but she pressed her lips tight.

Tully slapped his hands on his lean thighs and stood. "That's clean rain falling now," he said. "We can move."

Ryan's nose had already told him that the lethal acid downpour had halted. The sound of drops falling on the asphalt-covered overpass and the cracked pavement beyond its shelter didn't change.

"Are you quite certain about that, young man?" Doc asked. "A return of the acid precipitation could quite spoil one's day, were one caught in the open."

Tully frowned at him a moment as if sorting out his words. Ryan got the impression the lanky man was no stupe. He just wasn't used to hearing that sort of talk.

Well, in the Deathlands, nobody was. It had taken Ryan some time to get used to Doc, too. And that was just in his lucid moments.

"That's how it goes here," Tully said. "Fresh rain always follows the acid. Dilutes it and washes it away. That's one reason the settled villes survive."

Ryan looked at Krysty. She had her limited doomie moments, but more important, she was better attuned to the natural elements than anybody Ryan had met. Whether it was her link to the Earth Mother, Gaia, or just a natural ability, he couldn't say.

She nodded. "I feel he's right." Then she flashed him that smile of hers that always made him realize how lucky he was. Even in situations as tight as this one.

"Best pick up your pal," Tully said. "We don't have to run anymore. But it's not healthy to hang around out here."

"Mildred?" Ryan said.

The physician was already kneeling over J.B. He was unconscious. Sweat sheened his forehead, more than what was due to the humidity.

"I don't like it," she said. "But it doesn't look like we've got much choice, do we?"

"No," Ryan said. "We don't. C'mon, people, let's get him up. We got places to go and people to meet."

Chapter Six

They continued south onto what looked like a largely intact highway that Mildred, who had spent some time in predark St. Louis, identified as Interstate 55, to make their way through a complicated tangle of broken concrete and twisted rail iron, fanged by nasty bent spikes of rust-red rebar. Evidently it was a collapsed bridge. A railroad-highway combo, by the looks.

No sooner were they past the collapsed ruins than Tully led the party down the brushy bank to the surface street that ran alongside the old highway. They jumped a little stream in the ditch at the bottom. Because there was just no way four people could cross it carrying the unconscious Armorer, and because the locals seemed uninclined to wade this soon after an acid downpour, Ryan draped J.B.'s limp form over his shoulders in a fireman's carry.

Everybody else hopped easily across. Burdened as he was Ryan didn't quite make it cleanly. The dirt gave way under his left foot. It slipped and went into the water to the ankle. Though he jumped clear as if J.B. suddenly weighed no more than dandelion fluff, Ryan felt a sting from the diluted acid in the little stream.

Krysty and Doc relieved Ryan of his burden. Tully tossed him a water bottle. "Best rinse that off before we go on," he said. "Just in case."

Ryan cocked a brow over his good eye. "Don't sweat it," Tully said. "We're not far from the ville. If we're not inside the perimeter inside half an hour, I likely won't be needing the water anyhow."

Ryan splashed water over his ankle and boot. It probably didn't do much good. It made him feel better, though. He tossed the bottle back to the patrol leader, who caught it with a grin.

"Why not use highway?" Jak asked as they started moving west between a stand of woods along the partially elevated, partially fallen-in right of way.

"Too exposed," Tully said. "Sometimes we get snipers in the rubble."

"And there's stickies, in those drowned warehouses and factories other side of the Interstate," another man said.

"Highway does get used by people passing through, Randall," Tully said. "Long-range traders and such."

"Things travel that road no human should meet or get to know anything about," a black-haired man with drawn gray-stubbled cheeks said.

"That's only by night," Tully said. "Anyway it's all superstition. Probably."

"I hear the screams, Tully. Can't hardly sleep none, sometimes."

"That's just stickies roasting rivermen or scavvies they caught," Randall said.

The companions found themselves toting the unconscious J.B. along a wide street. The rain, having seemingly washed away the remnants of the toxic rain, had stopped quickly. The air smelled fresh. Overhead the clouds had taken on the colors of an old bruise, gray and green and brown, an improvement over the tortured, boiling orange of not so many minutes before.

They passed beneath standing bridges where a railroad line swung in from the northwest to join a highway that crossed their route. A little farther south the highway they paralleled swung off west. Walking under an intact underpass, their captors went on triple alert. The guy who didn't sleep so well jumped when a pigeon boomed out from high up the embankment near the overhead and flapped out into the milky sunlight. His buddies laughed at him.

When the group emerged, the clouds were breaking up. Ryan blinked his good eye at the sight. As hot as it was, without clouds to filter the sun the day would only get hotter. And J.B. wasn't getting any lighter.

"How are you holding up?" he asked the others.

"Don't worry about us," Krysty said. "We'll do what we have to do."

He ginned at her. "Like always."

"Not much farther to go, anyway," Tully said. "We'll see about getting you some wheels for your friend when we reach the gates. We got people who can tend to him. Ace healer name of Strode."

Lonny muttered something about mollycoddling no-account outlanders. His leader ignored him. Though Tully acted like a good guy—and Ryan knew too well it could all *be* an act—and seemed to have his shit pretty much in one sock as a leader, he also seemed to allow the bulky brown-haired man an unusual amount of slack. There had to be some link here Ryan didn't see.

No way to scope it now, nor to know if the fact, if fact it was, had any use to him and his friends in their current predicament. Ryan filed it away and let it go.

Ryan saw Mildred's shoulders and upper back tense. She was a physician, a fully qualified preskydark doctor who tended to think not too much of what passed for doctors these days. Truth be told, she had met several healers whom she had to admit were truly gifted.

But whether it was more prudence than the freezie woman usually showed, or simple fatigue, she didn't make a point of the fact *she* could tend to J.B. as well as any and better than most. Besides which, if Soulard were the relatively large and prosperous ville a twelve-man patrol wearing reasonably clean outfits suggested, they probably had medical facilities better than the Deathlands standard.

Tully led them down the center of the wide street. His troops stayed crisply alert. Here, anyway, they seemed to be more worried about jump-out-from-cover attacks than coming under long-range aimed fire. More and more of the structures they passed were intact, which shortened potential fields of fire and favored blitz-style ambush.

"Wonder why these littler buildings held up so much better than the skyscrapers," Mildred said. Ryan was mildly surprised she had breath to talk.

It was more of a surprise when Doc answered; even after all their association Ryan had a tendency to underestimate his physical hardiness.

"Smaller surface areas," he said. "Being more compact, they proved more resistant to the blasts. The bigger buildings provided greater surfaces for the shock waves to push against."

As they marched through the ruins between increasingly intact-appearing structures, in the growing sunlight Ryan realized the black kid, McCoy, was no longer with them. None of the others looked concerned—about the youth's absence, anyway. Even here in what they evidently considered potentially hostile ground nobody seemed to assume he'd been snatched by someone. Or even wandered away into danger.

So Tully sent him ahead to spread the word they were coming, Ryan thought. He'd probably use some secret bolthole. Mebbe even one only a kid knew about, or could even get through. The patrol leader had to have spoken quietly to the kid when Ryan wasn't looking, or even flashed him an arranged signal. Or, hell, for all he knew it was standard operating procedure.

They were working in a dangerous information vacuum here. The bitch was, even though their escorts were proving neither hostile nor closemouthed—except mebbe the lout, Lonny—they didn't seem inclined to small talk right now. Ryan wasn't about to distract them, if they thought there was something here to look out for.

And anyway, he wasn't sure himself where Mildred and Doc found the energy for chitchat. He sure didn't have much to spare, right now.

"Biggest danger here is stickies," Randall said. "They infest the flooded warehouses and like to hunt up here from time to time. Plus sometimes scavvies think they can snag an easy score this close to a ville."

"There's also people from Breweryville," said Dowd, the haunted-looking dude who couldn't sleep. "They might attack us if they come upon us."

"Oh, crap," Randall said. "They can be dicks. But they're not coldhearts."

"Brother Joseph says they lack a true sense of community."

"Look alive, guys," Tully said hastily. "We don't want to get too caught up talking and wind up crawling with stickies."

That drove a shudder through everybody, companions and captors alike. There were numerous varieties of the needle-toothed mutants with the sucker pads on their hands and feet that could strip skin from meat and meat from bone. Most of them shared a love for human flesh, cruelty and fire, not necessarily in that order. Despite their pyrophilia they often colonized near bodies of water, and seemed to take to the water well.

Ryan couldn't help noticing that the patrol leader had

once again steered talk clear of the subject of Brother Joseph. Whomever he may be.

They came to a corner where a wire fence stretched down the street ahead of them and down the street west, backed by dense thorny hedges and topped with coils of razor wire that gleamed in the sun despite being pitted and stained by the acid rains.

"Soulardville," Tully said with evident pride.

"Didn't that used to be the farmers' market?" Mildred asked. "Those long shedlike roofs inside the perimeter?"

"Uh-huh," the patrol leader said, nodding his ginger head. "It's a farming-and-gardening center now. Our market's more centrally located."

"What'd you say your ville's name was again?" Ryan asked.

"Soulard," Tully said.

Doc perked up. "'Soulard,'" he said. "Why, bless my soul, but unless I misremember, that means 'drunkard' in French."

Tully shrugged. "Mebbe so, some time past. Sure not now."

"Bro Joe don't allow drunkenness," Dowd said gloomily. Perhaps he felt he'd sleep better for a good load on.

"Bro Joe?" Ryan asked.

"It's still the baron who rules in Soulardville!" Lonny bellowed. Ryan thought he was going way too red for Dowd's remark. Lonny turned an angry glare on Doc.

"What d'you mean by that, anyway, oldie?" he yelled.

"Back off the trigger there, fella," Ryan said.

"Why, nothing, my boy," Doc said. Though his forehead shone with sweat, he didn't seem to be flagging under his burden. "Nothing at all. Just passing the time of this lovely day."

Lonny gave him a narrow, suspicious glare. "You okay

there, old-timer?" Tully asked. "You want mebbe to get the white-haired kid to swap with you?"

"Not at all, young man, thank you kindly. I have resources unlooked-for."

They continued south along the fence. Ryan watched his people closely. There was nothing they could do for J.B. right now but shade his face with his hat, which they had. He was concerned about how the other three were holding up. Krysty's sentient hair hung limp over her shoulders, a sure sign fatigue was getting the better of her. Mildred would, from time to time, start to slump, then straighten. Usually at such times she glanced back at the unconscious Armorer suspended among them. It was as if she renewed her strength, or at least resolve, by reminding herself J.B.'s health and very survival lay very much in question, and depended on her ability to keep on keeping on.

Ryan also monitored Jak. The teen was volatile and obviously smoldering at the fact they'd been taken captive. He wasn't tracking too closely that their captors could've treated them far worse. In fact, under the circumstances, they could hardly have treated them better. Of course that could change at any instant; Ryan knew that as well as Jak did.

He just didn't want Jak flying off and *making* the locals treat them more harshly.

Visibility through the hedge-covered fence wasn't good. Ryan suspected that was part of the shrubs' purpose. Glimpses through gaps suggested that south of the garden sheds lay a cultivated field, a block north to south and at least three blocks east-west. Then the perimeter turned mostly to the fronts of what seemed to have been houses and small businesses, their doors and ground-floor windows bricked up. Razor-wire coils spiraled along rooflines. The streets between were blocked off by piles of big rubble chunks as well as the fence.

"That's a pretty fine defensive perimeter," Ryan said. Talking was hard, but it took his mind off the ache in his shoulders and lower back from lugging J.B.'s deadweight.

Tully chuckled. "Have to be triple-stupe not to be able to fortify out of the bones and guts of a dead city."

"That's true."

They passed a still-intact church whose white spire showed flaking remains of paint bubbling from the nuke strike's thermal flash on its north side. East of the street lay a wide expanse of grass, green but yellow-spotted from the acid rains. Farther along stood more ruins.

From just ahead came a shout. Square three-story-tall towers made of different colored bricks flanked a wide street leading into the ville. The black snouts of long-blasters poked out from underneath peaked roofs. A couple were trained right on Ryan and his little party.

"Almost over, people," Tully told Ryan and his friends. "We're at the gates."

Chapter Seven

The Soulardville gate was a stout, barred construction, topped with the ubiquitous razor-wire coils. It ran on a metal-lined track cut into the asphalt of the street.

The gate opened with a squeal of bearings as runners ran down the track. Inside waited a quartet of men in armless black jerseys holding longblasters. Long wooden truncheons hung from their belts. Sec men, Ryan thought.

The patrol headed inside. Big trees shaded the gate area, and Ryan was grateful for that.

As their escorts spread out around them, calling greetings to bystanders, the one-eyed man took stock of their surroundings. The church to the right of the gate seemed to have been taken over as a sec-man headquarters, or at least station. To the left lay an open area, with tables under canopies: a market or trading station, mildly busy today, with men unloading goods to a table from a light wooden land wag while others admired heaps of produce.

McCoy approached them, leading a stocky woman wearing overalls, with a gray braid wound around her head. Right behind came a wooden cart with steel-tired wood wheels. As the sec men covered the captives with their blasters, the woman bustled up.

"I'm Strode, the ville healer," she said. "We'll take over from here."

The bevy of assistants who had pushed the cart trotted

around to ease J.B.'s limp form away from Ryan and his friends. Predictably, Mildred bridled.

"What do you think you're doing?" she asked. Her voice rasped from dryness in her throat; she hadn't been following her own advice about keeping hydrated while carrying her wounded lover.

The Armorer had already been laid on a pad on the bed of the cart. Strode leaned over him. "Hmm," she said. "Competent job of field dressing."

"'Competent'!"

Strode looked up directly at the twentieth-century physician. "You did well by your friend, given the circumstances," she said firmly. "We have him now. We've got a clean infirmary and scavenged meds as well as herbs."

"Herbs!" Mildred sounded as outraged as if the gray-haired, red-faced woman had suggested using *vodoun*.

For a moment electricity seemed to crackle between the two female healers. Strode fixed Mildred with a piercing blue gaze. Mildred tensed as if about to go for the older woman's throat.

Krysty laid a hand on the other woman's shoulder. "Mildred," she said gently, "let it go. We're not completely ignorant savages. This woman obviously knows what she's doing."

Mildred set her strong jaw rebelliously. A pair of sec men stepped up to bar her way as Strode gestured. The acolytes set off both pulling and pushing the cart at a trot down the broad street that led into the fortified ville. The healer walked alongside at a brisk pace.

Tears welled in Mildred's eyes then coursed down her cheeks.

They were still hemmed in by a combination of their original captors and sec men, who weren't exactly wearing uniforms but all seemed to wear mostly black. Some of the men were relieving the patrol of their weapons and toting them into the old church. The patrol members surrendered their blasters and crossbows without protest.

Interesting, Ryan thought.

Krysty met his eye over Mildred's shoulder, gave him a quick smile and nod to show she was doing fine. He doubted that. But it was part of the reason he loved her: her fortitude and courage were the equal of any man's he'd known. She'd keep going and do what needed to be done until her strength failed her. Her heart never would.

A pair of sec men pointed their blasters—an M-16 and a Remington pump scattergun—at Ryan as he reached to his belt. With a sardonic smile on his chapped lips, he saluted them with his canteen, then took a long drink. The water was hot and brackish but refreshed him.

Doc had plopped himself down on his butt on the blacktop in the shade of a sycamore and sat with his knees wide apart and his sword stick beside him. Jak squatted beside him and panted like a wolf. Their captors had relieved him of the throwing knives with which he festooned himself, but Ryan would've bet his last swig of water the albino youth had a couple holdouts hidden on him. Again, it wasn't likely to help much, especially with J.B. trundled off to his friends had no idea where, but completely in the power of their captors. Even if they could break out, they weren't going to do so without the Armorer.

"We don't want to rush into anything anyway," Krysty said to him. Ryan jerked slightly. As often the case, the full-bodied redhead seemed to be reading his mind. "We don't know what's here."

"They could have treated us far worse, to be sure," Doc said, taking a swig from his own canteen and wiping his mouth with the back of his hand.

"Yeah," Ryan said. "Let's hope it stays that way."

Patrol leader Tully, now disarmed, stood to one side talking with a man a finger shorter than his own gangly height. The man wore a black vest open over a bare chest deep-tanned as leather, beneath a thick pelt of red-brown hair, black jeans over black boots, a gunbelt with a Ruger Security Six .357 Magnum in good condition at his left hip. He had a long deeply seamed face as tan as his chest, with a well-broken nose. Close-clipped reddish-brown hair was in full retreat from a freckled forehead. Mild-seeming brown eyes looked out from beneath eyebrows like smears of black paint. He wasn't so much wider than Tully, as he just seemed more solid.

A chiller for true, Ryan thought.

Tully walked over with the black-clad man beside him. "This is Garrison," he told Ryan. "He's sec chief for Soulardville."

Neither party to the introduction offered to shake hands. "Get your people together and follow me," Garrison said.

His voice was quiet but not soft. Neither his tone nor the sec boss's posture threatened. Ryan sized the man up as the kind who wouldn't bother with threats. Seen up close, he looked as unyielding and hard as a cypress knee.

Ryan nodded. No point butting heads when he'd only lose. "Let's go," he told the others.

"Where?" Jak asked. He showed no sign of standing.

"Where I take you," Garrison said. His tone remained matter-of-fact. The look he gave the albino youth was another matter altogether.

One time during his road-dog days with Trader, Ryan had seen an Ozark mule skinner give a chronically balky mule that look. The next time the mule acted up the skinner had shot it dead in its harness with a big old black-powder horse blaster he worse crosswise in his belt.

"Jak," Krysty called, "come give me a hand with Mildred, please. She's had a hard time of it."

Mildred had already reclaimed her composure. She was painfully aware of her relatively coddled and sheltered upbringing. Never mind her father had been murdered by the Klan when she was a child. Compared to people Deathlands born and raised she'd spent her life before her cryogenic suspension on Easy Street. She hated to show weakness to her friends. She frowned and started to say something.

Krysty held up a hand. "Save your breath," she said. "Let Jak help you."

The albino teen had got up and hurried to Mildred's side. Her eyes widened as she realized what the redhead was actually doing. Jak had followed her suggestion without the thought entering his head that she had given him an out from a no-win confrontation with the Soulardville sec boss without loss of face.

The look on the sec boss's sunburned face never wavered from...*composed,* Ryan reckoned the word was. But Ryan thought he'd caught just the slightest flicker of recognition in those dark eyes. Garrison looked to be shrewdly perceptive as well as in total command of himself and his surroundings. That made him triple-dangerous.

They set off down the street at an easy walk. A quartet of sec men flanked and followed them. Garrison let Ryan walk shoulder-to-shoulder with him without comment.

And that was the upside of dealing with a man like the sec boss. Ryan knew what he was. He knew at a glance what Ryan was. They understood each other perfectly with no need to jaw.

Houses lined the street, mostly in brown or maroon or yellow-tan brick, neat beneath pitched roofs with scrolled wooden eaves. Raised-bed gardens had replaced long-dead lawns, and interspersed with the houses were garden plots growing a profusion of vegetables and herbs: tomatoes and beans climbing up frames, onions, carrots, lettuce just sprouting. Down one block to the south Ryan caught a glimpse of an orchard of trees just beginning to fruit out. Big trees dropped pools of shadow at irregular intervals on the asphalt.

"My word," Doc breathed. "It looks as if war has never brushed this place with its wings."

"Does if you'd seen it before," Mildred said. "This is Russell Boulevard. Used to be a lot more buildings along here. Those gardens used to be houses."

"It's so green," Krysty said. "It's like a drink of water after the ruins."

"Too neat," Jak said. "Too crowded."

And in fact a fair number of people went about their business. Some carried crates or big ceramic jugs, or pushed loaded handcarts. Others walked briskly as if to appointments. Children played on stoops. Chickens scratched in front yards and cultivated patches. Pigeons cooed and bubbled from the eaves.

"We been building this place up for a hundred years," Garrison said with a note of pride in his voice.

"You've done well," Krysty said.

Ryan was reserving judgment. Krysty sometimes teased him he couldn't sniff a flower without suspecting there was a bee waiting inside to sting his nose. He reckoned that was about right.

He also saw no reason to change.

And speaking of flowers, they were there, too, purple and blue and yellow heads nodding from beds below windows and stout ceramic planters on porches. This place was easily as prosperous as Front Royal, where he'd grown up.

"Barely an hour ago the acid rain was falling fit to

bubble the skin straight off a man's face," he said. He gestured around with a hard hand. "How'd all this come through looking so pretty?"

"Special-treated tarps and cloths," Garrison said. "Special frames set out. The trees're pretty resistant. We usually get plenty of warning when a hellstorm's brewing."

"What happens when you don't?"

Garrison chuckled. "Ever know a man to leave this world alive?"

For a moment Ryan looked at him as they walked. Then he barked a short laugh. "No."

The street turned to what had been a commercial district. War's legacy was much more visible here. While many houses had intact windows, the big commercial picture windows had been blown in and were covered with plywood sheets or planking. From neatly lettered signs above the doors Ryan gathered they were now small stores and workshops. He heard the tink-tink of a hammer on metal from one door left open to allow the sultry breeze admittance.

The street widened out. "Lot of buildings here've been demolished," Mildred murmured. "If I remember right, anyway."

For her, Ryan knew, the memory was just a few years old. But sometimes she still had trouble coping with the brutal contrast between the world she'd gone to sleep in and the nightmare she'd awakened to.

Whatever had been before there was a wide square here now. Ryan saw that the extant pavement had been eked out with paths of crushed gravel, and mosaics of jagged, salvaged concrete slabs. It was handsome work, he had to admit.

In the center of the plaza stood a low platform made of one big concrete slab laid with little regard for leveling:

no finesse. It looked quite brutal by contrast to the almost unnatural primness of what they'd seen of the rest of the ville. A weather-stained tarp covered the slanted upper surface.

Garrison said nothing about the slab. Ryan didn't ask for an explanation. It didn't seem to bear on their continued survival one way or another.

Beyond it stood a sprawling two-story-tall block of pink brick, with a gabled slate roof and a brick chimney. It had a gaudily painted wooden entryway stuck onto the front, obviously a postdark addition. The garish gold and purple paint clashed with the ville's overall reserve as harshly as the strange slab dais in the middle of the town square.

"Baron's palace," Garrison said.

"Never would have guessed," Ryan commented.

Garrison led them down a side street to a gray brick house just behind the "palace." It was unremarkable except for black iron bars on the windows. Garrison unlocked an iron-and-mesh sec door and opened it. The barred door had a steel flap in the bottom section. A closed wooden door was inside.

"In here," he said.

"How long?" Ryan asked.

"Till you're sent for."

Ryan turned the knob. The inner door was one of the old flimsy predark plywood-sandwich variety that kept the wind and some of the cold out but a sturdy child could put her fist through. Of course with the outer door that didn't much matter.

Inside was gloomy, musty and hot. Dust motes floated in the light through the open door. Some lumpy-looking pallets had been tossed around the wooden floor.

"How about food and water?" he asked Garrison. "We haven't eaten all day."

"You'll be provided for," Garrison said.

Ryan went in, followed by the others. "You got the run of the place," Garrison said, closing and locking the outer door. "You might want to open the windows. Get some air."

"Yeah," Ryan said.

"What now?" Mildred asked when the sec boss went away.

"The usual. Scope out the house. See if there's any way out."

"Think there will be?" Krysty asked.

"Hell no. But we take nothing for granted."

They searched the house, quickly but cautiously. They weren't going to take for granted there weren't hidden dangers, either. Given the sort of things that wandered around a ruined city there might even be unpleasant surprises their hosts knew nothing about.

But the place was as empty as an old skull.

As they finished their quick but thorough recon, somebody rattled the sec door. They went down to find several locals carrying several gallon ceramic jugs as well as several large covered pots. Under the longblasters of a pair of hawk-eyed sec men they unlocked the outer door and passed in the jugs and jars.

"Water," Jak said, uncapping a jug and sniffing.

"But these are empty," Mildred said. She held up the lid of one of the squat pots as if to prove her point.

Ryan just looked at her. "Oh," she said, and replaced the lid with exaggerated care.

"So what now?" Doc asked.

"We wait."

"I'm worried about J.B.," Mildred said.

"Me, too," Ryan said. "But there's nothing we can do about it now. I'm going to sleep."

He stretched himself on a lumpy canvas mattress.

A CLATTERING WOKE HIM. Burly Lonny stood outside, kicking the door with a boot. He held a large covered blue metal dish.

"They sent me with some vegetable stew for you," he said. He set the dish on the porch, then shoved a bag through the flap-covered metal hatch in the bottom. Krysty retrieved it, opened it.

"Bowls and spoons," she said.

"Wood spoons," Mildred said, sitting up and blinking muzzily. "So we don't dig our way out, I guess. They're right on top of things, these folks."

Lonny had stood up, still holding the dish. He had a strange and ominous look in his eyes.

"You're gonna hunt her," he said. "They'll offer you supplies and jack, and you'll take it. Because you're just coldhearts who'll do anything for pay. I know your type!"

"Hold on," Ryan said, standing up. "Back up a couple steps. You lost me."

"The princess!" Lonny snapped. "You don't care about her. What they'll do to her. Your kind don't care!"

He snorted a deep breath through his lump of nose, drawing his head back on his thick neck. Opening the lid of the food dish he hawked and spit a big glistening green glob into the stew. Replacing the lid, he rocked the dish from side to side, to stir the mix up right. Then he bent down and shoved the dish through the hatch.

"There you go, coldhearts," he said. He turned and marched off.

"What that about?" Jak asked.

Ryan shook his head. "Slagger's a few rounds short of a full mag."

He picked up a chipped bowl and a wood spoon from

where Krysty had laid them out on the floor, went to the dish. Opening the cover, he spooned himself a bowl of stew.

Mildred gagged. "You aren't seriously going to eat that?"

Ryan sat down cross-legged on the floor with his back to the wall, facing the door.

"Had worse," he said, and dug in.

Chapter Eight

From the heaviness of the fist banging on the steel outer door Ryan knew who he'd see when he opened his eye.

"Garrison," he said, sitting up. His body felt as if mules had been playing kickball with it.

Around him the others roused themselves from sleep. Outside the shadows were lengthening toward afternoon. The light had gone mellow, softening the edges of things.

"Baron wants to see you," Garrison said.

BARON SAVIJ WASN'T what any of them expected.

His room made up pretty much a big chunk of the upper story of the baronial palace. The chamber was decorated lavishly. And also in what, even by Deathlands standard, was pretty dubious taste.

The chamber was festooned with swatches and banners of purple and gold silk. Giant velvet paintings, of bare-breasted women, Elvis the King, African warriors and, in close-up, a snarling tiger's face, hung from every wall. Candles and lanterns burned everywhere, hanging by chains from golden lamp-stands, on gold-painted stands by the walls, from a candelabrum overhead. Dominating all was a vast bed canopied in purple and gold and green satin, and hanging behind it, a giant tapestry—evidently also predark, since the figures were too precise and the colors too bright even after decades for handwork—of a black man with a ferocious Afro. He wore an abundance of gold jewelry and strode defiantly with an electric guitar in one hand and a panga not unlike Ryan's in the other, at the head of a retinue that consisted primarily of scowling, hypermuscular thugs with shaved heads, and beautiful women.

The curtains of the big bed were parted to reveal the baron, lying with his head propped on a green satin pillow.

He had been a big man. That was obvious from his frame beneath the purple satin coverlet. From the way his sallow, mottled cheeks had fallen in it was clear he'd suffered catastrophic weight loss. He turned his hairless head right to face the newcomers and blinked gum-encrusted eyes at them.

The room stank of incense and stale piss and shit. It even made Ryan's titanium-steel stomach restless.

A young woman in a green smock dabbed at the baron's eyes with a cloth soaked in some sort of a solution. He waved her away feebly.

"Let me see these people," he said in a slow, cracked voice.

Garrison and Strode had escorted the companions to see the baron of Soulardville. He blinked at them slowly. Though his complexion was mottled with greenish and yellowish bruiselike marks, Ryan guessed he had been a medium dark-skinned black man. His eyes were a dark blue, which would probably have been startlingly intense had they not been clouded and dimmed by his condition.

"You look…strong," Baron Savij said. "Reckon…you'll do."

Ryan just stared. Krysty said hastily, "Do for what, Baron?"

"I want my baby back," he said. A tear rolled down his right cheek to make a dark stain on the pillow. He stretched a clawed, discolored hand toward them. "Bring her to me. *Please.*"

His eyelids fell shut, his arm dropped like a dead bird. His hand dangled off the edge of the bed, palm up. The female attendant hastened to ease it back onto the coverlet beside him.

"He dead?" Jak asked. The words were horribly loud in the sudden deep silence.

Krysty shushed him fiercely. "What I say?" he protested. Doc took him gently by the arm and led him aside.

"You'd better go now," Strode said. She looked no more than usually concerned for the health of her prize patient.

"Is he?" Ryan asked as she led them toward the stairs.

"Is he what?" the healer asked a bit impatiently.

"Dead."

"No. Just exhausted." She seemed minded to say more. Instead she flicked her eyes toward the sec boss, who stood gazing down at his baron with a thoughtful frown rumpling his face.

They started down heavy stairs of dark-stained wood. "Rad sickness?" Mildred asked quietly. The ville healer had assured her J.B. was resting well and she and the others would get to see him once the bosses were finished with them. Mildred seemed to have accepted the healer's competence. She still was obviously none too pleased with their situation. But then, who was?

Lips pressed together, Strode nodded briskly. "Apparently he broke open a hidden rad pit while leading an expedition into ruins to the northwest of here. He took a substantial dose. Probably ingested some."

"Lethal dose?" Mildred asked.

"Only time will tell. At this point some random disease could swoop in and carry him off opportunistically.

Pneumonia's a real threat. Even with scavenged antibiotics, there's a limited amount we can do."

"Rad death," Jak said softly, and shivered. Not much scared Jak. But death by radiation exposure would frighten the balls off a brass statue.

"Hard way to go," Ryan said.

"Know any good ones?" Garrison asked.

Ryan shrugged. "Easier ones and quicker ones, sure."

"Wait," Mildred said, stopping dead halfway down the steps. "I know the man in that tapestry. That's Savij!"

"The first Baron Savij, yes," Strode said. "He founded Soulardville in the days just after the bombs quit falling. He and his posse showed up one day armed to the teeth and took over."

"I knew him," Mildred said. "Knew *of* him, anyway. He was a famous gangster rapper. Unlike a lot of them he was the real deal. Authentic street thug, been shot half a dozen times, suspected in a dozen murders but somehow never convicted. Supposedly kept his posse supplied with cocaine, hookers, illegal automatic weapons, explosives and rocket launchers."

"Sounds like our founder," Strode said.

Frowning, Mildred shook her head. "I remember reading once that Soulard was a totally white-bread little suburb. How would a bad-ass black man like Savij take over a place like that?"

Garrison chuckled like gravel shaken in a gallon can. "Who was gonna stop him?"

They came out onto the ground floor. A young woman was lighting kerosene lanterns against evening's impending arrival.

Two men stood on a dark brick floor near the landing. One was tall, erect in bearing, lean with just a hint of pot belly pushing out the front of a T-shirt tie-dyed in a red and orange and yellow sunburst, over which he wore an open sky-blue shirt. Sun-faded jeans and sandals completed the ensemble. He wore a three-lobed golden pendant, each lobe of which was engraved with a spiral.

Late-sun glow from the street gilded a round cheek and a head of neat dreadlocks just long enough to tie into a queue at the back of his neck. He was a middle-aged, relatively light-skinned black man with laughing eyes and a trim salt-and-pepper beard.

The shorter man was a little skinny white guy dressed in a red, green, black and gold T-shirt bearing an image of the original Savij. It had to be relatively recent scavenge by simple virtue of the fact it was intact. It was, however, filthy; Ryan, accustomed to the smells of himself and his friends after days of wandering in wilderness and ruin, felt a bit of a twinge at the sheer intensity of his body funk. He had a ratlike face, much of which was concealed, probably for the better, by big dark glasses. His hair hung over the shoulders of his shirt in tangled dreadlocks, so greasy they not only made it impossible to tell what color they might originally have been, but also actually left obvious stains when they brushed the already grimy fabric.

"I'm Brother Joseph," the tall man said in a rich baritone voice that flowed like honey. "This is my associate, Booker.

"I am the spiritual guide of this community of seekers," Joseph said. "I'm pleased to meet you all at last. I've heard a great deal about you."

"What would that be, Brother?" Krysty asked, putting some sugar in her voice. Men tended not to get suspicious when a question came out in that kind of tone from that kind of face and body. Krysty had a great many assets—mental, spiritual and physical—and she wasn't shy about using any of them to help her friends survive.

In this case, Ryan knew, it could be important to know whether their reputations had preceded them. It happened. If they had, it might give them leverage they wouldn't otherwise have. Conversely, if the saga of One-Eye Chills and his merry band *wasn't* known here in the rotted-out corpse of St. Lou, it might just mean potential enemies could underestimate them. And whatever the sentiment of the ville as a whole, they had enemies here: burly Lonny's bizarre behavior with their food demonstrated that.

"Why, your running battle and heroic last stand in the ruins of downtown," Joseph said. "You would be Krysty, would you not? Our patrol's reports scarcely do your beauty justice. Nor your obvious intelligence. And you, Mildred—"

He turned the considerable candlepower of his smile on Mildred. "Our own healer gives high marks to your field treatment of your wounded comrade. Had you not taken the actions you did, promptly and efficiently, we would not have had the opportunity to save his life."

"Hmm," Mildred said. But she didn't seem quite so full of piss and vinegar as she had a moment before.

"And you are Jak, the valiant youth," he said, turning and nodding. "And you, sir—Doc. I'm afraid our people made rather heavy weather of your full name."

"Dr. Theophilus Algernon Tanner, sir, at your service."

"An honor to meet you, Doctor. You are clearly a man of education. And last, the hero-figure, the leader-from-the-wilderness. Ryan. You must be a most remarkable man."

For once Ryan felt at a loss for words. He felt Krysty sidle against him and take his arm. "He is," she said.

Brother Joseph beamed more brightly. "Indeed! You are all remarkable men and women. Every man and woman is a star, the oracle tells us. But now you'll want to pay a visit to your fallen comrade. I trust you'll forgive me this brief delay. After an afternoon of praying and meditating over what your advent might mean to this ville, I found myself dying to meet you. You'll join us in an hour for supper, I hope?"

"Sure," Ryan said. That was an easy call, anyway. A free feed was a free feed. Neither the vegetable stew nor Lonny's loogie had been enough to do more than dull the edge of hunger long-honed by privation.

"Splendid. Come, Booker. We've business of our own to attend to."

"MILDRED," the man on the bed said in a rough-edged whisper. "Sorry. I let you down. Everybody…down. I… fucked…up."

Now wholly Mildred, and not even the least little bit the briskly professional Dr. Wyeth, the sturdily built black woman clutched his hand in both of hers. "Honey, no. Don't talk that way. It wasn't your fault."

"Bullet flies where it will, J.B.," Ryan said. "You of all people should know that."

The Armorer's eyes were closed. His cheeks were yellowed and sunken. He looked awful, for a fact. Though not a sensitive man, Ryan was too attuned to the realities of morale to point out the fact, even in any sort of fun. Fact was, his own heart ached to see his friend and battle brother reduced to this condition.

"Mildred's right," he said. "Don't fret yourself on nonsense. Rest. Get better."

"What he's trying to say, in his manly, near-inarticulate way," Krysty said, moving to the other side of the sickbed, "is that we need you, J.B. Rest well. Come back to us soon."

Although no breath of air blew through the open windows of the neat, almost dazzlingly clean infirmary, in a former storefront across the big plaza from the palace, her sentient hair stirred around her shoulders as if in a slight breeze. It showed the agitation of her own spirit.

"Heh," the Armorer croaked in what seemed to be an attempt at laughter. "Mebbe I'm chilled already and all them stories about heaven weren't the lies I thought they was. I'm surrounded by angels…"

He sighed and relaxed. Ryan's hard heart skipped a beat before sense took over and he realized his friend had simply passed into sleep, not caught the last train west.

Strode made a sound in her throat. "Strange as it seems I think that last remark was probably a favorable sign," she said. "Making a joke shows he's keeping his spirit up. That's important to healing."

"I know," Mildred said. "Back in my day—when I was studying the healing arts, I mean—some people claimed it was all a myth that your feelings could affect your physical health. But most of the people I knew who actually did healing knew better. And so do I."

"Whitecoats," the stocky woman with the gray braid said, shaking her head. She wore an old-fashioned stethoscope around her bull neck. "They know so much about facts and figures and so little about what matters, where people are concerned."

"How you know whitecoats?" Jak asked suspiciously. He was always suspicious. Mention of scientists tended to make him more so.

"We have some of our own," she said. "I have to admit, they're helping us to make new medicines from herbs and plants. And of course Breweryville is full of whitecoats. The brewmeister fancies he's a scientist himself."

"Brewmeister?" Doc asked.

Strode shrugged. "Their baron."

"You don't sound too fond of him."

"Well, he's not lovable. I'm not as down on the ville itself as…some of our people here. I wouldn't want to live there myself, that's certain sure, even though they're richer than we are."

A look passed among the companions. Compared to what they were accustomed to—their whole lives, in Ryan's and Jak's and Krysty's cases, not just their last few years of wandering the wastelands—Soulardville was all but unimaginably prosperous and peaceful. And clean. Ryan was actually becoming aware of his own stink through the carbolic-acid smell of Strode's domain, and the way his unwashed clothes chafed, the way every fold and crevice of his lean hard-muscled body itched. He realized he'd begun scratching his ribs unconsciously.

Mildred had stepped to Strode's side and was discussing J.B.'s treatment. All traces of rivalry or suspicion between the two women had disappeared like a pinch of dust thrown to the wind. Each recognized in the other a true professional in her field. Now they talked shop.

"—antibiotic powder in the wound," Strode was saying.

Mildred's eyebrows rose. "Your whitecoats make you antibiotics?"

"Not yet," Strode said. "Brewmeister claims his have cultured and refined penicillin. Mebbe so. They got all kind of fancy gear down there, from the days they really were a brewery, back before the big cull. Claim they reworked some of it to make antibiotic. Me, I don't trust 'em that far yet. This stuff's scavenge. Old as it is, it still retains some potency. It's better than nothing."

Mildred nodded.

"So, what's the deal with this Brother Joseph?" Ryan asked the ville healer.

Her face shut down. "He served the current Baron

Savij the last five, six years as a combination guru and right-hand man," she said. "Now that the baron's incapacitated and his daughter's…missing, he's stepped up to run things."

She didn't sound too happy about that. From her body language Ryan guessed that fact wasn't anything she wanted noised around. Fine with him; she was taking good care of the Armorer, so he didn't want anybody jogging her elbow.

"Is Brother Joseph a native of Soulardville?" Krysty asked.

Strode shook her head. "Turned up nine, ten years ago. Claimed to have wandered the wilderness for years seeking spiritual answers. Lotta people who listened to him seemed to think he found some."

"And what do you believe, O dear and glorious physician?" Doc asked.

Whether she was exhausted or just had heard it all already—both occupational hazards for a busy healer—Strode didn't even give him a "you have got to be shitting me" look.

"I'm agnostic, myself," she said. "Some of what he says makes a lot of sense. Some of it doesn't. He does seem to help some people. But what he brought with him…"

"What?" Jak almost yelped. "He sickie? Plaguer?"

"Not in any physical sense."

They stared at her.

"I've already said too much," she said firmly. "Obviously more of the people here agree with what he does than don't. And mebbe he does keep us safe. That's all I'm going to say."

She sighed. "All right. Your friend's a tough bird. He's in stable condition, and I calculate he's likely to recover soon. But he's going to be out of it for some days yet. And now I think it's best we all leave now and give our patient time to rest without being disturbed by our noise."

Curiosity itched Ryan like an armful of mosquito bites. He already knew there was no point peppering the woman with more questions. Fortunately the rest of his crew did, too. They allowed themselves to be herded none-too-subtly toward the door to the outer room.

Mildred, though, hung back, hesitating. Strode frowned. Of all the people in the small band of adventurers she clearly respected Mildred the most. Yet her expression also suggested she reckoned a fellow healer, of all people, should know better than to risk troubling the rest of somebody in the kind of shape J.B. was in.

"Thank you," Mildred said at last. "You've done right by J.B."

To Ryan's astonishment the burly white healer enfolded the stocky black one into her strong arms. They hugged each other fiercely. Krysty looked on, smiling slightly and nodding.

Ryan's eye caught Doc's sardonic gaze. "It is women, my dear Ryan. Some say they're a guild unto themselves. Men of science such as myself have often speculated they're actually a separate species. Do not bother your head trying to understand them. Men have tried that and failed for millennia before my time. No further progress I could see had been made by the time of the great killing. I doubt much has been made since then."

"Besides," Krysty said as Strode and Mildred broke apart, "the heads men actually *use* to think with are too small for really important stuff."

Chapter Nine

"So you see," the tanned and wiry man with long gray-brown hair was saying to Krysty and Doc, who sat across the heavy-laden table from him, "from the very outset we employed square-foot gardening techniques to maximize our yield. The founder, the original Baron Savij, was quite an enthusiastic proponent of organic gardening. He proved to be highly knowledgeable, as did various members of his posse."

"Yeah," Mildred said. "He was definitely known for his fondness for cultivating certain forms of herb. Smoking 'em, too."

The speaker, whose name Ryan didn't catch, turned red. Everyone else laughed.

The banquet hall was on the palace's bottom floor. The kitchen was in the back. Heat washed into the room whenever the double doors swung open to admit servers carrying laden trays and full bowls. Although the twenty or so diners gathered around the big table—made by pulling several smaller tables together—raised the heat level plenty by themselves.

Amazingly, it didn't stink. Not by Deathlands standards of stench. Cleanliness seemed the order of the day in the ville. It kept down disease, something every ville feared, especially since sickness spread like floodwater rising through concentrated populations.

Nor did Ryan and his friends contribute to the stink

level. They and their clothes had been freshly washed. They had bathed in metal tubs and water had been brought to them by order of Brother Joseph. Their clothes had been laundered by other ville helpers. Though the clothes were still damp, that actually helped cool Ryan a bit. It wasn't as if they weren't going to sweat their duds sopping by the time dinner was through anyway.

"I'm really interested in what you're doing here, Mr. Bulstrop," Krysty said to the long-haired garden guy.

The man smiled so big it seemed the top of his head would just open up backward like a hinged beer-stein lid. "Thank you so much, Ms. Wroth."

"Ms. Wroth," Ryan repeated aloud. "They got some bastard manners in this ville. Ow! Why did you kick me?"

"Because I'm not close enough to," Mildred said grimly.

"But I was impressed!"

"Ryan—"

The tone in Krysty's voice shut him right down. Since he'd finally gotten grown-up and hard-bit enough to stand up to Trader, who'd ridden him unmercifully during his early apprenticeship, Ryan would step down for no man.

Then again, only a blindie would mistake Krysty Wroth for a man.

"My friends!" Bro Joe's voice pealed like a bell from the head of the table. Booker sat at his side, stuffing a piece of bread into his face with crumbs cascading to the scarred wood table below him. Ryan noticed he'd managed to turn the bread gray just from briefly handling it. Ryan was glad that whatever breeze the open windows and doors gave didn't blow down from that end of the table. It would've taken the edge off even his appetite.

"As you know," the preacher continued when the burble of conversation stopped, "we are privileged to have guests with us tonight—intrepid wanderers of the wasteland!"

That brought out some discreet applause. Ryan wasn't sure how the guest list had been assembled. Most of the attendees were getting on in years, forties at least, looked well enough fed and well-scrubbed. He didn't reckon they'd been picked for opposition to Bro Joe; he noted Strode was absent. Tully sat at the far end of the table from the preacher and looked fairly uncomfortable. Didn't harm his appetite any Ryan could see.

Garrison was there, sitting up on the preacher's right across from Booker. Ryan admired the strength of his stomach. Unless, like some folks, he'd been born without any sense of smell.

Ryan caught Krysty's eye as she smiled around at everybody, playing the ideal dinner guest in a way that wouldn't have been out of place at a baronial party in Front Royal. Her expression hardened briefly as she caught Ryan's attention.

Guests, he knew she was thinking, as he was. Six sec men with hands behind their backs and sidearms and truncheons hanging from their belts stood at ease around the dining room. Brother Joseph might call the companions guests, but there were still blasters ready to come out if they started actually acting like them. They were prisoners, no matter how well they were being treated.

Fattened? Ryan didn't like the taste of that line of thought.

"In their honor, and in honor of our wonderful ville and the service rendered it by a succession of heroic Barons Savij, I propose that we bring out Saga to give us the story of Soulardville!"

That brought out another round of applause. It was louder and more enthusiastic than before, although Ryan thought he caught some eye-rolling, too. Apparently there wasn't unanimity on the locals' appreciation of this Saga.

The palace was a big place. Ryan had the impression it had expanded beyond the building's original footprint, possibly by breaking down walls between it and neighboring buildings. Though they might've built additions to the structure, too. They'd had plenty of time. He had seen the walls they'd built around their ville, to seal it off from the outside world.

So Ryan wasn't sure where the old man in the walker shuffled in from. He was tiny and wizened and the color of aged mahogany, with a thrusting blade-nosed face and a shiny egg of skull with just a fringe of white fluff like cotton puffs glued on. Bright green tennis balls, right out of the scavenged can, capped the front legs of his walker. He wore sandals and a brown-and-black-striped dashiki that hung to his knees, and a cap halfway between a skull-cap and a fez knitted out of gold, red, yellow and green yarn on his crown. Like Booker, he wore dark glasses.

"What with wrinklie?" Jak asked, gesturing with a roasted chicken leg.

"I think he's some kind of bard or chronicler," Krysty said.

"Looks like he could have come here with the first Savij," Ryan said, sopping up some beans bubbled with molasses and bacon from his heavy blue earthenware plate with a crust of bread.

The far end of the table from Brother Joseph had lacked a chair or place setting. Now Saga thumped his walker to the spot. At a gesture from Brother Joseph a chair was placed for him. He sank onto its cushion with a grateful sigh and with help from an attendant set his walker aside. Then he leaned forward and placed hands that looked like claws carved from aged hardwood on the table.

"Hear me now, children of Soulardville and visitors from the wasteland!"

Ryan almost jumped out of his chair. The old man's voice was triple-loud and trumpet-brassy, especially coming out of such a dried-up old cicada-husk of a body.

"Hear me as I tell the tale of Savij, the gangsta who made the ville! Out of the very flames of the big nuke he strode into Soulard. Him and his posse. And the people of Soulard cowered in fear before him.

"But he didn't bring destruction. He brought life. Life! Because he was a prophet and had seen the end coming. He had studied and he had calculated. He knew. He knew!"

The ancient paused to lubricate his aging vocal cords with a healthy slug of wine from a glass jar.

In the hiatus in the old man's oddly hypnotic rhythmic shouting, Mildred leaned toward Ryan across the table. "Savij was a big conspiracy theory buff," she said quietly. "He got into survivalism and all kinds of crazy stuff."

She shook her head, making the beads in her plaits rattle.

"Guess he wasn't so crazy after all, was he?"

"The S-Man!" Saga exclaimed. "In his wisdom he taught the people of the ville how to survive the fire and the poison that fell from the sky. But the travails of the bad old world outside weren't over. Oh, no! The New Mad rid! The New Mad rid the earth of tens of thousands who had lived through the blasts and the fire and the invisible death! The earth shook, the buildings fell down, the mighty river jumped its bed!

"And then the sky went dark. Earth grew cold. And so it was for many years.

"But the first Baron Savij bade the children go forth into the ruins, amid the cold and the darkness, and seek out the means to live. And so we did, over those terrible, terrible years of shadows and ice.

"And when the skies at last cleared, he led the children out into the healing rays of the sun and said, 'Yeah, motherfuckers, can you feel it?' And verily they said, 'Fuck yeah!'"

"Fuck, yeah," the other diners echoed reverently.

Mildred's left eyebrow rose. She looked around at the others. Doc stared amiably into infinity at a point just above the others' heads. Jak was fidgeting in his chair like a little boy who needed to go pee. Krysty maintained a suspiciously frozen expression.

J.B. wasn't there to grin and shake his head and perhaps mutter a wise-ass crack under his breath. For the first time Ryan really missed the runty little bastard, keenly felt the hole his absence left.

He hadn't had luxury to do it earlier. To miss his friend and hard right hand, even during their hours locked up, when other needs like eating and drinking and sleeping took priority.

"Fuck yeah," Ryan said loudly, hoisting his mug in salute. Then he took a swallow of beer to cover his grin. Mildred shot him an outraged glare. It went right up her back for him to go along with this mumbo-jumbo. That was part of why he said it.

And partly, he thought, as he swigged the beer, it was because these Soulard fusies had given them good grub and better beer, and also they outnumbered them and took their blasters. It didn't cost him anything to say crazy shit if that made his hosts happy.

He hoped Mildred would chill out before she got them chilled, period.

"So the days passed. We waxed and grew strong. Strong! The first great Baron Savij, the founder, set us to work on the building of the walls and fences and the planting of the hedges that protect us to this day. Praise him! Praise his memory!

"Came the day for him to lie down and give his bones to the earth. But from his studly loins he had brought forth a fine, strong son. The new Baron Savij was good and wise and strong. He carried on his father's mighty work.

"Thus we built our strength and built our wealth. We came to trade with the others who had somehow managed to survive, despite lacking the wise firm hand of Savij to guide them. The scavvies in the ruins, the haughty opportunists from Breweryville, we traded with them. Lo, people came from as far away as Fort Zellich and even Camp Knappenberger, far in the wooded mountains to the west. They crossed the perilous river from Eastleville. Because we had the good shit. The best food, meds, wine, the best pottery, the best salvage. We were for real! And we still are, praise Baron Savij!"

He hoisted his wine jar, which a young boy kept topped off from a large ceramic jug. A seismic wave of the red fluid slopped over the side and splashed onto the tabletop. The diners, who had finished eating, by and large, moved their chairs back with scrapes on the brick floor to avoid getting splashed or dripped on. Beyond that no one paid any attention.

"But something was lacking." He drank deeply, belched in satisfaction, wiped his mouth with the back of his hand, belched heroically and set the glass jar down with a clunk on the tabletop.

"Something was lacking, my children. We had soul, but that soul cried out for nourishment. Then one day, one glorious day, a wanderer came to us. A man who quenched our thirst for the spirit. A man who brought us the compact, just in time to protect us from the new menace from the sky—Brother Joseph!"

The diners burst into wild applause. It seemed to Krysty there was an overstretched quality to some of the smiles, a glassy look to certain eyes. But no one seemed willing to let his or her neighbors out-do them in zeal.

"Wait," Jak whispered, as Joseph rose, smiling. "What menace from sky?"

Krysty pressed a finger urgently to her lips.

The ville's spiritual leader spread his hands before him, palms down, for silence. As though he were stilling the waters, the frenzied approval ceased.

"Thank you, Saga," he said. "An inspired performance."

Saga's jaw dropped. "But I'm not done."

"You must be exhausted. My acolytes will help you to your rest."

The wrinklie went ashen. "I'm goin', Bro Joe! You know me! I'm your biggest fan!"

"Of course," Joseph said, nodding magnanimously. "And I yours."

A couple of husky young men in T-shirts tie-dyed similarly to the preacher's appeared. They lifted Saga to his feet, planted him gently but firmly in his walker. Then with him clutching frantically to its metal bars they lifted him by his matchstick arms and hustled him out.

When Saga and his unwelcome attendants were out of sight and earshot, Brother Joseph swept the table with his pale amber gaze.

"And now, if our guests would be so kind, I think we're all dying to hear the chronicle of their undoubtedly strange and terrible journey that has led them here to our garden of peace and prosperity."

Chapter Ten

In the book-lined study Brother Joseph sat leaning back in a secretary chair with his hands folded across his bit of paunch. When a quiet female acolyte wearing the signature tie-dyed T-shirt ushered them in, the preacher seemed lost in thought or meditation.

Or asleep, Ryan thought.

The self-proclaimed holy man kept his offices in the back of an erstwhile commercial space across the plaza from the palace, which he had converted to a temple of sorts. The front room had chairs arranged in forward-facing rows, as well as tables around two sides of the room. A couple of those seekers Joseph had mentioned at dinner sat poring over books by the light of candle lanterns. From the smell Ryan guessed the candles were made out of animal-fat tallow.

Bro Joe's inner sanctum was snug and modest. A slow sluggish breeze blew in through the window. It carried smells of some night-blooming flowers that competed with incense remnants that permeated everything, especially the shelves and shelves of books arranged around the room. The volumes were mostly histories or inspirational and religious titles, Ryan saw with a cursory skim of his eye. The shelves were interspersed with predark posters sandwiched between plastic sheets, the sort that showed pictures of flowers and sunsets and carried inspirational messages in flowing script. Ryan ignored them, too.

He did flick a glance to Krysty and wondered how Brother Joseph kept hold of these people if weak beer was all he had to offer.

To all appearances these people had it triple soft easy. But this kind of prosperity drew predators and scavengers the way a fresh corpse did. Soulardville's occupants hadn't laid down the enormous effort and sweat it took to build, much less maintain, the perimeter around the ville without mighty powerful incentive, more than either the most charismatic or coercive baron could supply. There had to be threats. Clear and ever-present ones.

Plus, the tactician in Ryan knew walls like Soulardville's meant dick without manpower to keep eyes skinned on them. And blasters to back them. The razor tangles, fences, hedges and stone barriers wouldn't have kept him out ten minutes; they'd barely make feral child Jak Lauren break stride. And Ryan and company knew for a fact the Soulardites had weapons and knew how to use them.

No, no matter how soft they had it, these people weren't soft. It took grueling work to grow the food and perform all the other more mundane tasks of keeping a settlement this size alive. So he had to ask himself what kind of hold Brother Joseph had on the Soulardites.

The guru's eyes opened. They were amber, unremarkable eyes…you'd think. But somehow he had a trick, a bit of theater, that made it seem as if spotlights had come on in the lantern-lit dimness, augmented by a smile whose whiteness argued that predark toothpaste was a prized item of salvage hereabouts.

"So, my friends," he said. "Welcome to my *sanctum sanctorum*."

"We couldn't very well refuse the invite," Ryan said. The invitation had been relayed by a soft-voiced acolyte. Given the way Garrison sat at the preacher's right hand at dinner—and the alarmed way Saga reacted to having some of Bro Joe's beefier acolytes called in on him—Ryan had been under no illusions it had been anything but a command.

"After your wonderful hospitality at dinner," Krysty added, giving Ryan a quick admonitory lash of her emerald gaze.

Brother Joseph's smile, which had relaxed a bit, expanded once again. "It was truly my pleasure," he said. "Our pleasure, I should say. Obviously, entertainment is at a premium in a community such as ours. And our people naturally hunger for news of the outside world—unrelievedly grim as it tends to be. We all found your accounts of your travels riveting. Although, I don't doubt, unduly modest."

Ryan caught a grin tugging at the sagging corners of Doc's mouth. He could read his thought easily enough: *My boy, you don't know the half of it.*

The one-eyed man certainly hoped Brother Joseph didn't know the half of it. By now they had a canned account of their doings and goings, recent and otherwise, down as pat as any professional con artist. It was every syllable dead-center true: no point risking getting tripped in a falsehood, however minor. And you could never tell what bizarre bit of rumor or news might have filtered in here.

"It is always our pleasure," Doc said, "to sing for our suppers. All things considered, it's one of the lightest prices we pay to eat."

Brother Joseph nodded. It wasn't news to him, likely, if it was really true he'd wandered the Deathlands himself before drifting in here.

He leaned forward across his desk. "I have a proposition for you," he said.

"We're listening," Ryan said.

"As you may have gathered, the baron's beloved daughter, Princess Emerald, has disappeared. Roughly two weeks ago."

"Princess?" Mildred all but snorted.

Brother Joseph shrugged. "It's what everybody calls her. She enjoys a certain popularity among the citizens of our commune, notwithstanding her definite willful streak. As for her going missing, there's no mystery as to how or even why. She left on her own power, in order to escape certain civic obligations."

"And the baron wants her back," Krysty said. "As any father would."

Brother Joseph nodded. "Naturally," he said. "But I emphasize there's more at stake here even than the wishes of our beloved, if tragically stricken, leader. Her return is imperative for the continued safety and security of this ville. I daresay even its survival."

"Want we bring back," Jak said.

Joseph smiled as if the youth had revealed a remarkable truth. "Precisely! And we are prepared to reward you most handsomely for her safe return."

"How handsomely might that be, Brother?" Ryan asked.

"We'd provide you ample supplies of ammunition, food and water as well as medicine. We can pay in local jack as well. And of course, there're the considerations of the meds and attention provided to your friend Mr. Dix, today and during his convalescence."

They dickered some as to specifics. In the end Brother Joseph gave in to most of their demands.

"We enjoy a degree of prosperity here," he conceded. "And our need is great. Lady, gentlemen, I believe we have a deal."

"Not guarantee princess alive," Jak said. "You know?"

Brother Joseph sighed. "I understand the realities of the world without our walls all too well, my friends. Princess Emerald is a highly intelligent young woman, however spoiled. She was obviously resourceful enough to slip outside the perimeter despite our vigilance. Despite her relatively sheltered life, I would expect her chances of surviving to be good. But as we all know too well, so much of survival in the aptly named Deathlands relys on mere chance."

"Yeah," Ryan rasped.

"So while obviously we should prefer that our errant child be returned to us safe and sound, we will accept conclusive evidence that you have indeed discovered her should she have met with some…misfortune."

"What does she look like, Brother?" Krysty asked.

"She's seventeen years old. Black complected, considerably darker than your Mildred or myself. She has straight black hair that she wears about shoulder length. She's perhaps five feet eight inches tall, broad of shoulder and rather…full of breast and hip. Beyond her tender years, one might even say."

"Fat?" Jak asked.

Brother Joseph chucked. "Not at all. She's most athletic. Muscular and agile. Her father, though perhaps a bit indulgent in many ways, insisted she be thoroughly trained in armed and unarmed combat starting as soon as she could toddle unassisted. Her most striking characteristics, overall, are her eyes. They are a brilliant green. Her mother named her for them."

"Where is her mother?"

"Sadly, she died five years ago. One of the earliest victims of King Screamwing's flock, in fact."

He rose. "And now I need to ask your indulgence to retire for the evening. We have an important civic ceremony tomorrow morning at which I officiate. I must get my rest."

"Sure," Krysty said.

"Some of Mr. Garrison's people are waiting to escort you to your quarters," the preacher said. "I bid you good-night."

"GUESS WHERE we stand?" Jak said as they walked across the plaza in the moonlight. A pair of Garrison's sec men toting longblasters followed them, not close enough to listen in but close enough to leave no doubt they were shepherds.

"What else did you expect, young Jak?" Doc asked, strolling grandly along with his cane, his straggle-haired head held high as if he were walking out on some high-society promenade back in his day. "In the end we remain at the mercy of our hosts. For myself, I find I quite prefer their gentle approach to whips and chains."

"I liked the subtle way he reminded us they've got J.B. hostage," Mildred said sourly. "Ryan, are you sure this is a good idea?"

"No," he said. "Am I a doomie, here? Can't read the future. Except if they give us back our blasters, and they turn us out the gates without food and water, we'll likely be dead in a few days. And if we turn down this gig, what chance is there that they'll keep nursing J.B. till he's back on his pins again? Doesn't seem like we got much of a choice."

"There's always a choice," Krysty said gently.

Ryan sighed. "Okay. Ace. Mebbe what I should have said is, I don't see that we've got any better choice. Fact is, I don't see this is necessarily such a great one. Others I can see're all worse, double down."

"I'm not trying to tear you down, lover," she said. "Never

that. I know we don't have any really appealing choices here. I agree that taking the preacher's job is probably our best shot. It's just that we should never forget that even when triple-huge events intervene, we always have a choice of what to make of them. Even if it's just to die rather than submit."

"I hear you," Ryan said.

Jak was walking along frowning, his head tipped to the side and his white hair streaming down to the right shoulder of his jagged-edged camo shirt. An unaccustomed smile split his lean lupine face.

"Hum's stopped," he said cheerfully.

"What's that, lad?" Doc asked. "What hum?"

Jak frowned and stared at him. "What mean, what hum? Same hum since we hit the perimeter. Loud. Makes teeth buzz and head hurt."

"No offense, my hot-blooded young friend," Doc said, "but judging by the expressions of our associates, here, I judge you are the only one who hears any hum. Heard. Are you quite certain you were not imagining it?"

Furiously Jak shook his head. "What? Think I droolie? Heard rad-blasted hum. Made me feel funny."

"As we age," Mildred said, "we tend to lose both the upper and lower ranges of our hearing. And Jak's got unusually keen senses anyway. Is it possible he hears something that's really there, but that we can't because we're too old?"

"Mebbe so," Krysty said.

"But what can it mean?" Doc asked.

Ryan shook his head irritably. "We don't know. We don't have enough information. It's just another nukin' unanswered question about this ville."

A figure stepped from the shadows as they approached

their house with the wrought-iron bars on the windows. The moonlight glimmered on a curve of high forehead.

"Garrison," Ryan said.

"Cawdor," the sec boss said. He nodded generally at the others. "A word with you? Alone?"

"Yeah."

"Ryan..." Mildred said dubiously.

Jak had gone tense, as if prepared to leap at the sec boss's throat and tear it out with his sharp white teeth.

"Don't worry," Ryan said. "Both of you. Face it—these people've had us dead to rights since they yanked us out from under the noses of the coldhearts in the rubble this morning. Anything they want to do to us, they don't have to get tricky to do it."

A smile spread slowly across Garrison's face. "You're a smart man, Cawdor."

Ryan waved the others on. "Settle in. Start resting. We'll need all we can get and then some."

"I won't keep your friend long," Garrison said. "I promise."

They walked south along the street. A yellow glow was visible above the trees that masked the horizon to the south.

"Breweryville," Garrison said, noticing Ryan studying the glow. "They keep at it night and day. Brother Joseph calls 'em crass materialists and opportunists. All I know is, they're pretty powerful and pretty well-heeled."

"Why haven't they knocked you over yet?"

"Give me a break, Cawdor. You've seen the defenses. And you've seen our people know how to fight. I know as well as you do walls and wire tangles and all that shit just keeps out the amateurs and the not-so-serious-minded. Do you think any of us'd still be here if we were content just to sit on our asses and trust a hedge and some angle iron to keep us safe?"

"Point taken."

"Now I don't say the brewmeister couldn't take us, if he wanted us. But he'd have to want us awful bad. We'd make him pay triple anything he'd ever pry out of the smoking wreckage that kind of fight left of the ville. And whatever else you can say about the old b-meister, he's one sharp stoneheart."

Ryan nodded. That made sense to him.

Garrison stepped out to stand in the street squarely before Ryan. "Listen, Cawdor," he said, in the same calm, deceptively casual tone that was all the one-eyed wanderer had heard come out of his head. "I live for this ville. Nothing else. To serve it. To protect it. My daddy served Soulardville, and his daddy, and his daddy before him. Whether I like it or not I will do whatever is necessary to protect this ville."

He paused and his forehead creased in a scowl. He had good eyebrows for it.

"This ville may not be perfect, but it's order and peace. You've seen what's waiting out there in the rubble. All that and worse is hungering to get in, every hour, day or night. I'll die if I have to, to keep that out and preserve what we got. Scabs and all."

Garrison studied Ryan's face by the light of a crescent moon. "I suspect you're about the same with your bunch."

"Mebbe." A smile quirked Ryan's lips. "I'd rather do what it takes to keep us all alive. Me included."

"I hear you."

Garrison briefly gripped Ryan's shoulder. His hand was dry and strong, just as Ryan expected.

"That was it," he said. "I wanted us to understand each other."

"Got you."

Garrison said no more as they turned and walked back at a relaxed pace. Some kind of night creatures made noise in the trees that was more like a rhythmic whining or moaning than anything else. He knew that wasn't what Jak had complained of. They were natural night sounds; they'd never fool Jak Lauren.

Ryan found himself liking the Soulardville sec boss. It was a novel enough feeling to surprise him. He hoped it didn't come down to them squaring off. Liking the man and being unwilling to chill him at need were two very different things to Ryan Cawdor. Garrison wasn't one of Ryan's crew. That meant he was one of *them*.

But if it came to throwing down there was no certainty how it would play out between them. That was what bothered him.

Chapter Eleven

A pounding on the frame of their front door yanked them from what Mildred, remembering her residency days, called, "The sleep of the just—the just exhausted."

Ryan slipped right into deep sleep at every opportunity, but at any sign of threat he came full-on awake between one heartbeat and the next, ready to act or react on the instant.

Now was no exception. He was actually crouching by his pallet, ready to jump in any direction, before he was aware of even moving. From the pallet beside his Krysty was uncoiling, more like a waking cat than something spring-loaded like her mate.

Krysty flowed toward the door, wearing only a long pale green T-shirt. She tugged the shirt discreetly down before opening the inner door. Several young people stood waiting on the porch.

"Yes?" Krysty said.

The one nearest the door, a young man dressed in a T-shirt and baggy shorts, just gaped at her. A black girl of perhaps fifteen elbowed him aside.

"Pull your tongue back in your head, Henry," she said. "You'll step on it. We brought breakfast for you, ma'am."

"'Ma'am'?" Krysty repeated in a bemused tone.

Through the slot the youngsters passed covered pots containing bacon and sausage and scrambled eggs, a plate of yesterday's bread, sliced and toasted golden. They also handed in a stack of ceramic plates.

"Well, well," Mildred said, standing up and stretching. "This is a whole lot different from the last time we got fed in here. That actually smells good!"

"Yeah," Ryan grunted. A muscle twitched in his cheek as he remembered slab-faced Lonny hawking in their food. He still hadn't figured that one out.

He knew what to do about it. The only questions were *when* and *how*.

"Smells great," Jak said, helping take in the containers of steaming food.

"Eat fast," the girl said. "Ceremony begins in an hour." Despite her air of juvenile self-importance, her dark eyes seemed unnaturally wide and there was something strange in her manner. Something strained.

As the companions sat down in a circle and began to ladle the good-smelling food, obviously fresh-cooked in the baronial palace's own capacious kitchen, Doc's long haggard face grew thoughtful.

"Why am I so forcibly reminded," he asked the air, "of the expression, 'the condemned ate heartily'?"

WHEN PRESSED by Mildred, Doc passed the crack off as a joke. But Ryan was forcibly reminded of the phrase himself when the next peremptory hammering on the door frame led to Mildred opening the door on Garrison and no fewer than half a dozen of his sec men, each carrying a shotgun or carbine.

"What's the occasion?" she asked.

"Lottery day," he said. "You're attending the cere-mony."

"Lottery?" Mildred asked. "That takes me right back… don't we need to buy tickets?"

One of the sec men snickered. Turning his head fractionally, Garrison shot him a look that shut him off dead as a shot to his head. Instead sweat broke out all over his suddenly ashen face.

"As outlanders," Garrison said, "you're exempt. Be glad. Now, shake it up. We don't want to keep Brother Joseph waiting."

Although the companions had all undressed at least partially for sleep, to beat the humid heat as best they could, they had finished dressing hurriedly after they ate. Nor had they enjoyed their meal, despite the strong temptation to linger over the unaccustomed richness and deliciousness of it all. For reasons having not a rad-blasted thing to do with the convenience of Bro Joe or Soulardville they wanted to be ready to roll on a moment's notice.

The day was clear but for a few white clouds rolling east over the big river. Down here in the ville there was only a slight breeze. The sun wasn't yet halfway up the sky. But it stung Ryan's cheek when they passed out of the shade of a linden tree into the street.

The plaza was thronged. Ryan guessed there had to have been nearly five hundred people packed in there elbow-to-elbow. It took a surprisingly little amount of room to hold a crowd that big when it was that dense. The mob spilled down the big main street and the shady side lanes, even half a block down toward the house where they had spent the night confined.

But despite being jammed in the plaza like Vienna sausages in a can, the good folk of Soulardville gave way pretty quickly when Garrison led his crew straight into them keeping the five companions carefully surrounded.

"Like a hot knife through butter," Doc murmured.

A path opened clear to the center of the plaza, which Ryan observed to be devoid of spectators. In the middle of it the mysterious slab had had its cloth covering removed. What they saw was a big thick chunk of concrete with raw busted edges; it had to have been eight feet by ten and at least a foot thick. It had to weigh tons.

"It must have taken an almighty effort to bring that here," Doc said. "What for, I wonder."

"Got a feeling we're about to find out," Ryan said.

"Those rebars sticking up," Mildred said, nodding toward rust-red lengths of metal jutting from the slab. "They've been bent so they're like hooks."

"That took some doing, too," Krysty said.

Garrison led them to a spot roughly in front of the baronial palace. A combination of sec men and Joseph's tie-dyed acolytes seemed to have been holding it open for them. The crowd seemed no more minded to tangle with the unarmed, fresh-faced young men in the colorful T-shirts than their grim black-clad counterparts with the blasters and hardwood nightsticks.

No sooner had the companions taken up position, right at the edge of the ten-foot-clear circle around the peculiar tilted slab so they had an unobstructed view, than a chant went up: "Jo-*seph,* Jo-*seph,* Jo-*seph!*"

The man himself emerged from his storefront temple. This day he wore a white shirt and over it a long smock not unlike a whitecoat's white coat. Except it had been dyed streakily in a whole rainbow of colors—red and orange and yellow, green, blue, purple, even black and gray and brown. Or mebbe it had been woven in all those colors; Ryan didn't know enough about the making and coloring of fabric to make a judgment. The self-proclaimed holy man wore loose pants of unbleached muslin and his usual sandals. He carried a staff with a large head on it that seemed of all things to be made up of scavenged green circuit boards. Little LED light glowed from it like red and green eyes at seeming random.

"What the heck's that thing?" Mildred asked.

"No doubt an object of religious significance," Doc said quietly. "Possibly talismanic. When I was confined in your time, dear lady, I chanced to read about something called a cargo cult in the islands of the South Seas, where natives sought to bring back the goods that had flowed to them so freely during your Second World War, by creating mock-ups of landing strips, and making aircraft out of crates. Perhaps we're about to witness a ceremony of similar import, to try to recall the prosperity of predark times, or assure a goodly supply of salvage."

One of the sec men turned around and glared. Doc favored him with a bland smile. Mildred couldn't refrain from muttering under her breath, "It wasn't *my* World War. I wasn't even born."

Brother Joseph reached the cleared space around the platform…altar, Ryan found he was thinking of it now. Without hesitation the guru strode forward and climbed up to the top of it, finding a strong standing position immediately, with the ease of long practice, despite the canted surface.

"My children," he called in that voice like an old-style church bell tolling from the steeple. "People of Soulardville. Seekers after truth. You know why we are here."

Instead of shouting a ritual reply the crowd fell dead silent. Brother Joseph tapped the base of his staff three times on the blacktop at his feet. Hard hollow raps echoed among the building faces.

"Years ago," he cried, "the peace of Soulardville was broken by a terrible menace from the skies. A horror that haunted all the ruins of St. Lou. It haunts them to this day!"

Ryan was aware of his companions' eyes on him. He shrugged. *No idea,* he mouthed.

"The circle of daily life was broken. No longer could farmers work their plots. Carters could no longer move goods. Friend could no longer visit friend, daughter no longer visit mother. No longer could the people assemble together to seek their strength in one another. In community.

"I was among you at that time. I remember when the horror of the screamwings arrived. The terrifying attacks. The hideous wreckage they left behind, which had been healthy, vibrant human beings before the winged horrors descended."

"I don't think I like where this is going," Mildred muttered.

Ryan glanced around, a bit concerned at attracting attention. But everybody was staring at Brother Joseph as if he were telling the way to the magic jolt tree.

"I believe you speak for us all," Doc said, sotto voce.

"Long and hard I prayed. Meditated and prayed. Prayed for guidance from the divine principle and all the spirits of the earth, the fire, the water, and especially the sky. And then was revealed to me—the compact!

"I went forth alone into the wilderness of broken concrete and steel. There I met the King Screamwing himself. He whose majestic and terrible form you may see wheeling even now against the blue vault of the sky!"

He thrust his staff up into the sky toward the north, above downtown. The crowd gasped.

Sure enough, a great winged shape circled lazily, high above the rubble of the great city.

"Triple-huge!" Jak breathed, eyes wide.

"What does he mean 'King Screamwing'?" Doc asked. "They are animals. Mutant animals, to be sure, vicious brutes, by and large. But a king? Preposterous!"

"It could be he's the dominant male," Mildred observed.

"Let's hear what the man has to say," Ryan rasped.

Not that that posed any problem. The soft-voiced conversation had taken place while Brother Joseph stood poised, pointing at the monster in the sky. The assembled Soulardites stared at it with fear and terrible anticipation. Something didn't taste right on Ryan's tongue. Mebbe he was just smelling their fear. It wasn't the right kind of fear.

"They're not afraid of being attacked, lover," Krysty said. "It's something else."

"I brought you back—the compact!" Brother Joseph cried. He lowered his staff with another ringing impact of its butt on the ground.

"Since that time the screamwings have left us in peace. Do I speak true?"

"You speak true, Bro Joe!" somebody shouted from the crowd.

Shill, Ryan thought, glancing toward the outcry and spotting a gaudy sunburst pattern. But the rest of the crowd instantly took up the cry.

Brother Joseph gestured with his staff and the crowd shut up again. "But everything in life has its price," his said, pitching his voice low, although Ryan had no trouble hearing it. He reckoned he'd have heard it about as clearly had he been way off at the back of the crowd, instead of twenty feet away. The man was good. He had to give him that.

"And so we pay the price. Each of us a share. Each of us a chance. Each of us, all of us, entered in the lottery."

Something ran through the crowd in an almost tangible ripple. The word had that powerful an effect. Ryan could actually see the whole mob flinch as one.

"And now—" Joseph rang the butt of his staff four times against the concrete at his feet "—bring forth this week's lucky winner!"

"Win-ner! Win-ner!" the crowd began to chant.

To the east it parted. A group of six of Brother Joseph's huskiest young male acolytes approached, clustered around a young woman. She had long dark brown hair that hung in curtains that hid her down-turned face. She wore a simple lightweight smock of brown with black stripes. Her hands were behind her back. Her feet were bare.

Krysty gasped. "She's just a girl!"

Ryan saw it was true. Even if he couldn't see her face, the slim figure—far from fully developed into woman-hood, even the way she walked—told the story well enough.

Jak shook his head as if clearing water from his hair. He clapped his hands over the ears. Their escorts looked at him funny, but they said nothing. Only steered a little farther clear of the albino teen, as if afraid whatever kind of crazy he had was catching.

"Jak, what on earth are you doing?" Krysty asked, as quietly as she could and still be heard above the rising noise of the throng that filled the street ahead of them.

"Whine. Triple-high. Heard yesterday in circle ruin. Back now." He squeezed his eyes shut. "Hurts."

Krysty looked at Ryan. He shook his head.

"None of the rest of us hear anything," the redhead said.

"Whose fault that?"

The acolytes led the girl to the tilted slab. She raised her head and looked around fearfully, her eyes glistening, cheeks flushed. Krysty was right: she couldn't have been more than fourteen.

The crowd kept up its chant: "Win-ner! Win-ner!"

Brother Joseph stepped carefully backward off the slab. The acolytes hustled the slim girl up onto it and knelt. Quickly they secured a short, coarse rope to her slender right ankle. Then they tied it securely to one of the rebars curved into hooks. With one quick rip, her smock was torn away by one of the acolytes.

"It's an altar," Mildred said. "Oh, sweet Mary, what are these bastards doing?"

"And now," Brother Joseph cried, "the price! The awful price is paid, that all of us may live and thrive!"

He pointed at the sky to the north again. The crowd looked. Someone screamed.

The screamwings came.

Chapter Twelve

At least thirty of the savage flying muties came in a cloud. Ryan tensed as his pulse rate soared.

"Get ready to run for it," he said tersely. "If we get in among the crowd, we'll have better odds, anyway."

"Wait." Krysty gripped his arm. "Nobody else is running."

"Oh, shit," Mildred was saying, over and over. Tears streamed down her cheeks. "Oh, shit, no."

Jak was looking around wildly. He was used to being the hunter. But he knew too well what it was like to be the prey as well.

He'd been the intended prey of the flying mutant horrors called screamwings. They all had. That they had survived their previous encounters was due as much to luck as to their skill and zeal at fighting and fleeing.

These were a new kind of screamwing to Ryan's experience. They were about the size of big tailless seagulls, he saw as the cloud approached. They were brown above and a dirty white below. They had big staring eyes and snapping narrow beaks—but beaks lined with needle-sharp teeth.

As they swooped toward the girl, who stood staring fixedly up at them as if frozen in horror, Ryan saw they were covered in what looked like short, soft fur.

People screamed and ducked away as the horrors fluttered near them. But they circled the altar. They were as fixated on the girl as she was on them.

One darted down from above. Ryan heard a ripping sound. The sacrificial victim shrieked and slapped a hand to her cheek. A screamwing flapped violently upward with a strip of something streaming from its beak. It was skin, freshly torn from the helpless victim.

The muties swarmed the helpless sacrifice. Their screeches almost overwhelmed the girl's frantic pain-filled shrieks. They became a living whirlwind of wings and furs and claws. And always those slim, lethal beaks full of deadly teeth.

Blood sprayed in all directions at they darted in to nip at an ear or tear a strip from a quivering pale thigh. The girl managed to keep them at bay from her face temporarily by swinging her head desperately from side to side, whipping her long hair back and forth. Then one latched on to the top of her head with its claws and began pecking downward at her face.

"Ryan!" Mildred screamed. "We have to do something!"

But Ryan only shook his head. They were hemmed in tight by the sec men. The guards' eyes never left them. *Figures,* he thought. *They've seen this show plenty of times before.*

Around them the crowd bayed like hounds. Some seemed frightened, some exalted. But all seemed caught up in a frenzy of emotions.

With a lost-child wail Mildred turned to clutch the first available friendly human form. It proved to be the bean-pole frame of Doc Tanner. The oldie clutched the black woman against him with one hand, so tight the bones stood out on the back of his hand like a mummy's. The two were often bitter rivals in day-to-day life, scrapping like dogs over a patch of turf. Now they clung to each other for comfort in the face of unspeakable horror.

Jak stood with arms folded tightly across his chest and his face half lowered. His hair hung in white curtains, framing it. His eyes glared ruby-laser death at their hosts and captors.

Ryan felt a warm firm hand grip his. He squeezed Krysty's hand back. It wasn't like her to seek even that much reassuring comfort from him. But he didn't begrudge it.

He made himself watch it all. The girl, her body robed in blood, dropped to her knees as her strength faded. Six or seven screamwings had landed and were knuckle-walking around on stubby hind legs and folded wings, picking at scraps fallen to the blood-washed concrete or ripping greedily at exposed bits of skin with their beaks. Most of the swarm had settled onto the victim now, clutching with their hind claws, pulling up strips of skin and flesh with their beaks, shaking blood from their big-eyed heads before diving in again.

A shadow wheeled across the plaza. Spectators screamed in renewed fear and pointed skyward.

"King Screamwing! It's the king!"

The largest screamwing Ryan had ever seen settled down toward the slab with a thunder of wings. Unlike the lesser screamwings, which rose up and screeched protest at the approach of their monstrous overlord to fly upward in spirals around the altar and its terrible bloody cargo, a yard-long crest stabbed backward from its head, as if to counterbalance its huge voracious jaws. These snapped open and shut several times with pistol-crack sounds, rousting the rest of its underlings from their prey.

The girl had fallen to her side and lay curled in a fetal position. Her nose was gone, as were her ears. Great patches of skin had been ripped away; Ryan could see skeins and knots of red muscle and gleams of yellow bone.

The great flyer landed. It stood a good eight feet tall. It bent over the girl. Its bent wings hid its quarry like the vampire's cloak in a predark horror vid. Ryan heard a crunching noise.

The girl uttered a last scream of pain, unearthly and unendurable. Then the great mutie monster unfurled its wings. With a boom like thunder it rose up. Wind that stank of blood and spilled bowels hit Ryan's face with tangible impact as the King Screamwing rose.

The girl's limp form rose with it, clutched in its great rear claws. The giant screamwing circled up into the painful blue sky. Then with vast slow beats of its wings it flew toward the single intact skyscraper that dominated all the ruins, carrying its prey to its aerie. The lesser muties followed it in a fluttering, squabbling cloud.

"Oh, God," Mildred said brokenly.

She pointed. The girl's right foot lay on its side on the altar. The rough rope that secured it to the bent iron was still tied about it.

Ryan drew in a deep breath. "Fuck," he said.

"We in mess of shit," Jak said.

"And then some," Ryan said.

"I DIDN'T THINK anything ever lived that could carry off a human being in its claws," Mildred said. "There were some awful big dinosaurs…flying reptiles…whatever. But it's hard to imagine a creature big enough to fly away with that poor girl."

"She was only a wisp," Doc said. "She probably weighed less than young Jak."

"Leave me out!" Jak snarled. He was walking bent over himself, clutching himself as if he'd taken a gut punch.

"How can you even talk about shit like that at a time like this?" Ryan demanded.

He felt Krysty squeeze his hand, briefly this time. "It's their way of coping," she said. "Just let them. All right?"

"Yeah."

They were being marched under guard down broad Russell Street toward the main gate through which they'd entered, only yesterday. A full ten sec men and Garrison himself surrounded them. Another six or seven civvies marched along with them, including Tully and Lonny from yesterday's patrol. The tall ginger-haired patrol leader looked ill. Lonny looked like a century-storm about to bust.

Brother Joseph brought up the rear, striding proudly with a quartet of acolytes, two males, two females, in attendance.

"I thought Tully and our pal Lonny were big fans of this Princess Emerald," Ryan said, putting his head close to Krysty's as they walked side by side.

"Brother Joseph's rubbing their noses in their own impotence," she said.

"Huh. Mebbe so. Just for meanness?" He'd long ago learned not to judge books by their covers, especially where any kind of power came into play. But even he was shaken by the depth of Brother Joseph's duplicitous cruelty.

"Probably layer upon layer of political games going on here we have no clue about," the redhead said, her voice husky with controlled emotion as well as held low. "Plus, yeah. Meanness."

They reached the gate. The market space was empty. "Reckon they shut it down for sacrifice day," Ryan remarked as gate guards moved the black-iron gate back with a metal-on-metal squeal.

"Or they find themselves short of customers on the regular occasions on which flights of screamwings wing their way hence," Doc said.

"That, too," Ryan said. "I think."

Under the blasters and glowers of Garrison's guards they were marched out onto 7th Boulevard. They found themselves at the center of a circle of blaster muzzles, facing Brother Joseph.

"Seems to me," Ryan said, "that you broke our little deal."

"Indeed?" Brother Joseph cocked an eyebrow. "How do you reckon that, Mr. Cawdor?"

"You said Emerald ran away to avoid her civic duty," Krysty said, her voice as low and dangerous as a mother wolf's growl. "You meant to sacrifice her, didn't you? And you still do!"

The holy man shrugged. "Like everyone in Soulardville—like myself—her name is entered into the great lottery. Her name was duly picked. It was her responsibility to accept her fate as that brave girl did today. Caitlin McDowell, her name was. A sweet child."

"You bastard! You fed her to those monsters alive!" Mildred cried.

"Such is the compact. Every moon we sacrifice one of our own to the king. In his turn, he keeps the lesser screamwings from hunting us the rest of the time. Believe me, I don't like it any better than you do. But it saves lives. Is that not worth sacrifice?"

"Does anything justify such extremes of barbarity?" Doc demanded.

Brother Joseph smiled thinly. "Evidently, to the people of Soulardville, it does."

"We never agreed to bring anybody back for human sacrifice to a bunch of flying muties," Ryan said.

"Indeed?" Brother Joseph cocked his head as if curious. "It seems to me you made no preconditions to your acceptance of my terms. And it was made clear to you, I distinctly recall, that Emerald had fled to evade her civic duty."

"Ryan," Krysty said, "we can't—"

"Then, there are issues such as the return of your weapons, not to mention your freedom," Brother Joseph said. "It does not appear you're in the strongest of bargaining positions."

"Mebbe not," Ryan said. "All right."

"All right?" Mildred said. "What do you mean 'all right'?"

"There's something else you're not thinking about," Ryan said.

"Not leave J.B.," Jak said.

Mildred's eyes got big and round. So great had her outrage grown that she'd forgotten all about her lover, however temporarily.

"Speaking of which," Brother Joseph said, "I made mention that the lottery takes place every four weeks. Should you not have successfully brought the princess back, or certain evidence of her death, within twenty-eight days, I very much fear your friend J.B. will be required to pay for his treatment by serving as sacrifice in her place."

"You wouldn't!" Mildred blurted.

"Dear lady, I watched young Caitlin grow up from a most delightful child. She was scarcely more than a toddler when I arrived. Her parents were among the first to hearken to my message. Yet I presided over her sacrifice. What does a man who is, after all, a stranger matter to me?"

"Enough," Ryan said. "I said we'd do this. But you still

held out on us when you bargained. We bring back this lost princess of yours, or her head, you pay us twice the amount agreed. Ammo, grub, meds, jack. The wag-load."

Brother Joseph drew in a short but deep breath and sighed it out. "Very well. Her return is most important to this ville."

"Why?" Krysty asked bitterly. "How can it matter so much to you who you feed to your pet monsters?"

"Dear lady, they aren't *my* pet monsters, I assure you. It has to do with the cohesion of the ville. The heart and soul of our community. The people must see that even the baron's own flesh and blood is not exempt from sacrifice. Otherwise, how can they be expected to continue to pay the blood price necessary to keep our commune alive?"

"Give us our blasters and gear," Ryan said. "Daylight's burning. Jawing won't bring your girl back."

"Excellent," Brother Joseph said. "Mr. Garrison, if you please."

While sec men trained their weapons ostentatiously at the five companions' heads, their gear was brought to them. Tully himself handed Ryan his pack. There were tears streaming down his freckled cheeks.

"I wish it didn't come to this, Cawdor," he said.

"Yeah. Well, you and me both." He dropped the sack to the ground and broke it open to check inside. The appropriate portion of the agreed-upon payment was inside. The pack felt almost twice as heavy as it had when he last hefted it.

The burly Lonnie brought Jak his rucksack. He and the albino teen exchanged furious glares. Lonny backed away.

"If all these guys with blasters weren't here," the slab-faced man said, "none of you'd walk away alive."

When the five had shrugged into their packs, Garrison

nodded. His sec men returned the travelers' weapons. Each carefully checked the pieces before stowing them.

"All right," Ryan said, slamming home a fresh magazine in the well of his SIG-Sauer P-226 and racking the slide. "Just one more little bit of business before we go."

He flung out his right arm to full length and fired.

Chapter Thirteen

Lonny's pig eyes went wide as a hole appeared between them. Pink mist made a brief halo around his brown top-thatched head. He fell with a sound like a sack of wet grain dropping out of a wag.

With much ostentatious clacking-off of safeties the sec men shouldered their longblasters, all aimed dead at Ryan's head.

"Hold!" Garrison barked.

The color had left Brother Joseph's face. "What is the meaning of this outrageous act?"

"Ha!" Ryan said. "You got some stones, Your Reverence, talking about outrageous acts after that shit you just made us watch. Lonny there thought we might like our food better yesterday when we were penned up if he hocked a big fat one in it and stirred it around. *Nobody* spits in our food and lives to brag about it long."

Ryan put the safety on and deliberately holstered the SIG.

Brother Joseph's eyes stood out from his face, which had gone from mocha to pale gray. "Y-you killed him just for revenge? For a petty slight?"

"Nothing's petty about fouling helpless folks' grub."

"Yes," Mildred said. "You grew up in this world, Brother. You should know. People have to learn they can't afford to screw with us. Or we'll have nothing but grief."

Brother Joseph shook his head. "You disappoint me,

Mildred. I'd expect a healer—and a woman—to have a more…humane outlook."

Doc laughed. "The gentler sex is gentler indeed," he said, "but only relatively."

"I keep my deals, Brother Joseph," Ryan rasped. "Even the ones that aren't spoken aloud."

Standing just behind the guru's left shoulder Ryan saw Garrison produce a rueful grin and a head shake. "Lower the pieces," he ordered his men.

He looked Ryan square in the eye. "You folks have five seconds to pick a direction and head that way like you mean it. And once you're started, if you so much as look back I'll give the word to ice you in your tracks. Understood?"

"Yeah," Ryan said.

Without a look aside he set off walking briskly south.

He heard the others following him. When they had gone a couple hundred yards with the heat of the sun bouncing back up off the asphalt in their faces, Jak asked, "Why not chill Bro Joe, the fuck?"

"His sec men would have avenged him instantly, lad," Doc said. "They might not have mourned his loss themselves. But they would have been quick to make up for the fact they failed to keep him alive by chilling us."

"Fat bastard Lonny needed to die," Ryan said. "Nobody pulls that shit on us and lives."

"What about Brother Joseph?" Krysty asked.

"We chill him," Ryan said. "Later."

"And how do you propose to accomplish that eminently laudable goal, my dear Ryan?" Doc asked.

Ryan hitched a one-shoulder shrug. "Work it out later. Right now we have to find Emerald."

"He'll never pay us," Mildred said.

"I know that," Ryan said. "He gave in way too quick

when I doubled the price. At that, I was only confirming what I already reckoned. Anyway we made a deal. We've got to keep it or J.B.'s dead."

"Happy shaking that place from boot heels," Jak remarked. "Big hum back. Makes bones itch."

Ryan frowned and scratched his cheek thoughtfully with his thumb. Bristle made a rough sound.

"I take it you have a destination in mind?" Doc asked.

"We're going to Breweryville."

"You think Emerald's gone there?" Krysty asked.

"No," Ryan said. "Think about it."

He felt safe glancing at her, since she'd pulled up alongside with swinging, confident strides of her long, strong legs. He took Garrison absolutely at his word they'd be gunned down instantly if they so much as glanced back.

Anyway the cracked, heaved pavement had begun sloping beneath Ryan's boots. In a few dozen steps they'd be out of sight of the Soulardville sec posse.

Krysty's smooth brow creased in a frown of concentration. "Despite the fact they trade," she said, "there seems to be some hostility between Brewery and Soulardville."

"That's how I read it," Ryan said.

"They seem to be the powerhouses of this vicinity, which means they're automatically rivals to some extent, even though we've seen no sign of overt conflict. That means there'd be too great a chance this brewmeister would use Emerald to strike against his rival, her father."

She glanced up at Ryan. "Or misuse her."

"Yeah."

"On the other hand, and paradoxically, he might try to buy Soulard's favor by shopping her back."

"Uh-huh," Ryan said, nodding.

"So, why are we going there, lover, since it seems pretty definitely the girl we're after didn't?"

"Double-easy. Information. From what we heard back in Soulard, B-ville's the biggest ville around. Does lots of trade." He shrugged. "Also, they've got no reason to cover for Emerald."

"And what might we have to tender in exchange for the desired information, my dear Ryan?" Doc asked.

"Information, for one thing," Ryan said. "People're always hard up for news of the outside world. Even in a place does a lot of trade like B-ville. I'm sure we know something we can swap to this brewmeister. And if not, mebbe we can do him a service. Something."

"Serenely confident as ever, I see," Doc said.

"Or overconfident," Mildred said.

"Whichever," Ryan agreed.

What was obviously the southern boundary of Soulardville approached on the right. To the left, more or less intact industrial and commercial buildings marched down the bluff into the green water of the Sippi. Ahead Ryan could see the great redbrick walls and towers of Breweryville rising above green treetops.

"Enough jibber-jabber," he said. "Jak, you swing out point. Krysty, take our left side." Those derelict buildings made him nervous. Anything could be denning in them, from stickies to coldhearts armed to the teeth and looking for unwary prey to wander past between the two rich villes.

"Mildred, you wing out right. Doc, you come up ahead of me. I'll pull rear-guard. Now, double-fast march!"

THE EIGHT-YEAR-OLD boy squalled as the sec man broke his right upper arm with a sickening thud of a lead-loaded truncheon.

"In order to achieve the maximum potential of government to do good," the man with the stained apron and fringe of white hair said, mopping his round, jovial face with a scarlet handkerchief, "it has to achieve respect. Right? Right. Nobody argues that."

Crying, the small boy fell to the ground.

"And what's one inarguable component of respect?" the baron—or brewmeister, as he insisted on being called— asked. He sat on a beer keg in the shade of a tree growing in a little courtyard, in font of a tall redbrick structure Ryan guessed was his headquarters. The building was big and square and looked kind of like an old-time church, complete with a crenellated tower with a clock in it. The clock's black iron hands seemed perpetually frozen at midnight. The upper third or so of the tower was made of a lighter, yellower brick than the rest. The boundary was uneven. Ryan guessed something, probably the nuke blast to the west, had knocked the original top off the tower.

Their host spoke as casually as if he were discussing nothing of significance. Perhaps the petunia that nodded bright heads in the exquisitely tended beds to either side of the entry steps. Or the other flowers growing in the beds inside the little courtyard fenced with a waist-high railing of spike-topped black iron, their fragrance doing little to dispel the pervasive stink of rotting hops. The ville still kept up its traditional occupation, along with farming and various forms of manufacture.

"Fear, of course," the brewmeister said as if nothing unusual was happening. "Fear. I prefer not to rule by fear. You can ask any of my people—ask 'em yourself, Ryan. Be my guest. But the time comes around occasionally when it is necessary for a benign ruler to reinstill fear in his subjects. So that they can be reminded of the consequences of failure and disobedience, before going back to the grateful and happy fruits of the good governance I provide them.

"Now, what can I do for you ladies and gentlemen?"

Ryan spoke fast to overwhelm Mildred's growl behind him. "We could use some information," he said.

The baron nodded and smiled. "And what have you got in exchange?"

Chapter Fourteen

"Why, Baron," Doc Tanner declared, throwing his arms wide in a theatrical gesture, "we bring news of the great wide world beyond these magnificent walls."

He held his loaded sword stick in one hand. His pale blue eyes had a faraway look in his tanned and weather-beaten face. Ryan wondered if his mind had gone someplace else—someplace where kids weren't eaten alive by flying muties, or had their arms broken by a cruel baron.

The brewmeister pulled a face and tipped his head left and right. "We get plenty of news," he said, "what with all the trade caravans who come in here. Plus we have a secure dock for rivermen to tie up. Still, you look as if you may have an interesting story or two to tell. What information do you want, exactly?"

Breweryville was a vast compound of tall redbrick walls and towers, surrounded by fields lined with crops in neat rows. Laborers in shabby linen smocks and woven straw hats worked the fields under the eyes of watchful sec men, who sat in the shade of parasols slapping the palms of their hands with their long oak truncheons. The workers' clothes looked homespun, mebbe a product of the big ville itself, mebbe brought in via trade. One way or another new-condition clothes scavvied from the ruins of the great city seemed to be considered too valuable to waste on the grunt laborers.

From inside, the walls showed different colors at various heights, ranging from near ground levels to up near the top. Apparently the inhabitants had rebuilt and repaired damage done by the bombs and quakes. They had plenty of material to do it with, Ryan reckoned. And time. It did suggest they'd been here a while. As Soulardville had.

The towers on either sides of the huge gates through which the companions had been escorted bristled with the barrels of what Ryan suspected were actual full-on machine guns.

The sec men hadn't even bothered relieving the outlanders of their weapons. Ryan was too canny to be reassured. They were being told, not subtly, they posed no threat.

The fact was, as far as he could see, that was true. This ville had a lot more activity than Soulard, a lot more people doing a lot more bustle. And a shitload more sec men.

"Got questions concerning Baron Savij of Soulardville's daughter, Emerald," he said.

The baron's eyebrows rose like fuzzy white caterpillars arching their backs. "Ah," he said sagely. "That will be pricey information indeed. Why do you want to know about her?"

"What do you offer us for that information, Baron?" Doc asked. "Nothing is free in Deathlands. Except of course, death itself!"

Yeah, Ryan thought, *thanks loads for reminding the baron of that. Plus all those sec men standing right behind us who suddenly don't have anything much to do.*

The brewmeister goggled at the old man. Ryan wondered if he got so little back-chat he had trouble understanding it when it came his way. But then the stout old baron laughed heartily and slapped his apron-covered thigh.

"By the days of the smoke clouds!" he exclaimed. "I must admit you're an entertaining bunch. Very well."

He leaned forward with a shrewd look on his face. "Let's get down to talking beans and bullets," he said. "I understand you are a skilled healer, Mildred?"

Ryan looked around at Mildred, who was still upset about the child with the broken arm. Her face was purplish and her eyes looked like boiled eggs.

"Yes, she is," Krysty Wroth said quickly.

She'd recovered her composure before Mildred. Of course. She was Deathlands-born. She knew how things went. No matter that even she sometimes had trouble swallowing them.

Somewhere, deep down inside, Ryan reckoned, Mildred still figured she was just visiting this hellacious future, so completely unlike the sparkling, clean-smelling world she'd known. Or mebbe that this was a dream, a horrible nightmare, she'd awaken from one day.

The brewmeister nodded. "Then there is something you can do for me," he said. "There's a little girl, delightful child. She was struck this morning by what our own healer calls a bout of appendicitis. Now, our healer unfortunately lacks the skill to treat that condition, since cutting is required. He's sorry for that now. Very, very sorry."

He turned his bright smile on Mildred. "Can you perform the necessary operation?"

Her color, which had begun to return to normal, went all purple again, and her eyes bugged out.

"What makes you think I'll—"

"Tell me, dear Mildred," Doc said brightly, "did you ever learn the old oath—what was it?—the Hippocratic oath that physicians used to take?"

Mildred went dead still. The color dropped from her face. Krysty was by her side, her bright red hair obscuring her face momentarily as she leaned close to Mildred's ear to whisper something. Ryan didn't need any psychic powers to guess Krysty was reminding the overamped doctor that whatever horrors went on in this ville, a little sick girl had nothing to do with perpetrating them.

"Yes," the stocky black woman managed to reply. Then as professionalism took over she continued in tones that became progressively more controlled and businesslike as she spoke.

"I can perform an appendectomy if the patient is not too far gone. If the appendix has burst, and she's got peritonitis, there's nothing I nor any healer in this world can do for her."

"Our ville healer says that crisis is still a few hours off," the brewmeister said. "Fact is, he bet his life on it. Such invasive cutting, however, lies unfortunately beyond his competence."

"Do you have antibiotics?" Mildred asked.

"We do. Prime quality salvage."

"What about painkillers? This is going to be hard enough without trying to do it without anesthesia."

In fact, even Ryan knew it was fairly simple surgery. He approved of Mildred not tipping that. Of course, the baron probably knew that as well as he. But why give anything away free?

"We have various opium extracts available," the brewmeister said.

"Good," Mildred said. "They can help treat shock in the patient, too. If she isn't too far gone I can do this. But you'll have to answer all our questions, not bargain over every syllable. You understand?"

The baron spread his pink hands wide. "It shall be my pleasure. You shall be performing me an invaluable service."

Mildred looked at Ryan, who nodded.

"Then I better get right to it," Mildred said. "Time's blood, as they say these days. Where is she?"

The baron gestured. "Some of my sec men will escort you. They'll ensure you have everything you need to perform a successful operation."

"Doc," Ryan said, "go with the healer. Give her a hand."

"Certainly, Ryan."

Mildred frowned again, but they were comrades. Ryan didn't want anybody going off alone in this latest nest of adders if he could help it. Having something urgent to do would keep Doc focused; and of all of them he probably had the knowledge best suited to help the physician. Anyway, Ryan wanted Krysty to hear what the brewmeister had to tell them.

Mildred got it, too, in just about two heartbeats. She nodded briskly. A pair of sec men with stone faces led her and Doc out the little gate and across the compound at a brisk pace.

"Not to check a gift blaster's bore for rust," Ryan said, "but I got to ask—isn't it a bit coincidental that this daughter or granddaughter of yours falls sick the very day a triple-skilled healer happens to stroll through your gates?"

The brewmeister laughed. "Why, whatever gave you the impression she was any relation of mine?"

Ryan frowned, confused. "Well, you're so all fired to see her cured. She's one of your big wheel's kids, then?"

"She is the daughter of my bitterest and most vocal critic in the Breweryville council," the baron said.

"Then why the nuke do you want Mildred to save her?"

"Why, to put him in my debt, of course. Plus it will piss

him off to no end." He laughed again, as happy as a child with a new toy.

The brewmeister looked up at the clouds. "Let's repair to the shade of the pergola," he said, nodding his shiny dome toward a wooden-frame shelter built in the middle of the little garden courtyard, its sides and rafters overgrown with fragrant honeysuckle. "The sun's coming out, and there's no reason to be uncomfortable, is there?"

WHEN THEY WERE seated on wooden chairs in the shade of lush vines laden with white and yellow flowers, silent servants in linen smocks brought a jug with several stone mugs. The servants set mugs before the baron, Ryan, Krysty and Jak, and then poured them full of frothy dark beer.

"What can I tell you about the princess, then?" the brewmeister asked. He picked up a mug and drank deeply. Then he sighed contentedly, setting the mug on the table and wiping foam from his mouth with his hand.

"You know she left Soulardville, right?" Ryan tasted the beer. It was full-bodied and flavorful. It was also familiar: they'd been served the same at dinner the previous night in the current Baron Savij's palace.

The brewmeister got a cagey look in his eye, then he shook his head. "Yes, I do," he said. "Word gets around about that sort of thing."

"We're looking to bring her back," Ryan said.

He wondered if word got around about what the Soulardites did to keep clear of the menace of the screamwing colony up in that high skyscraper. He decided it wasn't worthwhile asking.

"Indeed. Savij has hired you, then?"

"He wants his daughter back," Krysty said.

"Yes. No doubt he does. You don't think she came here, surely?"

"No," Ryan said.

"Why wouldn't she, though?" Krysty asked. "It seems there's rivalry between you and Soulardville. Your ville might offer her attractive refuge."

"I don't know how much they told you about the so-called Princess Emerald in Soulard."

"Not much," Ryan admitted.

"She's no dewy-eyed innocent. She's seventeen years old with a reputation as a hellcat. It doesn't surprise me she left the place, frankly. By all accounts she's a young woman of some ability and enterprise, if lamentable decorum. No doubt she felt that Soulardville restricted her horizons too much to endure."

Or that the horizon of Soulardville was going to fill up with her own personal flock of screamwings, Ryan reflected. He certainly wasn't fool enough to trust this wily old baron. On anything, least of all that he wasn't fully aware of Emerald's real reasons for splitting.

But playing stupid was often smart. Trader'd had to pound that through his arrogant skull. People were always willing to believe it—believe they were smarter than you, especially. And being underestimated also gave you an edge. An edge a man like Trader could turn into clear profit.

Ryan had learned how to use that kind of an edge as well.

"Still, she would have felt safe here, right?" Krysty pressed, her green eyes wide. Ryan realized that he wasn't the only one smart enough to play stupid.

"She would've regarded that as walking into a trap. Oh, quite correctly, of course. She would be much too valuable a bargaining chip not to use. I have a responsibility to this ville and to its people. It's up to me to protect them, to make their lives as much better as I can. I could buy a lot of benefit for Brewery with Emerald Savij to trade."

"Do you know where she went?" Ryan asked.

"Only that it was somewhere other than here."

"Surely you must hear rumors," Krysty said with a brilliant smile.

"Well, yes, I admit we have. A young woman as...energetic as Emerald tends to make waves when she passes. We know she stayed a time with Horse McKinnick's scavvie band in the ruins of downtown. She didn't linger long, and I gather left with some acrimony. But they would know where she went from there, if anybody would."

"How do we get this McKinnick to tell us?"

"An excellent question, Ryan. An excellent question. If Krysty will forgive my lapse into vulgarity, the only means that suggests itself is to grab him by the balls. He is neither an honest man nor a reasonable one. He fancies himself brilliant, but all he shows is a degree of cunning you'd expect from a vicious animal."

"You trade with him?" Ryan said.

"Not with him, no. We'd shoot him down on sight. Anybody sane would. He's hard to miss—he's almost seven feet tall, with a great tangle of reddish hair and beard. And he also has a patch, over his right eye. I suspect strongly that is his only point of similarity to you, Mr. Cawdor."

The brewmeister shrugged expressively. "We do conduct trade with his people. What else can we do? If we had to pass favorable judgment upon all our trading partners before we did business with them we'd get scant commerce."

"Yeah." Ryan sat back in his seat. "So where do we find this McKinnick and his crew?"

"Last reports we received, their main hideout is the old museum near the stumps of the Arch."

"Lotta cannies there," Jak remarked.

"Oh, yes. It's what makes it profitable for Mr. McKinnick. He's jealous of anybody poaching on what he considers his salvage grounds. The cannies do an admirable job of policing it for him. Of course, that's not by intention on their part. They'd eat him as soon as anybody."

The brewmeister took a deep drink. "Ah. An especially fine batch. No doubt they'd eat him with extra relish, so to speak. McKinnick is not a lovable man."

"What about screamwings?" Ryan said. "Looks like you got a big colony of the bastards living up in that big old tower."

"Met One. Yes. Somehow it managed to survive both the blasts and the earthquakes largely intact. An impressive feat of engineering. What would you like to know about them?"

"How to deal with them, mostly."

"As for that, all I can advise are keen senses and staying near overhead cover. They dislike going into restricted places. And luck. That never hurts, of course."

"Of course," Krysty said. "Don't they bother you here?"

He laughed. "We—my ancestors, rather—were lucky enough to come into possession of a number of machine guns, including a .50-caliber Browning. I admit the smaller-caliber machine guns are more effective, with their higher rates of fire. But like everyone, the screamwings have a most healthy respect for a .50."

A crunch of footsteps on gravel made Ryan turn. Mildred and Doc were coming back through the gate into the little courtyard with their sec men escorts trooping after. Mildred's face ran with sweat, but she looked calmer than she had since J.B. had been hit.

"What?" demanded the baron with a hint of querulousness. "Was there something you needed to complete the operation?"

"The appendectomy? No. That's done. You think you could scare us up some chairs and some of whatever you're drinking, Baron? Your sick-bay room is on the hot side."

"Seriously? You've finished already?"

Mildred frowned. "I said I did, didn't I?" She was still in full-on physician mode, meaning she brooked no shit from anybody.

"Efficient, is our Mildred," Doc said.

The brewmeister clapped his hands. Servants appeared to pop out of the ground, bring chairs and mugs. Mildred and Doc took grateful places in the cool, sweet-smelling shade and drank deeply.

The brewmeister smiled. "I'm impressed."

Mildred set her mug down. She had a foam mustache. After a moment's hesitation she wiped her mouth with the back of her hand. A hard thing for her to do, just coming out of the mind-set of a doctor trained in the late twentieth century, when sterility wasn't just a principle but a religion.

"It was an appendectomy," she said. "Aside from the fact you've got to open the body wall, it's about as simple an operation as there is. Your people had the stuff all ready. The girl was healthy enough, if a little undernourished, when the inflammation started. But your healer was right—the appendix hadn't burst yet, so it was just knock her out, slice her open, find that bad boy and snip it off. Then a quick cleanup, sew her up, done."

"Of course I'm impressed at your manifest skill, Mildred," the baron said. "What really impresses me, though, is how you tried neither to draw the procedure out nor to make it seem more involved than it really was."

"Why would I do that?"

He laughed. "This is a treasure you have here, Mr. Cawdor," he said. "A real gem. I'd be tempted to try to hire her out from under you if I didn't know better."

"The girl's doing all right, then, Mildred?" Krysty asked.

She nodded. "Unless something unexpected happens, she'll be fine."

"Excellent," the brewmeister said. "You've abundantly paid me for the little information I was able to impart. I'll consider that credit to your account. Will you stay for the night? We can offer excellent accommodations. On the house, completely."

Ryan didn't even need to poll the others with his eye. "Thanks, Baron," he said. "We want to move as quick as we can on this. From what you say, hunting this Emerald is going to take some doing."

"Indeed it shall," the brewmeister said. "If I may offer a word of advice—don't allow her so much as a whiff of suspicion that you are hunting her. Or she'll vanish like a snuffed candle flame."

Ryan nodded. "We'll keep that in mind."

The brewmeister tipped his head to one side. "If I might ask one favor of you," he said.

"Go ahead, Baron," Krysty said, ever the diplomat.

"If you find her alive, please tell Baron Savij I helped find his missing child. I reckon it's time to reach out to Soulardville, warm up relations."

"You got it, Baron," Ryan said. "No problem."

The aproned man smiled and nodded. "Splendid."

With a little grunt of effort he rose. Ryan and Krysty

stood up. Mildred and Doc finished off their mugs and joined them a beat later. Jak sat gripping the white-painted metal arms of his chair and frowning up at the tower.

"Clock," he said. "Why hands don't move, eh?"

Ryan looked up. The tower clock said 12 straight up. He realized it had said the same when he first came close enough to make it out.

The brewmeister chuckled. "It's absolutely right twice a day," he said. "What else do you know in this disordered world of ours that can offer such precision?"

Chapter Fifteen

The enormous red-bearded man jumped to his feet as Krysty strolled through a gap in the rubble. The city wreckage here ran to chunks of stone and concrete as big as a compact predark car, all jumbled up as if they were toy blocks a giant child had petulantly kicked aside when through with them.

About a dozen other scavvies sat around the fire in the middle of the bowl-like depression in the lumpy gray dust. She wondered why they bothered to start it so early. The sun was just approaching the jagged western horizon, a fat red face half obscured by the rampant fang of the tower that gave the screamwings their nesting place. The flames were still so pale in the slanting yellow-orange light as to be almost invisible. And the ruins didn't need any more heat. In the unlikely event the air temperature dropped significantly after dark, the sun-warmed blocks would keep releasing their stored heat until the sun rolled back up over the forests and tall tangles of industrial wreckage across the river.

"Don't trouble getting up, gentlemen," she said, smiling. "I just have a few questions."

"You!" the huge man bellowed. He had a nose like a mutie potato with an eye patch on one side of it. "I know you! You're one of the coldhearts that cost me half my people!"

"You shouldn't be so hostile to strangers just passing

through," she said. "We weren't bothering anyone. Except the cannies whose dinner we were busy trying not to be when you jumped us. You're not worried about their tender feelings, are you?"

"And your screamwings!" he shouted. "They scratched shit off my face. And look—" He held up a side of the befouled denim jacket he wore. "They tore my jacket."

"They weren't our screamwings. Believe me. Now, this will all go much more smoothly if you all just sit down and take deep breaths and we discuss this calmly."

The man shot an arm in the air. It looked like a tree growing in fast motion in an ancient vid. "Take her! The train leaves the station tonight! And *she's* a-pullin' it!"

But his men—Krysty didn't see any for-sure females among the bunch, anyway—were smarter. They kept their seats.

"Listen, McKinnick," said a gaunt man with long stringy blond hair and a raw-looking gash down the right side of his dirty face. "You don't think the bitch would just walk in here without backup, do you? Nobody's that stupe. Unless you say triple-stupes and droolies coulda handed us our asses like she and her pals did a couple days ago?"

McKinnick's face crumpled like a fist. "You're too smart an ass for your own good sometimes, Sanchez," he said. But he studied the lone woman with a frown and his one good eye. As good as an eye that consisted of a yellow iris peering out of what seemed to be a pool of blood could be, anyway.

"Yes, he is a smart man." Doc's educated tones echoed sourcelessly among the canted blocks and chunks of hot stone. "We have the drop on you gentlemen. So softly, softly!"

"That's right," Krysty said. "So why don't you keep

your hammers lifted, boys? If we wanted to chill you, you'd all be staring at the sky this moment."

The giant scavvie leader grubbed in his dark tangle of beard at what Krysty guessed was probably his chin.

"What about Louie?" he demanded suspiciously. "You chill him?"

"Louie?" she asked. "Skinny kid, brown hair? He's fine. Taking a little nap with his wrists and ankles trussed up."

"Sleeping on the job? The little fuck-snake. I'll chill him myself!"

"For shit's sake, McKinnick," Sanchez said. "She means they knocked him out and tied him."

"Damn," McKinnick said. "What about that one-eyed fucker? Where's he?"

Krysty shook her head. Her hair had curled into tight ringlets that didn't hang down to her shoulders.

"He didn't make it," she said sadly. "We ran into some trouble on our way back up here."

"Why'd you come back up, anyway?" a black guy with a red handkerchief knotted around his head so the ends stuck up like little nub-ears to either side of his head said. "Couldn't keep away from us?"

"We got some questions, is all."

"Well, I got the answer to 'em *right here,*" McKinnick said, grabbing the permanently dark-stained crotch of his blue jeans.

Krysty put her hands on her hips. "That's not getting us anywhere. Why don't you just sit down and—"

With speed truly stunning for a man so huge the scavvie leader crossed the twenty-odd feet of uncertain footing between them in less time than it took an eye to blink. Krysty Wroth had superb reflexes, but the sudden move took her so off guard that she was unable to react before he had a huge arm wrapped under her right armpit and had her hoisted up so her head shielded his. She felt something sharp prick her neck and looked down to see he had the tip of a monstrous knife with a vicious saw back pressed under her jaw.

"All right, you droolies out there!" he yelled. Even from behind the back-eddying carrion stench of his breath enwrapped her head, overpowering even the stink of his gross, unwashed body. "Throw down your blasters and step out where we can see you! Or I'll cut the eyes out of this bitch's red head and skull-fuck her to death."

"DAMMIT, KRYSTY," Ryan said out loud, struggling to keep the big scavvie boss centered in his scope. He didn't worry about the scavvies hearing. He was lying on his belly two hundred yards away, on the second story of what had been a parking garage that had had its higher floors planed right off. "I warned you not to get fancy!"

McKinnick's followers scattered like roaches. A yellow flash came from the right of their camp. A scavvie with a dark scalp lock suddenly arched his back like a cat hit by a speeding land wag and spun down to a cloud of dust with his yard-long braid flying up in an arc through the evening air. A boom reached Ryan's ears. He recognized the sound of the short-barreled scattergun underneath the main barrel of Doc's outsized monster handblaster.

A brighter flash in the gathering twilight told Ryan that Mildred had weighed in with J.B.'s M-4000 shotgun. A Mex-looking scavvie trying to point a single-action revolver toward the hidden attackers suddenly had his face punched into a blood cave by an invisible fist. Having taken the whole double-00 shot column to the bridge of his nose, he folded like a suit of clothing slipping from a hangar.

As the 12-gauge's even more thunderous boom echoed through the ruins, in the midst of all the noise and dust and scrambling stood McKinnick, roaring, with his god-awful big blade shoved up against Krysty's neck. By cunning or instinct, the scavvie chieftain had the struggling woman perfectly positioned so that Ryan, despite his height advantage, had no shot.

Not even the sneaky expedient of a thigh shot. Hit the bone, he'd go down. Hit the big artery, and he'd bleed out in seconds. It was as certain a chill shot as a brain or heart hit, and almost nobody remembered or even knew to protect their thighs. But Krysty's own long thrashing legs were in the way. Ryan didn't dare break the trigger.

"Krysty!"

FOLLOWING ADVICE from the brewmeister, the companions had departed Breweryville afternoon before last by a western exit. They'd worked their way farther west among what had mostly been modest residential neighborhoods, once upon a time.

Now the neat detached houses of yellow and tan brick stood long abandoned. Their windows were gaps as empty-black as skull eyes. Their doors were mostly missing, long-ago smashed in by scavvies, perhaps survivors of the first single great spasm of the big war.

The houses had long since been gutted of everything. In the years following, the war survivors had ventured out of Breweryville and Soulard, daring the cold and the dark of the black-sky years, seeking canned foods, meds, weapons, ammo, usable clothing. After skydark ended, the looting had grown, extending even to the copper wires in the walls and the metal pipes and plumbing fixtures. Ryan guessed wars had been fought between the two neighboring villes, as well as freelance scavvies, over the loot in those thousands of formerly neat houses.

Now the roofs were missing slates. Some sagged where rain had gotten in to eat out the rafters. The one where Ryan and company forted up for the night was in pretty good condition: no point risking their hides if another hellstorm blew in, or even getting wet and miserable when it rained, as it did for an hour around the middle of the night. There were dark stains on the floor, but the place just smelled of dust and wood rot. The blood or shit or piss that marked the hardwood floors had desiccated to nothing decades before and blown away on the winds that blew unimpeded through the gaps that had been doors and windows. There seemed to be some bats dwelling in the attic, but otherwise it looked as if even animals gave the place a pass these days.

There was nothing for them. They'd even eaten the insulation in the attics, probably years before any of the party but Mildred and Doc had been born.

Next day the companions had worked their way around Soulardville's west side. They stayed on triple-red alert. They didn't expect Soulardville patrols to be hunting them, especially not there. But they didn't want to chance an encounter with them.

Neither did they want to risk a run-in with any of the other two-legged predators that still infested the corpse of the dead city. Even if this area was thoroughly picked-over, hope springs eternal. Somebody desperate enough might decide there might be treasures somebody had missed in the blocks of nearly intact residences. And nobody knew what motivated muties. The particularly virulent breed of stickies that infested the St. Lou area liked to stick close to the Sippi and the flooded buildings that flanked it. But none of the companions was willing to risk getting pulled apart by suckered fingers and needle-toothed jaws by taking anything for granted.

And always there was the threat of the screamwings that laired in the great tower.

So the five friends worked their cautious way downtown. They moved carefully for fear of stirring up rad pockets. That danger was very real, as both the Soulard patrol that captured them and the brewmeister assured them, whether or not whatever had happened to Savij was any accident. And of course there were still the cannies and the well-armed, ruthless scavvie gangs vying for control of still relatively rich ruins.

Now they ventured back into the hunting grounds of their former persecutors. But this time there were crucial differences. The companions, even one down, were well-fed, well-rested and, perhaps most important, well-hydrated.

And now *they* were on the hunt. Their ammo stocks had been restored. Evidently Bro Joe really wanted Emerald back. Their packs were stuffed with all the cartridges, shotgun shells, black powder and caps they could carry.

McKinnick's mob denned in the ruins of the old Expansion Memorial Museum, but scavenging parties were usually abroad. They worked the downtown rubble inland from the stubs of the blown-away Arch itself. It had been the companions' bad luck that the cannies who first jumped them had chased them right through the heart of McKinnick's hunting grounds.

With the clues given to them by the Soulardites and some of the brewmeister's sec men, the companions located the giant scavvie boss and a dozen of his people inside a day. Partly that was just luck. Partly it was the fact that McKinnick had gone out of his way to let the cannies know the high cost of fucking with his crew.

Assorted rotting body parts had been impaled on jutting rebar or simply placed on rubble cairns. The presence of fresher heads, hands and, most revoltingly, boobs clued the searchers they were nearing their prey.

In late afternoon they found the scavvie band. The companions held brief debate, huddled on the second floor of an office building. They'd picked a vantage point that offered a mostly intact overhead as well as view of the scavvies' campsite.

"Oughta sneak up and blast good," Jak said.

Ryan raised an eyebrow. When they'd found him, Jak had been a guerrilla leader of sorts, at the tender age of fourteen. He'd been quite a success. He was smart, keen as the blades he loved to carry, but he was still a youth despite lifelong seasoning as hunter of beasts, muties and men.

And sometimes he reminded Ryan of the old saying Trader used to quote: When a man's got a hammer, every problem looks like a nail to him.

"Begging your pardon, Master Jak," Doc said, squatting like a big improbable bird on the bare concrete floor of the former office building, "but is not the objective to get information from these people? Unless you have come upon a way of extracting data from corpses which you have neglected to share with us."

Jak shrugged. "Always takes somebody time die. Plenty time question."

Mildred scrunched her face up. "That's not what I'd call optimum information-gathering technique, there, Jak," she said. "Not even interrogation. For one thing, people who've suffered severe wound trauma have a bad habit of up and dying on you, when even a skilled physician can't really predict it."

Jak shrugged again.

"Why not just ask them?" Krysty asked.

Even Mildred looked at her as if she were crazy.

"Don't mean to pick nits here," Ryan said, keeping his eye on the unsuspecting scavvies as they assembled their campfire in a pocket of the ruins, "but last time we saw this particular bunch they were trying their level best to chill us."

"I believe, Ryan," Doc said, "that, speaking precisely, they were running for their lives from the screamwing swarm. These, of course, being the ones who succeeded."

"Yeah. Well. Before that they were sure keen on seeing us cool down to air temp. How do you reckon they want to talk to us now?"

Krysty smiled. "We approach them and ask nicely."

Doc's eyebrows went north and the edges of his mouth went south in a look of contemplative surprise. "Well, the sheer novelty effect should at least buy you several seconds. Before they attempt to rape and murder you, of course."

"Well, that's where the old concept comes in," Krysty said. "Mildred knows."

Mildred raised an eyebrow. "I'm all about avoiding bloodshed when it's possible, which so far seems to work out once a year. In a good year. But I'm drawing a blank, here, girlfriend."

"You know the one," Krysty said. "I've seen it on old posters and bumper stickers. 'Peace through superior firepower.'"

A corner of Mildred's mouth stretched open, showing closed white teeth. "I don't want to burst your bubble, but I think that the end result of that particular way of thinking was—"

She swept a hand around, encompassing not just the

half-collapsed and gutted office building, but the whole shattered ruins of St. Lou and the entire world beyond.

"—this. The big nuke. The earth-shakers nukes and the killer quakes. The storms and skydark. The muties, the pain, the acid rain. The Deathlands."

Ryan rubbed his chin.

"I see your point, Mildred," he said. "But I calculate mebbe Krysty's onto something. If we get the drop on them, they might just be reasonable. *Might*."

"It does make sense, my dear Ryan!" Doc exclaimed. "After all, these are coldhearts we are speaking of. What are the scavvies, after all? Why, *traders*. They must engage in commerce to translate their salvaged goods into wealth they can use. And commerce entails the ability to engage in peaceful exchanges."

"Were plenty willing to take us down," Jak said.

"To be sure. But we had intruded on their territory, which as you know scavvies tend to protect as vigorously as wolves. And, frankly, they saw us as prey. They're compelled to act differently under the blasters of a place like Soulardville or Brewery."

"But we aren't in Soulard or B-ville," Ryan said.

"Hence we return to Dr. Wyeth's splendid point."

"Wait, it wasn't my—"

"Forgive me—the lovely and lethally talented Krysty's point. A momentary confusion."

"So, you're in favor of the 'peace through superior fire-power' thing?" Krysty asked. "Got me confused now."

"Why not?" Ryan said, slapping his thigh. He was careful not to do so loud enough to make a noise that would carry beyond the walls of their hideout. Dust rose from fabric stretched taut over his thigh where he squatted. "They're careless. We can get close double-easy, set up a cross fire. Then I step out and open what we might term negotiations."

"Perfect plan, lover," Krysty said. "Except for one small detail."

"What detail?"

"Not you," she said. "Me."

"AND I WAS triple-stupe enough to go for it," Ryan muttered from behind the scope of his Steyr. He lay on his belly atop the truncated parking structure, with the long-blaster's forestock propped on his backpack.

He had to use all his iron will to keep from squirming in impotent frustration at what he saw through the scope. He didn't dare drop the hammer for fear of hitting Krysty.

It had seemed to make sense. Krysty had pointed out that this particular bunch—just a part of McKinnick's band, they gathered, even after the multisided battle of a few days before had thinned their ranks considerably—was exclusively male. What with one thing or another, they might just leap reflexively into action if Ryan strolled from nowhere into their midst. He cut a pretty threatening figure.

Whereas, as Krysty pointed out with her usual blunt appreciation of reality, when a woman who looked like her strolled into their camp circle, immediate fighting to the death wasn't the first thing that would cross their minds. And Ryan had to admit, she had powerful skills of persuasion. It might even work.

"Yeah," he grunted. "Like she used on me."

And it had been a fair enough plan. He knew Krysty had a point, both about the scavvies' lesser likelihood of jumping to code red if a woman appeared in their midst and her implicit point that she would be more diplomatic than Ryan.

But they'd all overlooked one thing: the asshole factor.

And McKinnick was definitely one *huge* asshole.

Krysty screamed.

Chapter Sixteen

Ryan's finger tightened on the trigger. He almost risked a shot through Krysty's shoulder, hoping the blow-through would wound McKinnick somewhere vital, or at least make him let her go so Ryan or one of the others hiding in the rubble could chill him.

Instead the huge scavvie dropped the struggling redhead as if she were hot. Krysty went flat on her face. Redfaced, the giant scavvie leader roared as he reached to his crotch and ripped something free. It drew an arc of red skyward as he flung his arm up.

Krysty's little hider knife. The coldheart's grip had pinned her right arm, but she'd put her left to good use.

Without thought or even correcting aim Ryan triggered a shot. It was pure luck he didn't pull off target. The scavvie lord roared as the 7.62 mm slug plowed through his right shoulder in a spray of blood. The little lockback folder knife dropped from his grasp.

The three companions still hidden in the rubble had been trading shots with the surviving scavvies, who had all gone to ground the moment festivities began. Now all three opened up on the suddenly exposed McKinnick. The giant reeled back as a charge of double-00 buck hit him in the capacious belly. Dust puffed from the front of his grimy outfit as Jak's .357 blaster joined Doc's booming black-powder blaster.

A new color began to join the urban camo grays, blacks,

whites and urban body-filth browns of McKinnick's shirt: red. Dull red patches, glistening moistly in the near-horizontal rays of the final sun, grew all across the vast front of the man.

He went to his knees, then he reversed grip on his huge saw-backed Bowie and prepared to plunge it into Krysty's exposed back. The redhead was facedown, hugging the dust-covered ground. So much as raising her head would be instantly lethal in the horizontal lead storm going on in that little cup of rubble.

As the huge knife descended, the top rear of McKinnick's keg head came off. A vast swatch of filthy tangled red hair fluttered like a broken bird wing and flipped right into the little campfire, where it began to send out a cloud of green-ish smoke.

Ryan imagined he could see Krysty's eyes go wide as the knife clattered harmlessly off a chunk of rubble six inches from her nose. Then most of her was obscured from sight as the mountain of man, filth and malice fell atop her.

Most of his brain promptly plopped out of the gap in the crown of the scavvie chief's head. It was a sort of dirty white, like none-too-clean bread dough.

Silence landed like a dud rocket. Ryan had jacked the bolt of his Steyr and sought targets, but none presented themselves. The surviving scavvies were hugging to the rubble.

He heard a plaintive voice rise up. "Who *are* you people? What the fuck do you want?"

The big man stirred. Instantly Ryan centered him in his telescopic sight, but he wasn't sure exactly where to aim. If having his brains blown out didn't chill him, where was he supposed to shoot him? he wondered.

Then the big body flopped limply to the side, raising a

billow of dust about the same color as his voided brains. Apparently unfazed, Krysty rose to her feet and dusted herself off.

"We want to talk," she called. "Nothing but. If you'd just listened to me the first time, none of this would of happened."

A hand waved nervously above a block of concrete that was smooth on the two visible sides and uneven on the tilted top. "Don't shoot," the same voice said, more pleading than anything.

"If you behave yourselves," Krysty said. She had drawn her own snub-nosed .38 and held it before her in a two-handed grip. It was angled toward the ground but ready to whip up and cut loose in an eye blink.

The scavvie's other hand came up. As if the owner was chinning himself on the sky, a whole lanky shape unfolded from concealment. It was the blond dude with the angry scar whom McKinnick had called Sanchez.

"Wasn't us who started this," he said. "Was him. That outsized piece of glowing night shit."

"Handy excuse," Krysty said, "although, yeah, technically it was. So don't you make the same mistake he did."

"Somebody's out there with a longblaster," the blond man said accusingly. "Sniping."

"That would be Ryan," Krysty said. "My man."

"Thought you said he was chilled."

"I said he didn't make it," she said. "And he didn't. He's still a couple hundred yards short of here."

"All right. Triple-funny. Can the rest of us stand up?"

"Slowly, carefully, hands in view at all times. Cross us and die. You know the drill."

"Yeah." He stepped around and plopped his lanky butt on the block he'd taken cover behind. Nine or ten comrades stood up, then stood looking sheepish with hands in the air.

"So," Sanchez said, "how can we help you?"

"We heard a woman came here," Krysty said. "Black woman. Young, mebbe seventeen. Good-looking, strong built. Green eyes."

"Oh, shit," a short skinny guy with a huge nose said. "I knew she was trouble."

"We all did, Grip," Sanchez said. "Except that fat ass-cheese McKinnick."

Sanchez hocked and spit. The phlegm glob traced a high green arc in the evening air and landed with astonishing accuracy on the middle of the fallen leader's upturned rump. Of course, Ryan admitted to himself, that made a double-wide target.

"Emerald, right?" Sanchez said. "Out of Soulardville? Turned out to be the baron's daughter. That the one?"

"Yes."

He sighed and slumped. "Said she wanted to throw in with us. We were cool with that—most of us. She carried a .44 Mag blaster and looked like she knew what to do with it. Looked like she could, you know? But then McKinnick had to go and try to rape her in the middle of the night."

"What happened?" Krysty asked.

Sanchez laughed uproariously. "Sorry. She did the same thing you did, Red. Stuck him with a little hideout knife. Didn't nail him in the balls like you did. Only got him in the gut."

He shook his head in disgust. "All that fucking belly flab, he might's well have been wearing a steel vest. Didn't do more than set him to bleeding like a pig and screaming like a little girl. She went bounding off into the night like a jackrabbit."

"Which way?"

Sanchez jerked a thumb over his shoulder. "East. Toward the riverfront."

"That was her second mistake," another scavvie said, "after trusting McKinnick. Stickies that way. Lousy with 'em."

"She's chilled now, sure," Sanchez said.

"You saw her die? Seen the body?"

"Well, no. But stickies don't usually leave much identifiable, you know what I mean. But no, ma'am, we didn't see her die."

From behind them came Jak's voice. "That all," he called. The scavvies jumped and turned. "No holdouts."

"All right, Jak. Ace. You all can come out."

Doc rose from the rubble like a scarecrow on a pole, grinning over his colossal handblaster. Mildred stepped out holding the scattergun at her waist, a fierce, determined look on her face. Jak appeared at the far side of the depression in the rubble and perched on what was probably a short length of wall foundation, holding his Python tipped skyward in his hand and a thumb on the hammer spur.

Sanchez's eyes were flicking this way and that. He reminded Krysty of a mouse caught in a corner, looking for which way to bolt.

"Look," he said, "it ain't healthy to be out here after the sun goes down. We want to get back to our base before it comes on full night and the stickies and cannies all come out to feast."

He paused. "You folks enjoy living more than screaming, you might consider doing the same."

"Looks like you intended to camp out right here," Mildred said.

"That was McKinnick," Sanchez said. "Notice where he is now."

"Suppose you tell me exactly what happened," Krysty said. "Then we can all go make our respective sleeping arrangements. You can start with after Emerald stuck your boss and ran."

"All right. We chased her. We were working down around Olive Street. Some sweet salvage around there—anyway, she lit out north across Washington, that's the street that leads off over the Eads Bridge. She cut down toward the river, under 70 to LaClede's Landing."

"Crazy," the little dude with the nose said. "That's like Cannie Central. And then all them stickies, live up in the old *Admiral*. Fucked-up place to be anytime. Worse after dark."

"We saw cannies skulking around, then we heard her scream." Sanchez shook his head. "Listen, not even McKinnick with the hole in his gut, not to mention his pride, wanted to press on any further. Girl's dead, and that's a fact. Or she wishes she was."

"When was this?"

"Couple weeks ago, mebbe. I swear, Red, that's the truth. And it was never our idea to try to run you people down. That was McKinnick right through."

"Bullshit," Krysty said. "We all saw you. You were eager as cannies to run us down. But that bullet's long since left the blaster."

She studied him a moment. "All right," she said. "What you say about Emerald rings true, and you have no reason to lie about that I can see. So go ahead and clear out now. And one word of advice—stay out of our road from here on. Your shadow falls across our path again, you'll wish the stickies had you. Forget the cannies."

Sanchez moistened his lips with a pale tongue. "I believe you, Red," he said. His eyes flicked toward his boss's prone body. "Can we, uh—"

"Don't press your luck," Mildred said.

"Right. So—"

"Pick up your traps and feel lucky we're in a forgiving mood," Krysty said.

"You got it. And—have a nice day."

"SO WHERE DO we stand?" Ryan asked.

They'd rendezvoused back in the partial structure from where they'd first scoped the scavvie camp. It had only a single intact stairwell, and a good enough roof, protection against things like acid rain and screamwings. It offered a readily defensible place to hide.

As they talked they ate dried fruit they'd brought from Soulardville. Krysty and the others filled Ryan in on their conversation with Sanchez and the others.

"So that's it," Mildred said. "She's dead."

Ryan arched a brow at her. "Really? You know that for a fact?"

Mildred blinked. Her face was just visible in the last blood-colored light of day.

"Well, they said the cannies caught her."

Ryan looked at Krysty. "You asked if they'd seen her body, right?"

"Right. And they hadn't. I'm thinking the same thing you are—our girl isn't going to be easy to kill."

"But—cannies." Mildred shuddered. "They're pretty serious about keeping hold of their food, once they catch it."

"Like scavvies said," Jak added. "She hopes she dead."

"If she didn't escape," Krysty said.

"Isn't that a big assumption?" Mildred asked.

"No more than that she's chilled," Ryan said.

"Come on. We know she's smart and tough. She's still a girl."

Ryan, Krysty and Jak all looked blankly at her. Doc chuckled.

"Never forget," he said, "we are just visitors here. Our boon companions grew up in the Deathlands. However pampered Princess Emerald may have been, however much the hapless baron may have wanted to hang on to his little girl, she was by contemporary standards an adult. And may very well be alive."

"You seriously think she had a chance to escape from cannibals?"

"She got away from McKinnick and his playmates," Ryan said. "Let's all remember something—we've got a job to do. And that job doesn't end until we lay hands on either the princess or irrefutable evidence she's no longer among the breathing."

"You're not saying you still take this job thing seriously?" Mildred said in tones of disbelief. "After what that monster Brother Joseph did?"

"Don't forget he's got J.B.," Krysty said.

"But we have to try to rescue him anyway! Why not, why don't we just throw over this nonsense and head back and break him out."

"That's a mighty well-secured ville," Ryan said.

"But Brother Joseph's feeding the people to those muties one at a time. Wouldn't they be eager to help us if we saved them from that?"

"Seems to me you got it exactly backward, Mildred."

"What do you mean?"

"You saw those people," Krysty said. "When they sacrificed that poor child, they seemed…eager, ecstatic. They think Brother Joseph is saving them from that. Allowing the few to pay the blood-price for the many."

"Anyway," Ryan said sharply, "we're letting our barrels

wander way off-target, here. The point is, we took the job. We sealed the deal. So we deliver. Simple as that."

"But the deal was tainted!" Mildred exclaimed.

Ryan shrugged. "I tried that argument and lost. In the end we took the jack and we took the bargain, even if it turned out to be the devil in disguise on the other side of the counter. It's still our word given. That's our bond."

"What now?" Jak asked. "Into cannie-land?"

"Just wandering around their turf seems like a poor proposition," Ryan said.

"Succinctly put," Doc said.

"Out there!" Mildred called.

Everybody looked toward her. A faint silvery glow was streaming in the open spaces where wall-size windows had been, molding her round cheeks and forehead in mercury. The crescent moon was rising over the bluffs across the big river.

She pointed. "Lights. Down there toward the river."

Ryan duck-walked up to hunker at her side. "Bonfires," he said. It seemed figures were moving across the brightest fire, about a quarter mile off in an area of buildings that seemed, at least in the thickening darkness, mostly intact. After a moment he turned back to his circle of friends.

"We need information," he said. "So we don't just skip in blind."

"What?" Jak said. "Just find cannie and ask?"

Ryan felt a slow smile cross his face.

"Shit, yeah," he said. "That's exactly what we're gonna do."

Chapter Seventeen

Scratch scratched.

Names among cannies tended to be like life: nasty, brutish and short. Also intensely literal-minded.

It was hot and humid here in the late afternoon. The air was thick and smelled of the river, and also the shit and piss and decomposing body parts in the vast stickie nest a little bit to the north. The buildings right down by where the brown water lapped up against the top of the old river wall had most of their walls standing, mostly in brick the color of a human liver. A color Scratch knew well.

The pack had enjoyed a big feed a few days back, when they chased some outlanders. They hadn't caught any of them. But several of the pack had been chilled. And so had four scavvies, at least whose bodies the Landing pack had managed to recover. So everybody had feasted until their bellies were round.

But that food would be gone soon. What didn't get eaten would go all liquid and slough off into the dust in another day or so of this wet heat. So Scratch had to come out here and forage.

He was by himself, considered too junior to be accorded a role running with the bulk of the pack, which was hunting richer grounds, on the heights of Highway 70, or south along the waterfront. The cannies were hoping to catch unwary wayfarers or even exiles from the big villes down that way, as they had half a moon ago. But that hadn't turned out too well.

He heard a scurrying and leaped after it into the dark interior of a brick building. There were rats down here. Catching even one of them would mean he didn't have to come back to the den empty-handed and face the unpleasant consequences.

In the gloom of what had been a corner room he saw a naked tail just disappearing into a hole. With a cry of anguish he threw himself on the floor, which was crusted with dried mud and crud deposited last time the Sippi had overflowed its banks and flooded the Landing. He stuck his hand in the hole and groped.

His fingers brushed the whipping tail tantalizingly. Then pain! Pain shot up his arm.

He squalled and yanked his hand out. Jumping up, he danced the dance of agony, waving his wounded hand in the air. Blood drops flew in the heavy air.

Then he calmed down. If he made too much noise, some other hunter would hear him. Early-rising stickies, his own pack—it almost didn't matter which. Either would be triple-bad.

He stuck his thumb in his mouth and sucked. The taste of human blood, salt and copper, heavy and hot, soothed him like mother's milk.

He looked around. He had to find *something*. If he went back empty-handed again, he'd go hungry and maybe get beat and bit for his trouble. And if the pack had had an especially bad day—or an especially good one—the senior males would use him.

Or they might just decide Scratch was more trouble than he was worth. Then the only question would be: raw or cooked?

He headed toward what had been a big window. A large

green tree grew outside, so big its roots had buckled up the sidewalk. Lots of trees down here near the river, anyway. That meant squirrels. Lots of squirrels. They tasted good. Much better than rat.

They were hard to catch, though, he admitted. Double-hard. He moved soundlessly across the dried muck of the floor.

And froze. He smelled something.

He had to stand there and take several deep sniffs to be sure. No mistake: human sweat, on relatively clean skin.

Clean human flesh was rare in the LaClede's Landing rubble and environs, a prized delicacy. If he could score a whole adult who'd bathed more recently than last cold-moon time he'd win full pack standing and go up over all sorts of rivals. That evil bastard Deadeye for sure. And Club-Dick—Scratch's sphincter tightened in remembered agony at the very thought.

He crept toward the window, hunkering down so as not to be seen if the prey was close by. Reaching the window, he lay down on his belly. The dried stuff on the floor itched his pecker. He ignored it.

His prey was a block to his left, down toward the river itself. His heart jumped. It was a woman, an oldie, but not wrinkled-old yet. She was plump with juice and muscle and the right amount of fat. Especially on her ass and bubbies.

He felt his dick get hard beneath him and didn't even mind the way the hard crust of crud sanded it.

She was middle-dark skinned. Her hair seemed to be done in short braids with beads. She carried a handblaster in a holster at her belt. She looked scared.

Lost. Had to be. Come off a boat put in to trade with the scavvies or the villes and wandered in the wrong direction.

Wrong for her, right for Scratch.

She disappeared down an alley. Scared as she was, she didn't think to look around much. Triple-stupe.

Scratch could barley believe his luck. It was good to be Scratch. He flowed like floodwater over the sill of the window, whose glass had been busted out so long ago not even glittering powder remained. Then he took off at a run down the cobblestone street.

He knew how to run pretty fast without his feet making flapping sounds. You had to be stealthy when tracking prey.

He reached the mouth of the alley, knelt, peered quickly around. The woman had almost reached the other end. She looked cautiously left and right as if there were anything to see but blank brick walls, with mud marks on them and a lot of old faded marks painted on. Never seemed to occur to her to look back.

Drawing his knife, which had a short, wide, almost wedge-shaped single-edged blade, he stole down the alley. His prey was headed toward the water, and that was a bad thing this time of day. It meant stickies might just be abroad. To have them grab her... The notion filled him with a burning, bubbling brew of fear and rage and frustration, to go with the hunger and blood-lust and adolescent horniness already boiling in there.

She paused at the alley's far end, hunkered down and looked with exaggerated care: first left; draw back; right. But still: not back. Never so much as a sign in the muscles of her upper back and shoulder, the brown sweat-sheened skin left bare by her green halter top on which Scratch's eyes were pinned, of turning to see the silent death running up on her.

He couldn't run balls-out, not if he wanted to stay quiet. He feared she'd hear the pulse that thundered in his ears as it was. So he didn't catch her before she'd straightened and walked into the middle of the next narrow street.

Scratch shot out of the alley mouth in pursuit. He'd time his leap to drag her right down on her face and those ripe big bubbies on the cobbles. Then his knife at her neck, and—

And nothing, it turned out. Because no sooner had he left the alley himself than something the size of a building hit him right in the back of his head. He felt pain, wide and broad, and lightning flashed through his brain along with an oddly musical note.

Then he was banging his own chin on the cobbles, biting through his tongue, rolling, flopping, as helpless as a beached fish with a world of pain, his head pushing hard to be let out.

He'd been took, he knew. Enemies! Enemies! But his vision was all blurs, and his limbs wouldn't work....

"NOT A VERY prepossessing catch," Ryan said. He stood over the stunned cannie, tapping the aluminum bat on the scuffed toe of one boot.

"Is he still breathing?" Doc asked. He stood on the other side of the mouth of the alley where they'd waited for Mildred to lure the cannie kid they'd been shadowing the past half hour. He still had his sword stick clutched near the tip with both hands to use as backup in case Ryan missed his stroke. But the one-eyed man had come through again.

Mildred bent over and pressed fingers to his neck. "Got a pulse," she said.

"Carry my bat, Krysty?" Ryan asked.

"Anytime, lover."

He looked at her, then blinked. He laughed and handed over the bat. They'd found it up in an apartment west of where they had chilled McKinnick the day before. Jak had said that they likely faced more close-in work and suggested they find some bashing weapons. Blades could get stuck in an enemy, and sometimes the most important thing to do to an attacker was just physically push him off you, so that you could bolt for it. Or so you and your buddies could chill him; whichever.

Given Jak's extreme fondness for knives, of which he carried at least a dozen, mostly concealed about his person at any given time, they took his advice to heart. So Ryan had the ball bat, Krysty a side-handle baton, Jak an ax-handle. Doc carried his sword stick, which he could wield with great skill. Mildred preferred to rely on the steel-shod butt of J.B.'s shotgun, which was designed for such work, unlike the precision tool that was Ryan's Steyr longblaster.

Ryan knelt by the semiconscious youth's shoulders and slid his hands under. "Whew," he said. "He smells awful."

Mildred hunkered down to grab his calves. She recoiled at once.

"Ew! He's all shit down the backs of his legs!"

"Want me take?" Jak asked. It wasn't that he was suddenly all-come-over solicitous for the freezie doctor. It was just that he, like the rest of them, was nervous about being caught on the streets by the cannie kid's pals. Or worse. He urgently wanted to move.

"Hell no!" she said firmly. "Thanks just the same, Jak. I hate these bastards, but I'll do what I have to. And I'll be damned if I give in to squeamishness about simple body wastes."

This time she helped Ryan pick up the limp form with perfect coordination. Ryan was surprised by the sheer deadweight of the slight youth. Still, deadweight or not, there wasn't that much to him: he was all sharp bone, barely covered by parchment-looking skin. Plus Mildred was strong for a woman, if not to the degree Krysty Wroth was.

"Sometimes," Mildred said as they hustled the now-moaning youth toward the hidey-hole they'd picked out earlier, "living in these Deathlands just gets the better of me."

"It does all of us, sometimes, girlfriend," Krysty said with a sympathetic smile.

"ALL RIGHT," Mildred said, pinching the cannie's thin cheek to rouse him. "You need to talk to us, boy. And talk fast."

He lolled his head. His blue eyes rolled in his pinched, foxlike face.

"Perhaps the boy's concussed?" Doc asked.

"I don't think so," Mildred said. "Pupils're the same sizes. Might take a while to manifest, though."

"Who gives a glowing night shit?" Ryan said. "So long's he doesn't die before he tells us what we need to know."

Mildred shot him a glare. Her patient-concern reflexes kicked in. He stared her down and she backed off, shaking her head ruefully, making the short beaded plaits swing.

"Nev-never talk," the boy said. A trail of drool ran out the side of his face. "Die first."

"That's a real possibility," Ryan said. He smacked the bat suggestively into the palm of his hand. He liked the little extra ringing sound it made. It sort of added something.

"Torture all you want," the boy said, a bit more clearly this time. Ryan guessed he'd never talked more than about halfway human at the best of times. "Landing pack don't break."

They had carried him into a back room of another of the long-vacant cafés or taverns in the old LaClede's Landing district, out of sight or easy earshot of the street outside the vacant doors and windows. There had been a venerable chair, heavy dark-stained wood, lying in a corner of the outer room. They'd tied him to that with rope from Ryan's pack.

Outside, dusk was gathering in almost tangible bluegray particles in the narrow streets between the buildings. These had suffered less gross damage than the buildings to the west in the downtown's crumpled core. The companions were all so wired on adrenaline they might as well have been jolt-walkers, for fear of getting caught down here after dark by the cannie's friends. Or worse.

"We aren't gonna torture you, boy," Ryan said. "You don't tell us what we wanna know, and make it triple-fast, we'll just clear out and leave you for the stickies."

"No!"

"Pipe down," Jak warned. "Or we choke some."

The youth's eyes were wide and standing out of his head now. Talk of stickies plainly terrified him.

"Your pack caught a ville girl two weeks ago," Ryan said.

"Yeah! Yeah! All water-fat and juicy. Dark meat! Like bitch there."

"Such a charmer," Mildred murmured.

"What happened to her?" Ryan asked.

"She fought. Too hard for ville bitch. Chilled two of us, then hurt Lumpy Balls so much he died two days later with his ball-sack all blue and swole up bigger'n his head! Balls really lumpy then, ha! But we downed her. We won. Chief Sharp-tooth said, tie her and take her. We make party with her at night by happy-fire!"

"Something tells me something went wrong with that little plan," Ryan said dryly.

"We built fire high. Then while we dance for to make happy, and for to make hungry, she gots loose! Cut ropes with hidie-knife. Sneaky ville bitch!"

"We seem to see a pattern developing here," Mildred said.

"I like this girl more and more the more we learn about her," Krysty said.

"Shut it," Ryan snapped. "What then? You chased her, right?"

Scratch's head nodded furiously, whipping the thatch of matted straw-colored hair. "We chase. She ran fast and we tired from dancing happy. But she triple-stupe! She ran up on old bridge. Right by big dry oldie ship stickies live in."

"Oh, shit," Mildred said.

"We so red, we nuke-red mad, we chase anyhow. Out on bridge. It all slippy, fally, and black black night! Black as stickie heart! And here come stickies all buggly eyes! Stickies in front! Stickies behind!

"We fight big fight with stickies then. Long-Dugs had her face and dug ripped off and fell in river. Stinky got tore open and guts stirred with torch. Did he howl! We had to make run then. Ran back home!"

"And the girl?" Doc asked. "What befell her?"

The boy blinked at him. "Huh? You stupe? Talk English!"

"What happened to the girl?" Ryan said.

"What else?" he said with a brown-toothed smile. "Stickies ate her."

"You saw that happen?" Krysty asked. "Saw her die?"

"No. Busy make fight so not make stickie food. What else? Bridge triple-dangerous all time. Stickies everywhere. She die! She had to die! Serve bitch right for what she done to pack!"

"Yeah, my ass just bleeds for your pals," Ryan said.

The youth blinked at him. "Others bitch you? Thought you chief, bitch them!"

"I think you're lucky I didn't really understand that."

"You were talking about a pattern?" Krysty said.

"Yeah," Mildred said.

"Surely you ladies do not entertain the possibility that Princess Emerald might have survived?" Doc said.

"Why not?" Krysty said.

"She survived the last impossible situation just peachy, seems to me," Mildred said.

"Yeah," Ryan said. "I wouldn't bet anything against this rad-blasted girl that I don't care to lose!"

From somewhere in the dusk came a long, nerve-freezing howl.

Chapter Eighteen

Scratch put back his head and howled back.

Ryan backhanded him across the face. "Shut that shit off!"

In a sinister fluid motion Jak drew and leveled his big Colt Python at the cannie's head. Krysty knocked his hand up. His red eyes flashed, but his reflexes—and for once his self-control—were so good he never triggered a shot.

"Why do that?" the albino teen asked with vibrating outrage.

"No time," Krysty said. "Just run!"

Ryan drew his panga. The cannie flinched. Ryan stepped behind the chair and brought the big knife down fast.

The rope that held the prisoner's hands parted and fell to the floor. The big knife never made a mark on Scratch's filthy hide. Then Ryan backhanded him with the fist that held the knife and knocked boy and chair sprawling and clattering into a corner.

"Why cut loose?" Jak asked.

"We had a deal," Ryan said. "Now run or get eaten!"

SEVERAL BLOCKS AWAY they paused and ducked into another building to catch their breaths and bearings. It had been a tavern. There was still an area on the floor they could see by the failing light where the bar once stood. It had to have been broken up for fuel long ago.

"Perhaps your mercy was misplaced," Doc said to Krysty. He was bent over with his hands braced on his rail-thin thighs. Everybody was winded. They were all in good shape from ceaseless walking but their sprint had been full-out, holding nothing back.

"Where are we now?" Mildred asked.

"Think it's the last building before the bridge landing," Ryan said, straightening. "The one the cannies chased Emerald over, if that little nuke sucker was telling the truth."

"I rather think he was," Doc said. "He seemed proud of the sordid affair, on the whole."

"Yeah. There's no accounting for cannies."

"Wait!" Jak yelped. "You mean big stickie nest ship other side building?"

"Reckon so," Ryan said.

"I don't see what a *ship* would be doing there," Mildred said. "Maybe it's some kind of boat, got stranded by a flood."

"We have to pass it," Krysty said. "Better do it now, before it gets full dark. Sun's setting now."

"Are we sure about this, people?" Mildred asked. "Shouldn't we at least look for a place to rest up, wait for daylight to try to cross? From what that kid said I get the feeling the bridge is half fallen down."

"Every cannie in Landing on butts now," Jak said.

"Well, how badly do we want to have every *stickie* in the damn Landing on our butts at the same time?" Mildred demanded. "I'm starting to wonder if it's not time to think about slipping back to Soulard and liberat— Damn!"

She whipped the heavy scattergun to her shoulder and fired. A huge yellow flame erupted from the muzzle. The noise in the closed quarters of the room almost imploded Ryan's skull.

The shot charge did worse to the stickie who'd suddenly appeared on the sidewalk right outside the window. His skull exploded. The slimy green body fell flopping to the pavement.

"Shit!" Jak cried. "They on us!"

"This way!" Ryan led them north through the building. Mildred brought up the rear. The shotgun boomed again as she turned and fired in a doorway to the next section.

"That got their heads down," she shouted to the rest as she charged after them. "We— Whoa! Holy shit, it's the *Admiral!*"

The others had crouched just inside a blown-out window on the building's north side. They were staring out at the landing that the big cantilever bridge took off from—or rather past it at the peculiar streamlined shape of a huge ship, four or five decks tall, tilted high in the air, its silvery superstructure bronzed by the last rays of the setting sun.

"Who?" Ryan said.

"The *Admiral,* an old riverboat. It was moored and used for a casino, last I heard. A big barge tow rammed it and knocked it loose."

"What it do *there?*" Jak demanded. He stood near the door through which they'd entered, watching their back trail.

"New Madrid Fault!" Mildred exclaimed. "Remember that crazy's story? 'New Mad Rid'? It's south of here, down on what used to be the Tennessee border. When all those big quakes cut loose right after the war, it must've gone up big-time. Probably sent a tsunami up the river that tossed that ship like a football."

"What do we do now?" Krysty said.

The .357 Magnum Colt Python had a peculiarly virulent muzzle-blast. Ryan felt the shocks hit him in the back of his head when Jak loosed two fast shots through the door across the building.

"Pick quick!" the albino youth shouted. "Company soon!"

"Fuck it," Ryan said. "We're going up the ramp and across the bridge."

"Right past the giant stickie nest?" Mildred yelped.

"I'm thinking more of the stickies we *know* are about to be crawling up our asses in fifteen seconds. Now, run like hell!"

Krysty set the example, vaulting the low sill and racing across the old parking lot and street, holding her trophy Mini-14 before her with both hands. Ryan gave Doc a hand. Meanwhile Mildred swarmed over next to them. She turned and knelt, training the shotgun back into the room.

"Go!" she shouted. "Jak, come on! Covering!"

Ryan paused only long enough to see Jak spin away, white hair flying, and dart toward the window. Then he ran for the long highway ramp.

They had to backtrack a bit to their left to get onto it. Krysty was already well up the sloping roadway. She stopped and swung the muzzle of her carbine down to cover the building they'd left as Mildred fired another blast into it. Then she turned around.

And froze.

The boat's blunt hull towered high above as if it were about to fall on her. The *Admiral* hadn't actually been thrown against the bridge by whatever had happened. Instead it had landed on a brick building and crushed it into a mound of rust-colored debris dense enough to prop its weight at about a thirty-degree angle. Ryan had seen bigger ships—in fact they all had—but he was bastard sure he couldn't recall one that *looked* so nukin' huge.

That wasn't what rooted Krysty momentarily in place. That would be the sight of stickies, dozens of them, swarming off the vessel like startled roaches.

"Well, fuck me," Ryan said, and scrambled up the ramp. "Krysty, move!"

As he ran, he realized it was getting dark fast. They had taken longer at their capture and interrogation of the young cannie than anybody realized. A glance over his shoulder showed him a tiny blinding arc of the sun just vanishing behind the cracked-egg top of the great dome that had housed some kind of arena for a sport unplayed in generations.

It also showed his other friends scrambling onto the ramp, and stickies streaming to meet them from the grounded ship.

Without breaking stride he hauled out his SIG-Sauer and fired a couple quick shots at the swarm. He saw one mutie jerk to a probable torso hit. It kept coming as if nothing had happened. Stickies were incredibly durable. Often only a brain-pan shot was really guaranteed to bring them down. Or a hit that broke the pelvic girdle. Nothing that stood on two legs could, when its support framework was busted.

But Ryan was out of position, and the range was long for a handblaster even if he were stopped and in a braced position. Shooting on the run was a low-percentage play at the best of times.

A flash lit the rapidly thickening twilight. A boom echoed between the buildings. Ryan saw one stickie fold over as it took most of the charge from Mildred's scattergun in the green gooey gut. It dropped to its knees and kept crawling forward. Another behind it reeled as a pellet or two ripped into it but wasn't slowed.

Another stickie's head erupted in blackish goo. It went

straight down on the ruin of its face and didn't move. Ryan tilted his head to see Krysty kneeling at the top of the ramp firing aimed shots from the Mini. It had been a hell of a shot for a carbine over open sights, especially in bad light, over at least one hundred yards.

Again and again the carbine spit flame. Ryan raced up the ramp and turned to throw himself on his belly beside the redhead. As he did, he unslung the Steyr from behind his back, disentangling it from the backpack with the grace of long practice. He twined the sling around his left forearm, braced the elbow on concrete still sun-hot and assumed a prone firing position.

"Go!" he shouted. Krysty didn't argue. She was up and running like a deer onto the cantilever bridge's first span.

Before shifting focus to his glass, which would crank his world down to a near pinpoint, Ryan took quick stock of his companions. Jak brought up the rear, blasting at stickies crawling on all fours out of the building they'd just fled. Mildred was stuffing single red plastic shells into J.B.'s shotgun and firing them. It was a difficult feat on the run, but she managed. Doc stood on the ramp's far side, nearer the great looming promontory that was the hull, booming away with his immense handblaster at stickies coming from that way.

"Doc, leave it!" Ryan shouted. "Everybody just run! I got it."

Without waiting to see if his commands were obeyed, he shifted the longblaster until it bore on the mass of stickies rushing the ramp in the face of Doc's aimed fire. With barely enough light to aim by, Ryan got a hairless head onto the top of the post in his scope. It was a hideous sight, something he never got used to: two sunken round black eyes like pits straight to hell, a nose that was little more than two vertical slits in a low mound of slimy skin, a round mouth ringed with teethlike needles.

He led slightly as he let out half of a deep-drawn breath, began to squeeze the trigger. The big blaster bucked and slammed into his shoulder with a stunning roar. When he brought the rifle back in line, with a fat fresh shiny yellow cartridge already cranked into its receiver, it was dead-on target. The stickie he'd aimed at was falling with the far half of its head simply gone.

"Get up from *that*, nuke sucker," he murmured as he sought another target.

He fired three more times. Two more stickies fell. The third one moved in an unexpected way just as the trigger broke. As far as Ryan could tell, that shot missed everything, even in that mob of the mewling monsters. Cursing, he snugged the steel buttplate back to his shoulder and sought a new target.

He had another problem: it was rapidly coming down to dead cave-belly dark. The Steyr's scope made it darker. Very little light came in the objective lens. All he saw were erratically bobbing blurs.

"Forget that, Ryan!" boomed a familiar voice from close nearby. He glanced up to see Doc high-stepping by, with his sword stick in one hand and the LeMat in the other, his coattails flapping behind him in the gloom like a heron's wings.

"They're coming, and the only thing now is to ride shank's mare as fast as she'll go!"

Ryan only understood that in the most general way. It was more than enough. He may not have gotten the exact words but it meant beat feet before they swarm you!

A glance over the top of his telescopic sight housing told him that was sound advice. Jak sprinted past. Mildred came chugging up the slope with a determined expression on her face, a few feet away. And about a hundred feet behind her came the first of the stickies, making disgusting bubbling squeaks and their sucker-toed feet slapping nastily on the pavement.

Ryan saw Mildred start to slow as if intending to provide covering fire while Ryan ran on. "Keep moving!" he yelled.

Her brow clenched rebelliously, and he felt a flash of fear she'd defy him. He pushed off anyway, snapping himself upright as fast as he could for all the weight of his heavy-loaded pack and the big longblaster. He was ready to grab the woman and tow her if need be. None of them was expendable, and he hated the thought of leaving a friend to face what the stickies would do to a person who fell into their suckered paws.

But for all the catching up she'd had to do as a twentieth-century freezie, Mildred had gotten more than a little seasoning during her time in the Deathlands. And one thing she was *not* was a slow learner. She powered right by Ryan, her short but strong legs moving in a blur.

He turned and ran after her. The Martin Luther King bridge was a wide roadbed supported by a sort of swooping angular cage of steel girders and strutwork. Such openworked metal structures tended to survive nuke blasts pretty well, unless they lay in what was called a radius of total destruction. The heat pulse of a thermonuclear weapon was over too quickly to seriously weaken the steel unless it went off really close. And there just wasn't much to a framework like that for the dynamic overpressure—the blastwave—to push against.

Something had done some damage, though. The highway buckled and cracked as if waves had been frozen in the asphalt. Girders were twisted like taffy. Some had broken and stuck out at odd angles.

Ryan didn't waste a lot of time on whys and wherefores. He turned, drawing his handblaster.

The stickies had fallen behind a bit. Some had gotten distracted ripping apart their fallen kindred. Not just the dead ones, either. He saw that a writhing mass of rubbery flesh beside the ramp was half a dozen stickies swarming the gutted one who had been crawling.

He aimed, shot. It was an easy hit now even at almost thirty yards because his targets were running right at him. He put two down with head shots out of three rounds fired and turned and sprinted on to find the others standing stock-still in the middle of the roadway several hundred yards along.

"What in the name of nuke death are you doing?" he shouted as he ran up on them. "Keep moving!"

"Perhaps not so easy a task, my dear Ryan," Doc said. He gestured grandly with his sword stick.

The central span was in ruins. It had simply fallen sideways, as if hinged on. Hundreds of feet long, it hung now by mere struts and beams along the side, like a mostly severed limb held only by tendons. The high girder-work still stood over it.

Right before their toes the Sippi was a southward moving uneasy blackness, like a living endless shadow.

"I didn't think a cantilever bridge was supposed to do that," Mildred said. "What now? We're stuck."

"Emerald made her way across," Krysty said. "We can, too."

"Are you so certain of that?" Doc said. "One might judge it likelier she fell into yon black waters yawning beneath our feet."

"There's ways across," Ryan said. "That metal framework's still up there. And whatever it is still keeping up the road. There's ways."

"Swim?" Jak suggested.

"We would more likely break our bones, hitting the water from such a height," Doc said. "A peculiarly unappealing form of death."

About a mile south, Ryan noted a yellow-orange glow that spilled off the bank to the river. Its actual source was obscured by trees.

"Must be Eastleville," he said.

Jak's Python cracked deafeningly from Ryan's left.

"Stickies come now," the albino teen shouted.

"Give it to them hard and fast," Ryan said. "We don't want them grabbing at us when we're crossing."

They turned and cut loose on the mob of stickies. The muties had shorter legs than norms and weren't especially good runners. Their hips seemed to be jointed-up. They were still a good fifty yards back, which wasn't good enough.

Ryan unslung the Steyr and shot, using his open sights. It was way too dark to see anything in the scope by now. Mildred was adeptly feeding rifled-slug shells into her scattergun round by round. Krysty fired rapid but aimed shots from her Mini with the folding stock extended and shoulder-braced. Doc stood with his LeMat held out at arm's length like a duelist; Jak knelt and aimed his own handblaster with both hands.

It was long range for handblasters, especially in the dark, but they had a lot of targets, jostling one another in their eagerness to get at their norm prey. Ryan blasted through a full magazine and started on another before the stickies broke and started milling back in confusion. By that time at least twenty shapes lay still or writhing in the causeway.

"That'll hold them for a few minutes," he said. "We better use them well."

They all turned and stopped dead.

Several dozen torches were approaching the far brink of the fallen span. They looked like flickering orange fireflies.

And beneath each torch was clearly visible the mis-shapen head of a stickie.

Chapter Nineteen

"One way or another," Mildred said, "this is really gonna suck."

Although this clan of stickies favored living right on water, like all stickies they loved and were fascinated by explosions and particularly by fire, to a degree approached only by the most dedicated of human pyromaniacs. Most especially they enjoyed experimenting with what fire would do to norms if they got their suckers on one. It could provide them endless hours of enjoyment.

The norm generally enjoyed it a good deal less.

"What now?" Doc said softly.

It was times like this when Ryan most keenly missed his friend and hard right hand, J. B. Dix. Quite rightly did old Doc Tanner call him the Master of Stratagems. He had a special gift for getting into—and more importantly, to Ryan's way of thinking, *out of*—tight places.

"We push on," Ryan said, coming to sudden decision. "Try down the side. Looks like the struts continue beneath the level of the old road."

"And the stickies?"

"We fight the ones ahead, or we fight the ones behind," Ryan said. "Or we go in the water and drown and die. I say we fight. Since we got to fight anyway, I'd rather do it moving forward."

"Better start now," Krysty said. To emphasize her words

she slung her handy little carbine and climbed over the railing. Her head dropped below the road level.

It was the controlled drop of a person climbing down, not an uncontrolled plunge to the concrete-hard surface of the Sippi.

"Ryan's right," her voice floated back up to them. "The struts do run across the gap."

The others followed her. Ryan snapped a couple more shots at the pursuing stickies and then replaced the depleted magazine with a full one. Stuffing the partially empty box in his pants pocket, he set out, too.

But he didn't take the low road. He took the higher one, scrambling up and down the zigzag girder-work bracing. His main intent was to outdistance his companions.

Nuked if I let Krysty be the first to face those muties on the other side, he thought grimly.

He made rapid progress. The rusted metal ripped at his callused fingers and palms. He had to wipe his hands frequently on his jeans to keep them from getting too blood-slippery, but he pressed on fast as he could.

Glancing down, he saw he was passing above his friends, just as he intended. Then he looked forward and his stomach did a slow roll inside him.

Stickies were climbing toward them. Both the way he was, along the angular network of girders, and along the struts that ran beside and beneath the original causeway like Ryan's friends. Only the muties had an advantage: the suction pads on fingers and toes that gave them their name.

They could basically crawl right along the *side* of the structure. Which they did, with needled grins.

He gritted his teeth. The temptation to let go and drop to a quick, clean death never entered his head.

He'd never abandon his friends, nor was it in Ryan Cawdor to give up without a fight.

He actually picked up his pace, scrambling reckless-fast, ignoring the pain and increasing slickness of his torn and bleeding hands, jumping heedlessly from girder to girder. Under normal circumstances that would have been triple-stupe. Now, what did he have to lose?

The stickies coming along the girders toward him actually seemed to pause, then they saw him speed up. Then, laughing their hideous gurgling giggles, they redoubled their pace.

When he got within twenty feet of the lead stickie, he hauled out his SIG and shot it through the face. Given the eyes were black lenses sunk in round pits, it was hard for them to show emotion. Nonetheless Ryan thought he saw surprise in the horror's right eye when the left one erupted in viscous black ooze. The creature broke away and plummeted without a sound.

The others chittered in consternation. Ryan halted, then shot two more off the girders. Looking down, he shot two that were fast approaching Krysty and the others.

Beneath him fire blossomed. Muzzle-blast whipped his pants legs against his calves. Krysty had drawn her short-barreled handblaster and was clinging with one hand and shooting with the other. The unexpected muzzle flare momentarily blanked Ryan's vision, but he heard a squeak of dismay and guessed she'd at least knocked her target loose from its perch.

Gritting his teeth and blinking away purple afterimage blobs, Ryan scrambled forward. Trying to cling to his SIG as well as the steel at the same time, he went down a slanted girder, trying to ignore the fact that to either side of him was an unobstructed drop to the water's black surface.

A stickie ran at him like a monkey on a branch. He shot it in the face. The mutie fell, but there was another right behind. His next shot hit that creature in the shoulder. It didn't even slow down. Instead it launched itself for him.

For an endless moment the mutie seemed to hang suspended in air. Ryan saw the sucker-tipped fingers reaching to pull the skin and muscle from his face; saw the gap of the monster's mouth fringed with narrow inward-curving teeth; smelled the abysmal stink of rotting flesh and intrinsic corruption that flowed out of that open gob.

Then he acted. He shoved the muzzle of the SIG-Sauer right into the black reeking gap of the stickie's mouth and fired.

The stickie's cheeks expanded comically, like a balloon being blown up. Its eyes stood out of their sockets. Ryan wondered if it was only his imagination that he thought he saw muzzle-flash glaring orange around them.

The stickie's left eye popped out of its skull. The skull itself burst open in the back, a chunk swinging right like an opening gate.

Ryan let himself fall back, catching himself at the last instant with his left hand on the girder. What remained of the stickie's face planted against the rusty steel with a squelching sound. Writhing, the horror brushed against Ryan's face as it bounced off, tumbling like a rag doll into the night.

"Ryan!" he heard Krysty scream. "Above you!"

He looked up to see another stickie posed on a vertical beam ten feet above his head, just about to spring for him. He tried to bring up the SIG, but his right arm had swung wide when he flung himself away from the girder to avoid being grappled by the dying reflex of the stickie whose head he'd blasted apart. He couldn't recover in time.

A bright white flash split the sky open right over his

head. The stickie squealed as something blasted through its skinny, rubbery torso front to back in a spray of black blood. It might not have been a fatal wound for a stickie, or at least not a wound that would stop it coming, but its convulsive reaction to the wound plucked both its hands off the beam. It fell.

Ryan looked farther up in time to see Jak in midflight, white hair streaming behind his head. He hit the beam the stickie had occupied, wrapped his left arm around it and clung like a baby lemur to its mother. A stickie gripped the outside of a girder that angled up from the base and swung itself at the albino teen. Jak pistol-whipped it across the face as it flew near. It back-flipped into a gibbering, shrieking cartwheel all the way down.

Ryan got his left arm around the pillar he clung to, extended his right arm and fired the SIG to slide-lock as fast as he could work the trigger. He guessed Jak's plan and was laying down covering fire. A couple of stickies dropped from the bridge. Others flinched long enough to allow the youth to make his move. Meanwhile the three companions still below, hanging on as best they could, added their own firepower.

With mad agility and utter lack of nerve Jak launched himself from angled girder to upright one to angled girder. Pausing to tuck away the big Colt Python, he gathered himself, a dozen feet up a vertical beam. Then he launched himself over the heads of the torch-bearing stickies crowding toward him onto the end of the bridge's level and intact cantilever arm. Performing a neat midair somersault as he passed through the flame of an upheld torch, Jak landed lithely on three points amid the third rank of stickies, scattering them like the sparks from his hair.

Then he sprang upright. He lashed out furiously with a fighting knife—a big clipped-point single-edge trench knife with a knuckle duster protecting the grip—in his right hand and one of his leaf-bladed throwing knives in his left. Black blood flew; stickies squealed in pain and confusion.

Clicking on the safety, Ryan jammed his blaster into its holster. He clutched the beam with both arms, drew his knees up and kicked out with both boots into the face of a stickie springing at him.

The creature got three suckers of its left hand stuck to the sole of Ryan's right boot.

"Ryan!" Krysty screamed again. This time he heard fear vibrate in her voice.

He let go, twisting his body. His boot came down on the horizontal rail that formed the side brace of the structure with the stickie's arm between sole and steel. Thin bones broke with loud snaps. The stickie shrieked, its suckers releasing Ryan's boot. He raised his foot to let it fall.

He hadn't quite recovered his balance and toppled backward. Jackknifing with all the power and speed of his core, he managed to whip his right arm over the horizontal rail that followed the roadway and arrest his plunge to doom.

A blur of motion. A stickie had slithered down an angled beam and was reaching for his face.

Ryan swung back his legs, then flung himself up and onto the rail. He wasn't sure how he managed to haul himself upright again without going over, but he did.

"Let's go!" he shouted, flinging himself forward. "Jak needs help!"

He plunged heedlessly the last few yards to the level roadbed. He swung himself over a yawning gap to strike the front rank of stickies boots-first.

His hurtling mass bowed the smaller creatures over. He

landed hard on his side, rolled over, then got to his feet with his panga in hand.

A stickie thrust a torch at his face. He heard the flame crackle and pop. Turning sideways, he leaned far back so that the burning torch-head went past his face. Then, seizing the torch between flame and rubbery hand, he thrust it upward while turning hard counterclockwise with his hips.

The fat blade of his panga whistled down and severed the stickie's arm just this side of the elbow. Black blood jetted.

Ryan kicked the howling mutie away from him. Blaster-fire crashed and flamed from close behind. His friends had begun to gain the roadway and join the fight from level footing. Slashing madly with the panga, clubbing stickies with the blazing torch, he smashed and hacked a path to Jak.

The albino youth had just gone down under a wave of the hideous muties, who promptly discovered they had a problem. He curled himself into a ball with his arms protecting his face from their lethal suckers. And when they grabbed at his back and shoulders they found their hands gashed by the jagged bits of metal, razors and glass he'd sewn into his jacket.

A stickie sitting atop Jak reared up, waving a blood-spurting hand and shrilling. Ryan thrust the torch into its face. The flame went with a hiss and a horrible smell. The stickie screamed.

Ryan kicked it away, then hacked down two more. A third, attempting to scrabble away on all fours, had Ryan's left boot come down hard on the small of its back, shattering its spine. It began to thrash and froth from the mouth.

With obvious effort Jak sat up. He planted the throwing knife in the gut of a stickie that closed on him from the

left, then smashed the trench knife's pommel into the face
of another attacking from the right.

Krysty waded in with her truncheon to the left of them.
To the right Mildred butt-stroked a stickie so hard its forehead caved in and it dropped straight to the asphalt. Doc
laid about left and right with his cane, then poked a stickie
neatly in the eye with its ferrule. Black blood and pale
aqueous humor spurted up its length.

Suddenly they were alone. The stickies broke and fled,
waving their suckered hands and bawling in fear. Some
were so panicked they ran straight between girders and
into space, to hang a heartbeat over nothing, windmill-
ing wildly before falling to their deaths. Others, in better
control of their tiny malicious minds, used their stickers to
swarm down the side of the bridge and beneath.

Ryan looked left and right. The way stood clear. He was
breathing like a bellows now. Blood and sweat ran in tor-
rents down his face. It trickled beneath the patch and made
his scar itch unbearably.

"Closing triple-fast behind!" Jak called.

Ryan looked back. The stickies pouring out of the
Admiral had torches now, too. They scuttled along the
girders and frame of the half-fallen suspended span without slowing. Some even held torches in their teeth to move
faster. The yellow flames glittered evilly in their black
eyes.

"Time to go?" Mildred said.

"Time to go," Ryan said. They sprinted across the
bridge for the eastern bank, soon leaving the chittering
horde behind. Even Mildred, with her relatively short legs,
easily outdistanced the pursuing stickies.

As they neared the descending ramp they saw, approaching through the woods, the uneasy glow of more
torches. Many of them. The companions slowed to a trot.

"Who do you think *they* are?" Mildred asked.

"I have no clue," Ryan said.

"I find myself disinclined to presume anything but the worst," Doc said. He was starting to puff some.

"Stickies don't usually like roaming the woods," Krysty said.

"You sure enough about that to bet your life on it?" Ryan asked. He was busy checking flaps and seals on his pack with his hands, making sure everything was secured.

"Well," the redhead said, "no."

"Great. Me neither. Make sure you got everything cinched down, people."

Eyebrows rose. But the one-eyed man's tone did not invite discussion. Everybody made sure their gear was sealed tight. As they did so they jogged forward, beginning to descend the long ramp. For whatever reason, ahead of them lay no visible sign of the highway that had once run from the bridge. Nothing remained now but a trail through dense brush into night-black hardwood forest.

"All tight?" Ryan asked.

"Yes," Krysty said. "But—"

"Follow me," Ryan said. He turned abruptly right, ran to the rail and jumped.

Chapter Twenty

"So whom do you suppose that was coming through the woods, my friends?" Doc asked. He stood in the brush that lined the shore, wringing out his frock coat. His sodden backpack lay against a gnarled tree root beside him.

Ryan hunkered by the softly sloshing water. He had his SIG-Sauer with the mag out and the slide open, blowing down the barrel to make sure it was clear of water.

Up on the bridge itself a tremendous fracas was going on. There were shrieks and chitters and the light of torches being waved furiously back and forth. Occasionally a body toppled over the rail on one side or the other to land in the sluggish Sippi with a resounding splash.

"Got no clue," Ryan said. He held up the handblaster so that the torchlight from the bridge shone through it. The bore was as dry as could be expected. He nodded, picked up the magazine, jammed it in the well and let the slide drive home.

"Wasn't it a little unfriendly to let strangers blunder blithely into a pack of ravening stickies?" Mildred ask.

"Mebbe more enemies," Jak remarked. He stood with his backpack on and arms crossed. He divided his attention between the bridge and the woods behind them.

"Yeah," Mildred said. "And maybe they weren't."

"Whoever it was," Ryan said, snagging the strap of his pack and standing up with it, "wouldn't you rather it was them who run into the stickies than have the mutie bastards still chasing us?"

"Since you put it that way," Doc said, "I do believe, better them than us."

Mildred shook her head. "Ryan, you are one cold article."

"You just getting around to noticing?" Krysty said with a smile.

"Anything in the woods, Jak?" Ryan asked.

The albino teen shook his head.

"All right. Take point. Mildred, left flank, Krysty, right. Doc, behind Jak. I'm pulling drag again. Head us straight into the woods mebbe thirty yards. We don't cut trail, cut right and we'll follow the river along through the brush."

"Where're we going?" Krysty asked.

"Lover," Ryan said, "we're going to *town*."

WELKOME TO EAST VILLE read the sign painted on a jagged-edged sheet of plywood and nailed twelve feet up an old wooden telephone pole, the words visible by the red light of a fire guttering in an ancient oil drum that was more holes than rusty steel.

Beyond it stood, or perhaps *slumped* was a better word, a good old-fashioned Deathlands pesthole. While it looked as if it were possibly built on a core of at least partially intact predark building, cinder block or prefab, it was mostly knocked together from tin sheets, planks and plywood scrap, and several tens of thousands of cans hammered out flat and tacked together.

They had come upon the remnants of a road that ran inland paralleling the shore. It lay close to an old rail causeway, whose embankment was evidently the only thing that kept the Sippi from washing out the buckled asphalt strip, or burying it in silt. The waters now came up right to the base of the railroad.

By the light of a rising moon the travelers followed a path cleared through a mostly fallen-down highway bridge. A few hundred yards south of that the road cut inland. It then turned south again to cross the ramp leading down from the combined railway-and-highway structure Mildred identified on the far side as the MacArthur Bridge, and continued south to the lights of what proved to be the booming metropolis of Eastleville. Population several hundred at least, or so Ryan judged.

The ville occupied a dirt crossroads in the midst of deep forest interrupted by sudden tall tangles of old tanks and pipes and other artifacts of once-major industrial activity. One road led a short ways west to the docks, a makeshift affair of scavenged blocks of concrete and platforms of warped planks. A couple of decent-size watercraft were tied up there, as well as a number of others all the way down to rowboats bobbing in the lights of lanterns suspended from poles on the dock.

The smells of burning kerosene, fish oil and rancid cooking grease emanated from the ville, as well as various shades of yellow and orange light, competing strains of music played on violin, slightly out-of-tune piano, guitar, flute, saxophone and enthusiastic banging of spoons on galvanized iron pans. The friends heard the blare of loud conversation and braying laughter.

Whatever it was by day, it seemed the postnuke rivertown gave itself over by night to drinking and debauchery of the most enthusiastic sort.

"I almost feel like I'm coming home," Ryan said, stretching his arms wide and arching his back. His shoulders and upper back ached from hiking—and running—

long distances humping the heavy pack. Plus the weight of his longblaster.

"I thought you had a more genteel upbringing," Mildred said.

He shrugged. "That was way back there. Seems like I really grew up in places just like this."

"Depending on one's definition of growing up," Krysty said.

They walked into the town. They were immediately hailed by barkers shouting the virtues of the establishments they fronted. With the ease of long practice they ignored them.

Jak stopped and pointed. "Looks interesting," he said.

It was a false-front two-story shack, not too sturdy-looking, whose front was ablaze with the lights of lanterns and candles. Painted grandly across the facade was the legend Hotest Gaudy Sluts Eest Of The Sippi!

"That's a pretty major boast," Mildred said, "given that we're all of what? Maybe two hundred *feet* east of the Sippi."

Doc whipped his cane under his armpit and straightened like an old-time gentleman out for a promenade on the town. "Come, lad," he said to Jak. "One thing this prematurely aged cavalier can assure you of—when an establishment feels it necessary to assure you of such a thing, it is most certainly lying!"

"But mebbe true!"

Being careful of the sharp bits sewn to his shirt—some of which had their glitter diminished in the garish light by a rust-colored matte coating of dried blood—Krysty grabbed the albino youth by the sleeve and towed him down the dirt street.

"Well, we aren't going to find out now," she said.

"Yeah," Ryan said. "We aren't splitting up."

"SO," RYAN SAID, leaning an elbow on the bar, "did you see a lone young black woman out of St. Lou come through here, week or two back? Or hear tell of such?"

The bartender was a tall, cadaverous party with a sort of long hound-dog face and long sideburns. He stood behind the plank-and-barrel bar rubbing dirt around in a mug with a gray bar rag.

"Lotta people come through Eastleville, friend," the bartender said laconically. "Don't all come through the Platinum Club."

"Oh, Louie," said the rather blowsy woman with the white-painted cheeks and the stiff bleached hair wound into an unlikely confection atop her head and whose bountiful bosom threatened to spill out of her low, tight, black bodice at any breath. She sat on a stool down the bar smoking a cigarette in a long black holder. Doc stood next to her, looking surprisingly debonair. They seemed to be paying a lot of attention to each other.

"Don't go fishing for bribes like that," the woman said. "Can't you see these people're quality?" She twined her arm around Doc's. "Especially Doc, here."

"But Madam Sally," the tall barkeep whined, "a man's got to eat. Not that you don't pay a decent wage."

"How many times do I have to tell you?" the woman snapped. "It's Madame Sallée."

"I'm sorry, Mad-Dam. It's just—I don't rightly know how to pronounce it."

She turned to Doc, sighing smoke through her nose. "These barbarians! *Ils n'ont aucune idée de la façon parler correctement.*"

"*Quel dommage.*"

She shivered and laid her head against Doc's shoulder. "Ah, Doc! You certainly know how to melt a lady's heart."

"A man of the world acquires certain modest skills— I beg your pardon, Jak? Are you quite well?"

Jak had snorted his beer through his nose. Mildred started to pound him on the back, then thought better of it.

"He'll live," Ryan said. "So. Black girl. 'Bout the height of Mildred here. Young, sharp-looking, big tits, green eyes."

"Hoity-toity type from one of those snooty villes across the water," Madame Sallée said with a sneer. "Won't have a dock themselves for fear we'll corrupt their precious peasants with our worldly ways. Oh, well, so much more business for us."

Krysty winced as memories returned like unwelcome house guests. "You know, Ryan," she said, "thinking about it, I can see why you prefer it here, too."

"Yeah," Ryan said. "Now, if we could stick to the subject. Please, somebody?"

Doc lowered his head to murmur something in Madame Sallée's ear. She laughed and tapped him lightly on the chest with her folded fan.

"Of course I'll forgive your friend's rough manners," she said. "He's obviously a rough-hewn adventurer type. Probably been all over these Deathlands. Could be a real heartbreaker to a woman who went in for the brutal type."

Mildred and Krysty turned and looked at each other, then started to laugh.

"In answer to your question, tall, dark and dangerous," the saloon proprietress said, "she was through here. Through Eastleville, anyway. She did not see fit to grace the Platinum Club with her custom. I chanced to encounter her one morning ten or eleven days ago, in Tank's Rusty Nail trading post down by the waterfront. She was inquiring about reputable scavenger outfits in the area. As if that ain't a contradiction in terms!" And she laughed through her charmingly *retroussé* nose.

"Wait," Jak said. "Why 'Platinum Club'? What platinum? Don't see no platinum nowhere."

"It is an honored name in these parts," the madam said, "with a rich tradition."

"Oh."

She fluffed her hair with her fingers. A couple strands snapped like dry straws. "You may take it as referring to my coiffure, if you wish," she said, then tittered.

She put her bleached head together with Doc in conversation that pointedly excluded the others.

"Thick as thieves, those two," Ryan remarked.

"Do my eyes deceive me," Mildred said over her beer, "or has our good Doctor Tanner made himself a conquest?"

Louie sidled down the bar. There wasn't a lot of custom at the moment, but a rowdy card game in the corner made it hard to hear more than a couple feet away.

"Not to contract the madam," the barkeep muttered, "but actually, there is a scavvie outfit working the area that got itself a pretty good rep."

Ryan cocked an eyebrow. "Truth to tell, I thought it was a contradiction in terms myself."

"Not always," Louie said, shaking his head. "This Daniel E. dude who runs the bunch seems like a pretty straight shooter. Drives a hard bargain, gives honest value. And nobody's ever bought anything off him that the rightful owner turned up looking for afterward."

"Mebbe just chills 'em," Jak said.

"You're young, boy," Louie said. "Otherwise you'd know word like that tends to get around."

The albino teen bristled. Ryan laid a hand on his arm. "Easy, Jak."

He turned his eye to the bartender. "Not a good call on the kid. He's been around the boneyard more than most men twice his age. The other thing though, about the rep—that's ace in the line. So, any idea where we can find this Dan E.?"

Louie's eyes, which already seemed to be mostly just slits in the seamed mass of his face, actually managed to get narrower. "Why you want to know?"

"We don't mean harm to him," Krysty said.

"We got no beef with anybody concerned," Ryan added. "Just want to find him."

"He don't seem like the sort who's eager to be found. Likes his privacy, know what I mean?"

Ryan slid a hand across the bar. Five 9 mm rounds stuck out just beyond his fingertips. "Like you said," Ryan said, "time's tough and a man's got to eat. This is live brass, and not reloads."

Louie moistened his lips with a gray tongue. "No comebacks."

Jak cawed laughter. Fortunately that wasn't uncommon enough to draw eyes. Except a single-barreled blue glare from Ryan.

"Who'd know?" Jak asked. "Ville like Eastleville full people eager sell skinny."

"He's right," Ryan said, turning back to the barkeep. "So why not take what's on the table now? Or would you rather we start taking bids?"

"North," Louie said. His eyes, or so it seemed to Ryan from the way the wrinkled lids shifted, cut toward his employer, who at the moment was having her hand kissed by Doc. Ryan raised a brow.

"His outfit bases out of a place up north. Three, mebbe four miles. Abandoned factory, I heard some of his people say. Big old brick thing not far from the river, woods all around."

"So he's scavenging there?" Mildred asked. "Say, this beer isn't bad."

"Comes from Breweryville," Ryan said. "Couldn't you tell?"

"Right about the beer," Louie said. "Not about the salvage. Nothing there but floors and a few walls. Legends say it was abandoned years before the megacull. Old Dan, he likes it 'cause it's triple-easy to defend. Does his salvage work in other old industrial areas. Or just heads inland a bit. There's tens of thousands of houses there, many of them still untouched. Same as down here."

"So why don't you live and work in those houses, instead of out of a bunch of thrown-together shacks like Eastleville?" Mildred asked.

"Lotta people think the old burbs're haunted. Rad dust, they *are*—same as over the Sippi. Not all the scavvies workin' them are near as ethical as Daniel E. Cannies like to lair there. And worse things."

"I hear you," Ryan said.

The bartender hunched up a stooped shoulder. "Anyhow, I reckon the real reason is, here's where the docks are. Lot shorter distance to walk to work or trade. Even if a quake does shake your own roof down on your head, ain't as if it's very substantial."

"Got it." Ryan opened his hand to the right. Louie made the stacked ammo disappear with a speedy efficiency that impressed even Ryan.

"So," he said to his companions, tipping up his glass

mug and draining the last drops and bits of foam. "We better see if someplace can rent us a room tonight. We've got weapons to clean and make sure they're full dry before we sack out."

He didn't think anything of mentioning the fact, nor did Louie show any sign of thinking anything of the fact that he did. That was life in the Deathlands.

"You won't get a better deal or cleaner bedding anywhere else in E-ville," Louie said. "That's straight-up. I don't take home extra whether you den here or go sleep in some bushes. And, uh, it looks as if the management has taken to looking upon you with a kind eye."

"Is that what they call it here?" Krysty asked with a twinkle in her eye. Little pink spots actually appeared high up on the man's gray and sagging cheeks as he turned away.

Ryan looked over to where Doc and Madame Sallée were, to all appearances, joined at the hip. The proprietress was a bit generous in that department, but notwithstanding that, nor even the mileage the thick face paint couldn't hide, she was a fairly handsome woman. Any scavvie or boatman or caravaneer who forked over his crib fee would count himself lucky to draw a gaudy slut who looked half so good. Or smelled half as clean.

"Doc?" he said, pitching his voice to be heard over the card game, where a vociferous dispute had broken out over who was a greater donkey, the man who raised with seven-deuce off or the man who folded to such a weak-ass bluff.

From a back room three tall, thin, middle-aged black men filed in. Like Louie they wore ruffled white shirts, black trousers and scarlet cummerbunds. An upright piano, blond wood-stained and battered and sporting a bullet hole visible from where Ryan leaned against the bar, stood against the wall. A battered but shiny saxophone and a stand-up bass in decent shape leaned in racks next to it. One man sat down at the piano. His partners picked up the other instruments and started doing musician-looking things to them.

Madame Sallée sank long fingernails painted the color of fresh blood into the lapel of Doc's frock coat in a highly proprietary manner.

"You people got yourselves a cut rate on our finest room," she said, "if you'll just be sweethearts and not rush Doc off. The band's good. I want him to hear them."

That wasn't all she wanted from him, Ryan thought. He held back a grin.

"He'll be fine here," Krysty said. "Won't he, Ryan?"

"Reckon he won't get into too much trouble."

"Reckon he will," Mildred stage-whispered behind his back, and snickered. As fatigued as she was, a single beer seemed to be having a disproportionate effect on her. Not that she was a big-time lush to start with.

With a languid gesture of red-nailed finger Sallée summoned a pot boy of about eight, dressed the same as the other male employees and with his round face scrubbed and his straight brown hair parted neatly in the middle, and told the solemn-faced child to lead their guests to their accommodations.

"What happen to 'we aren't splittin' up'?" Jak asked in disgust.

"If I got to spell it out for you," Ryan said, "Doc got lucky. Which, you got to admit, doesn't happen often."

"Come along, Jak," Krysty said. "You'd want us to do the same for you."

Mildred sniggered again at the look on the teen's paper-white face.

"Oh. Almost forgot." Ryan turned back to the bar and

signaled the bartender. Louie finished filling a tray full of mugs for a serving girl. The bartender came over.

Ryan pushed across a single bullet. "One more thing. We're going to need a boat."

Chapter Twenty-One

Lying on his belly in brush damp with the dew of recent dawn, Ryan held the navy spyglass to his good eye. A young woman stood naked in an open section of wall, three stories above a gravel yard dotted with a few dandelions just opening yellow heads to the daylight. As Ryan watched, she ran her hands back through her kinky black hair. She appeared to be gazing off across the river, possibly at her lost homeland.

He heard the slightest rustle of sound and turned to see Krysty elbowing up beside him. They hid in the dense undergrowth of a hardwood forest, not a hundred yards from the river, at the verge of a wide cleared space that, they knew, surrounded the long-dead factory on all sides.

"Borrow?" she asked.

Wordlessly he handed the glass over. As she focused it he carefully scanned their surroundings, looking for details they might have missed. Or possible threats.

The friends had traveled here in the boat they purchased in Eastleville for the rather exorbitant price of the Mini-14 Krysty had recovered from McKinnick plus its banana magazine. She'd mostly exhausted the .223-caliber ammo while fighting off the stickies anyway. The craft, a simple twenty-foot-long whale boat with a little two-stroke alcohol-fueled mill, lay hidden on the riverbank among thick thorny wild blackberry bushes covered in pink and white flowers.

The past two days they had spent skulking in the nearby woods and scoping out the gutted factory building that was Dan E.'s headquarters. They had been all around the perimeter, spending hours split into teams observing the stronghold from various angles. They even shadowed work parties as they tramped toward the woods to their current scavenging grounds amid a big development of long-empty tract homes roughly a mile to the northwest. They slept under makeshift tents, moving their campsite every night to reduce the odds of a bad-luck discovery.

For all the seeming wildness of its woods, marsh and grassland, this particular stretch of country was either occupied or traversed enough by relatively settled humans that many of the Deathlands' more alarming denizens had been hunted back. The unexpected appearance of whoever had fought the stickies on the east side of the bridge a mile or so south was yet another reminder nothing could be taken for granted.

"Pretty," Krysty said, studying the girl. "I can see why you don't mind this part of the surveillance."

He grunted a brief laugh. "She does love her routine."

"We have enough information now to move on?"

"Mebbe so," he said. "Longer we stay out here, worse we're asking for something to go south on us. And I'm itching to get back and check on J.B."

She made a distressed sound. Glancing at her, he saw her lips pressed together.

"I don't like this, lover," she said in a low voice. "Not any part of it. From everything we've learned, girl's smart, tough and resourceful. And that she has triple-good reason not to want to go back. The fact she's so pretty doesn't make it any easier to think of...that happening to her."

"The little girl who got given up to the screamwings didn't have it coming, either."

"No, but we couldn't do anything to help her. This one…" She shrugged.

"I'm not leaving J.B.," he said. "You don't want to, either."

"No, I don't. I won't. But you also know if we go back, even if we bring the princess, Brother Joseph and his creepy acolytes will never let us leave alive."

"That's true," he said, wiping sweat from his face. It was a beautiful morning, with birds singing and flowers blooming and the air thick with the smell of moist green growing things, as if the big nuke and skydark never happened. But it still got nuke-red hot in a hell of a hurry here, a long spit from the great river.

"But like a man said in a book I read as a kid, it's also irrelevant. We made a deal. We take this girl back, and we leave with J.B., regardless of whether they want us to or not."

"You make it sound so easy."

"You know better. Know *me* better."

"But Jak even managed to sneak inside the scavvie stronghold last night. Surely he can find us a secret way into Soulardville, so we don't have to carry out this…this horrible bargain!"

"But we do, like it or not," Ryan said. "That's the part everybody always keeps forgetting. We made the deal. We honor the deal. Like or dislike don't come into it. Now, let's get back with the others and calculate what comes next."

"THEY WOULD APPEAR to have created a formidable defensive system," Doc said.

He sat beneath a tree in his baggy boxers, his bony white knees drawn up, wearing a sort of hat he'd contrived out of leaves against the heat. He had spent the past three days painstakingly creepy-crawling at the edge of the two-hundred-yard cleared zone, making detailed sketches of the former factory, its defenses and what he could observe of the structure's interior and movements of its occupants inside. It was considerably facilitated by the fact that much of the outer walls were simply gone. There wasn't much by way of internal partitioning left, either, although the scavvies liked to define their own personal spaces with movable screens or hanging curtains. Apparently they liked being able to catch such breezes as stirred the hot, humidity-heavy river-valley air.

How they liked it during winter's snow and hard-driven sleet was, to Ryan's mind, a different question entirely. Krysty suggested either they migrated somewhere a little more airtight when the weather started getting serious cold, or they'd only set up shop here earlier this spring.

"They have people on watch for twenty-four hours of every day," Doc said, sounding like a teacher lecturing his pupils. "By night guards patrol the roof, in pairs, which are spelled every two hours. They enjoy a clear field of fire in all directions, with sandbagged hard-points spaced throughout the open area in the walls to protect riflemen. They set out long strings hung with bells or cans with rocks in them, in different locations each night, both inside the structure and in the cleared zone surrounding the building, to provide warning if intruders approach. When they travel to and from their work site, they take a different route through the woods each time. They do not appear overly comfortable in the woods, and they do seem to stick to the same few trails in what appears random rotation."

Any well-educated man of Doc's time, it turned out, had been trained to draw accurately and well. He'd covered many pages of one of the notebooks Mildred was forever scavenging—and scribbling in—with his diagrams and sketches and notes. These were strewn out among the companions in a little clearing in the brush a quarter mile south of the abandoned factory. If there'd been people in this spot in the past hundred years they saw no sign of it.

"They primarily appear to expect either wholesale assault, or attempts to purloin their salvaged goods by stealth. For those reasons they occupy the ground and third floors. The second is where they keep the fruits of their labors. They have numerous locked strongboxes for the most valuable items."

"Which don't concern us," Ryan said.

Doc nodded. "Quite so. The fourth floor is mostly vacant, although they store less valuable items up there. The ground floor is rather heavily fortified, with sandbag emplacements, makeshift ramparts of brick and concrete and coils of the ubiquitous razor wire."

He looked grandly around. He seemed to be enjoying himself hugely.

"In sum, my friends, they would appear to be a most difficult nut to crack."

"But they sloppy," Jak commented, crunching into a preserved carrot from Soulardville.

"Always happens," Ryan said. It gave him a pang: it was just the sort of pithy and pertinent observation the few-spoken Armorer would pipe up to make. Ryan was pleased to have come up with it on his own, not that it was any earth-shattering revelation. He was good and knew it. And his other companions were triple-sharp, too.

He just wondered what his eye was missing that J.B.'s eyes wouldn't.

"No matter how keen you are or think you are," he said, "enough time without anybody making a serious play for you, it all starts to get routine. You get bored, complacent. Your guard comes down."

"Did that happen when you and J.B. were with the Trader?" Mildred asked.

Ryan chuckled. "Didn't have enough downtime between people and muties making plays for us to ever get slack."

"In this case I suspect this particular band's rather formidable reputation works against them as well as for them," Doc offered. "Coldhearts are less likely to attempt to avail themselves of the fruits of their labor by force because they know they will be competently and fiercely resisted. Because people seldom prove willing to take the risks, the scavvies are not kept as alert as your Trader's caravan was."

"Don't think anybody ever accused Trader's crew of being slack in the self-defense department," Krysty said with a twinkle in her eye.

"Nope," Ryan said. "Trader just had kind of a knack for pissing people off. Drew trouble like flies to shit, basically."

"So we've talked out a plan, the last couple days," Krysty said. "Do we run with it?"

"Seems complicated," Jak said.

"Straightforward don't seem likely to work with these people, does it?" Ryan asked. "Much less a cagey little critter like Emerald. Anyway, it's as simple as I can see us making it."

"Only question now is, will it work?" Mildred said.

Doc slapped his skinny thighs and laughed and laughed. Ryan feared the oldie was losing it again.

"Oh, it will work, my dear!" Doc exclaimed. "The real question is, at which point will it run off the rails?"

As SILENT AS THOUGHT, Jak slid down the rope in blackness.

His long white hair was wrapped in a dark bandanna. His hands, neck, face and feet were carefully blackened with charcoal. His wolf-keen senses were stretched to their fullest.

He heard the sounds of human habitation. Far off, a hum of earnest conversation, indistinct, came from behind some kind of screen illuminated by low lantern-light, away at the far end of the factory's third floor. Nearer, he heard snoring in several voices, echoing ever so slightly between the concrete floor and ceiling. And almost directly below came the rhythmic soft sound of a person of middle size sleeping. A young girl, by the sound.

Somewhere down on the ground floor a pair were having sex. They were trying to keep the noise down out of consideration to their fellows. Their success was indifferent. Jak suspected the others were accustomed to tuning out such sounds. Just like the snoring.

Their noise was unlikely to help him. From his own experience, and observing his companions, he guessed any out-of-place sound louder than a fart would bring scavvies instantly awake. With, it hardly needed saying, weapons in hand.

But he excelled at stealth. He'd been inside the dead factory by night before. Then, as this night, he had scaled the outer brick wall like a gecko, although that first time he hadn't carried a coil of light, strong nylon rope about his narrow waist, as he did now. The climb itself wasn't as triple-tough as his friends made it out to be, not much of a thing at all to the albino teen. The ancient walls still stood mostly strong and firm despite the wag-size holes yawning in them. But lots of mortar had fallen out from between bricks over decades of neglect and weather, not to mention the odd earthquake and thermonuclear blast in the vicinity. He found plenty of grips for fingers and toes.

Double-easy. A breeze.

It was during the previous night, that first recce, when he'd found the hole in the floor of the fourth story that let down within a dozen feet of where Princess Emerald slept soundly on her pallet, hidden from the rest behind a scavenged silken screen.

The scavvies had a weakness. No surprise: every defense did. As smart and tough and resourceful as Dan E.'s crew was, there were too few of them to secure the whole structure completely. What they overlooked was what most people did: the possibility that somebody might try coming at them from above.

Well, that and one other thing. They did, after all, split their people both above and below their treasure storeroom. The thing they totally never reckoned on was that they might face intruders who didn't give a spent brass for even their most precious salvage.

The rhythm of the girl's breathing was interrupted. Jak froze. She produced a soft snort, a rustle and her regular breathing began again. Watching carefully in the starlight filtering in the open wall, he saw her turn over and settle back in.

He let out his own breath. Double-close, he thought, willing his heartbeat to settle down. Too close.

He slipped the rest of the way to the bottom of where a loop of rope he held on to hung and swung an inch above the bare concrete floor. The end was tied on his waist to keep it from dragging and possibly making noise. It poised a certain fouling danger, if you were clumsy. Jak was as graceful as a cat.

He set both bare feet flat on the floor simultaneously. They made no sound at all. Here, near the floor, the air was thick with the smells of bodies, smoke, some kind of incense or herbs, as well as the dense, moist vegetation outside. Close up the strongest scent was girl sweat.

Princess Emerald slept naked. She was astonishingly beautiful lying there on her side with her head pillowed on her arm, the soft dark contours of her firm young body outlined by fugitive light from stars. Her privacy screen now masked the far lantern glow from Jak's sight. Jak was a healthy young male; he felt himself getting hard inside his jeans.

Noiselessly he walked up behind the sleeping girl. As he did he wadded a handkerchief in the palm of his right hand. Kneeling carefully, he reached out and stuffed the balled cloth in her mouth, covering it with his hand. At the same time he slipped his left arm under her neck, then grabbed his own right wrist.

Instantly she tensed and tried to fight. Instead of her first instinct being to scream she tried to bite his hand. He admired her fighting spirit for that, but it wasn't the best response from a survival standpoint. That would've been the scream, despite the makeshift gag.

He'd suggested holding a knife to her throat to discourage her making noise. The others nixed that at once. Emerald had a habit of reacting badly to that sort of thing, and just because she slept nude didn't mean she didn't have her favorite nasty little hideout knife concealed in her bedding where she could get at it double-quick.

Instead he applied strong pressure to her carotid artery with his forearm, just as he'd been drilled by Mildred. The cloth handkerchief muffled the noises she made struggling with him. Keeping his right hand slightly cupped prevented her getting a grip on his palm with her teeth. He really didn't want that to happen.

Just as he had done when Ryan demonstrated the

sleeper hold on him, the girl suddenly slumped into the limpness of unconsciousness. Not trusting her deep cunning—another thing he admired about her—he kept up the hold for a slow count of ten after she went under.

Pulling another handkerchief from inside his shirt, Jak quickly folded it thin, looped it over her mouth and tied it at her nape. He took a black cloth bag from his belt and pulled it over her head, cinching it around her throat and tying it off just enough so it wouldn't come up over her strong chin, not tight enough to interfere with her breathing. He was glad her coarse, slightly kinked black hair was tied back; otherwise he'd have had a triple-bad time trying to corral it. He drew her limp arms behind her, fastened her wrists together with a noose of triple-strong predark nylon fishing line and tied that off.

His first thought, as he jumped to his feet, was to hope she hadn't noticed his boner pressing against her bare back through the fabric of his fly. The very thought embarrassed him ridiculously.

The way her large breasts lolled on her rib cage when he pulled her onto her back didn't help any. Steeling himself, he undid the tail end of the rope from around his waist, made a quick loop of it beneath her arms and her breasts, then putting hands under her armpits, dragged her over beneath the hole.

He tugged the rope three times, hard. In a moment it tautened. The princess was drawn slowly up through the hole in the roof.

He didn't even try to stop himself staring at her nude, limp body as Ryan and Krysty, waiting overhead, hoisted her up. Some things were just too much to ask of a man.

For an eternity he waited while his friends untied the climbing rope from the hopefully still-unconscious captive and made sure she was securely bound and gagged for extraction.

He heard them come back to the hole above. He crouched by the pallet, looking up in anticipation of seeing the end of his lifeline snake back down toward him.

And from just the other side of the screen a young male voice said, "Em? You asleep? There's something Lana and I'd like you to take a look at."

Chapter Twenty-Two

Jak froze. Without a whisper of sound he drew his big trench knife with the studded knuckle bow. If he could cut the newcomer's throat with one swift stroke, then hold him tight enough to keep him from breaking away or noisily kicking over stuff as he bled to death, there was a chance they might still get out of here alive and with their captive without the alarm being raised. Sure, it was the same chance as a moth caught in the middle of a forest fire, or close. But a chance.

He heard the scuffle of leather on concrete as the man approached the end of the two-sectioned privacy screen. Six heartbeats more and he'd peek around and see Jak.

"Em? You there?"

The guy was clueless. Jak gathered himself to strike. Any instant...

Away off in the night a woman's shrill voice screamed, "Stickies! Help! Stickies got me!"

Jak just had time and presence of mind to flatten himself behind the princess's now considerably disordered pile of bedclothes. He blanked his mind and tried to think himself part of the floor. It was an old hunter's trick. He'd known it to work, too. Not just on animals or even muties. Men, too.

Jak made himself relax. He believed an enemy could feel his tension that close up, if not smell fear. But he was ready to snap into action at the first sign of discovery.

Chilling or running like hot nuke death was after him, whichever.

Instead he heard a gasp. Then, "Shit! She's gone!"

"That must be her!" another male voice asked, as the terrified woman screamed again, wordlessly this time, rising and falling and quivering with terror.

Footfalls pounded away from Jak. Men and women shouted. He heard clacks and clatters as scavvies snatched up blasters and checked for chambered rounds.

Jak didn't wait around, nor did his two friends, who were crouching on the vacant floor above. The rope came wriggling down. He leaped and caught it. Rather than have them haul him up he scaled it like a squirrel up a beech tree.

Just before he vanished up through the hole he saw scavvies clutching blasters running toward a stairwell at the far end of the floor. The screen that had stood between him and the lit lantern was down. He saw the scavvies wore whatever they slept in, from fully dressed to T-shirts and skivvies to skin. He noticed one girl with ash-blond hair hanging to the small of her back and carrying a lever-action carbine, who had a triple-nice rear.

"No time to sightsee," Krysty said from right over his head, her voice low.

Without comment Jak scrambled up to the fourth floor.

GRUNTING, Ryan paid out line.

"This girl's been eating regular, anyway," he muttered. Even with Jak's and Krysty's aid, lowering her deadweight the thirty-some feet to the ground was a challenge. "Ought to call her Princess Lead-Butt."

"Shh," Krysty said.

The line went slack. Ryan held up. A tug, and he let

out more of the rope. A brief delay, then three sharp tugs on the rope. With a sigh of relief he felt the rope go completely loose.

Peering over, he saw Doc's scarecrow figure kneeling to lower the nude and still-unmoving form of Princess Emerald to the gravel of the yard against the foot of the factory wall. Along with darkening his face, Doc had chosen to apply lamp-black to his silver-white hair as well. It made it stick out in weird random spikes, as if his head were some kind of glistening mutie burr.

From just a few feet away it wasn't easy to make out even that little detail. They'd waited for the moon to set and the night was cave-dark. Also clouds had started to roll in from the east as the companions watched Jak do his human-fly routine up the blank wall.

Though Ryan didn't much care for doing it that way, Krysty and Jak belayed for him while he slid down the rope. He was heaviest, and it was best to have both the others on the line, even if it was tied off to a pipe coming up through the floor that had somehow escaped the ravages of over a century of scavvies. Possibly because cast iron was such a triple-bitch to cut.

Next came Krysty, dropping the last few feet like a leopard. Then Jak rappelled down, having quickly untied the rope and looped it around the pipe so it could support his weight on the way down.

As he let go one end and pulled the line down after him rain suddenly dumped on their heads.

"It will help cover our egress," Doc said helpfully.

"Still sucks rads." Ryan stooped, folded the still-unconscious captive over his shoulder and set off running. Wet gravel squeaked beneath his boots. The raindrops looked like little artillery shells going off when they hit the ground.

"But the plan…" Krysty called softly, running up alongside him. He heard both Jak and Doc thudding after him. Jak could actually have bounded past like a deer had he cared to; he guessed the kid was taking it on himself to pull rear guard.

The original plan was for two of them to carry the captive. While certain other things were supposed to happen that were now unlikely.

"It's shot in the head," he said. "We go to Plan B."

"There's a Plan B?" Krysty asked.

"Run for the boat," he said, "and hope like hell Mildred doesn't dawdle!"

"FUCK," THEY HEARD, muffled but unmistakably by the brush and the rain. "Fuck, fuck, fuck."

"Actually, it's a sort of pleasant accompaniment to the rain," Krysty said. She was kneeling with her not inconsiderable weight on the small of Emerald's back, pinning her bare belly on the now slimy mud and grass a few feet from the river.

With a splash Ryan, Jak and Doc finished manhandling the whaleboat back into the water.

Mildred emerged from the brush. She was soaked, as they all were. Her plaits stuck out. It looked as if somebody had been slapping her in the face with branches. Which, Ryan reckoned, had more or less been the way of it.

"Fuck," she said a final time. "So much for getting them to waste a bunch of time tramping through the woods. When I couldn't light the bonfire, they figured out they'd been jobbed right away. They're heading straight here."

"They spotted you?" Krysty asked.

"No."

"The river!" Doc exclaimed with a snap of his long,

bony figures. "If they suspect a raid of some sort, the natural escape route lies…right here, actually."

"Sound like buffalo herd stampeding," Jak said critically. As if the boat going in the Sippi hadn't been even louder than the racket Mildred made approaching their rendezvous point.

"It's nothing compared to the noise the scavvies're making," she said, stopping to bend over, brace herself and wheeze. "They couldn't hear an elephant stampede with a brass band playing on their backs. They make me look like Jak in the woods."

"Hey, now," Jak said.

"Relax, Mildred," Krysty said. "Not your fault it decided to piss down rain."

The plan had called for Mildred to augment her phony screams for help with a big fire set out in the woods, to put visions of stickie kidnappings in the heads of Dan E.'s scavvies. Fortunately she'd screamed convincingly enough to get much of the crew to turn out and cover her friends getting clear of the derelict factory with their prize. Less fortunately the sudden downpour had trashed all hopes of starting a good fire.

"Help me get the girl in the boat," Ryan told Doc. "You settle down now, Princess. You try to kick me again, I'll put a shotgun butt up behind your ear in a none-too-gentle manner."

"I'm impressed you managed to find your way here so quickly," Krysty said, enfolding the panting physician in a quick fervent hug. "I admit I was worried."

"At least it's not raining so hard I didn't have the lights of Soulardville to home in on," she said. "Never thought I'd be glad to see sign of that shithole."

Emerald emitted a squeal of outrage. By way of

retribution Ryan let her drop double-hard on her tailbone in the boat.

The companions got in cautiously after. The most experienced small-boat handler among them, Jak took the stern. He started to rev up the little motor.

"No," Ryan said. "Cast off and let the current carry us. Use the oars to fend off the bank or the bottom if we have to."

They did and began to drift south down the Sippi. The angled stubs of the Arch showed gleams of the lights from Soulardville beyond. There were no sounds except the splash of rain in water and patter on skin and wood, and the changeless, ever-changing voice of the mighty river.

Then there was a commotion like an elephant with its tail on fire, not far north of where they had cast off from. They heard voices calling to one another.

"Mmm!" Emerald said urgently.

Krysty sighed. She handed her oar to Mildred. Ryan had the other, although for the moment they drifted a good fifteen feet from shore. Carefully she removed the hood, revealing the bulging cheeks and furious eyes of a triple-pissed girl.

Krysty drew her snub-nosed Smith & Wesson Model 640 and pointed it at the bridge of the captive's nose. Emerald's green eyes went saucer-wide.

"No sounds," the redhead murmured. "Got that?"

Emerald nodded vigorously.

A quarter mile or so upstream somebody uttered a cry of triumph.

"Found where boat went in water," Jak said.

The grass had been thick enough that no tracks would show, Ryan knew. But sliding a big boat up and down the bank crushed the grass in a swath so wide even wilderness-challenged types like the scavvies could never miss it, even in the dark. And the sweep of a pale yellow beam across the river surface showed they had lights, probably bull's-eye lanterns such as the companions had observed them carrying before.

Their pursuers' calls quickly turned to consternation and then frustrated fury.

"Fire up the mill," Ryan called softly to Jak. The rain continued to fall, although not at so vigorous a pace. "It's not loud. And even if they hear there's not much they can do about it now."

"Head across now?" Jak asked.

"No," Ryan said. "Keep driving us along the shore. The scavvies got some scoped longblasters. If they spot us, one of them might get ideas."

"Would they chance a shot hitting their friend the princess?"

"Depends on how much she told them of her family history, Doc," Krysty said. Ryan couldn't miss the note of sadness in her voice.

"Damn straight," Mildred declared passionately. "If I was being carried off to be sacrificed to those awful things, I hope one of you would put a bullet through my cranium."

That dampened the jubilant mood their successful escape had engendered in them worse than the rain. They putted along south at about twice the current's speed. Before they reached the Martin Luther King bridge Ryan had Jak make for deeper water, farther from the bank.

They knew there'd been stickies around the east end of the bridge. Also Ryan was getting a prickly feeling along the back of his neck about keeping too close to shore, where anybody might nail one of them with an arrow or thrown rock, or even try jumping into the whaleboat from a low overhanging branch.

Just because they had Dan E. and his scavvies on their tail big-time now didn't mean no one else would make a play for them. In the Deathlands night there were no friends.

Emerald sat amidships with Ryan's coat around her shoulders. Her gag had been removed, but her hands were still tied. Her ankles had also been close-tied to thwart a leap overboard to freedom, which everybody suspected she'd do if given a half-chance, even if freedom only meant a quick inhalation to fill her lungs with water, and sink down where the most determined screamwing could never get at her....

She saw Ryan looking at her and shook her hair back defiantly. "You real proud of yourselves now?"

"No," Ryan said. "So, what were you after over there with Dan E. and the scavvies, Princess? A power base to plot your return? A ticket out?"

"Friends," she said. Suddenly she hung her head. "Just friends. I never had any growing up. I couldn't. I was the baron's daughter, and always had to remember how important I was. Although everybody was nice to me all the time. Like they had a choice!

"But Dan and his crew took me in. Treated me nice. Said as long as I pulled my weight and didn't whine too much I was welcome aboard. They were my friends."

A tear dropped from her eye. Ryan was actually torn between cry-me-a-river contempt for a spoiled little girl who thought she had it tough, to feeling a certain pang for her genuine depths of loneliness. That and the fact that, nuke dust, she *did* have it tough.

But then she snapped her head up. Her cheek was wet but her eyes blazed like green fire.

"You wouldn't know anything about friends, would you?" she railed at him.

"Yes," Krysty said. "He would."

"They'll never rest until they track you down!"

"Sweetheart," Ryan said, "I'm counting on it."

"So what did Bro Joe offer you, anyway?" she demanded. "Jack? Ammo? Meds? Some of his opium?"

"All those things," Ryan said. "Plus one more—the life of one of our friends who got hurt and wound up in the care of your healer, Strode."

"Strode? Is she still all right? What am I saying? Of course she would be. Joseph would never dare fuck with her. He's a chickenshit at heart. The people love her too much to let him do anything to her. Anyway, he needs her and he knows it."

"Needs her for what?" Mildred asked.

The girl uttered a wild laugh. "To rule the ville! Duh! He's no good without a healer, even if he does have some kind of deal going on with King Screamwing like he says."

"Some kind of deal," Ryan said with a thin grin. "Yeah. That about sums it up."

"You know Bro Joe arranged to have my daddy dosed with rad dust, right? I think it was his nasty little monkey Booker set the trap. Little prick's a lot more nimble than he looks."

"Reckoned as much," Ryan said. "About your daddy, I mean."

"You did?" The captive wasn't the only one who looked surprised. So did his companions. All except Krysty, who sat right behind the girl. She gave him a little nod.

"So mebbe you know all that about Joseph wandering in the rubble and getting some kind of spirit vision where he walked with King Screamwing's a load of dud rounds, huh?" Emerald said. "He's got some means of controlling them. He can call 'em, and he can keep 'em away. How, I got no clue. But it's true. I know it is. Screamwings're nothing but a bunch of nasty mutie animals. Even that triple-big triple-bastard king. Although mebbe he is a bit smarter at that. Got a head on him like one of the Clydesdales they got at Breweryville."

Slowly Ryan nodded. "Kind of worked that out, too."

This time it was Krysty who said, "You did?"

"Yeah. Tell you later. Right now we need to keep eyes skinned. Got bridges coming up. Good place for trouble, if trouble wants to happen."

Emerald was shaking her head. "I don't get it," she said. "You people actually seem like you got something in your skulls other than dried-up horse shit. So how come you're so triple-stupe you don't realize Bro Joe's never gonna pay you? Except mebbe with a bullet in your heads. If he doesn't feed you to those flying shitbird friends of his."

To Ryan's surprise it was Mildred who answered.

"Girl," she said, "do we look to you like people who got a choice?"

The captive folded her arms beneath her bare breasts and scowled. "You always got a choice."

"That's just facile bullshit," Mildred said.

"No," Ryan said. "She's right. There's always a choice. You can always choose to die. Or you can choose to live and pay the freight. You can choose to break a deal and make your word worth nothing to anybody, or you can choose to keep a deal no matter how hard it runs or how deep it cuts. You can choose to run out on your hurt friend and leave him to his fate among enemies, or you can do whatever it takes to get him clear, even if in the end it means you all die. We know we've got choices, Princess.

"And we know which ones we made. So, it sucks to be you. That's a right damn shame. But it's just how it is."

Chapter Twenty-Three

Dawn was rising out of the tree-lined bluffs along the far bank and spreading like fog over the river when they pulled the boat in between two warehouses at the little makeshift landing not far from the Soulardville gate. When Madame Sallée whined about Soulard and Breweryville not allowing docks on account of moral pollution from the notorious east side, she either didn't have her story or her facts quite straight. Even the crippled wrinklie Saga had mentioned that Soulardville traded with riverfolk, which meant they had to have a place to tie up. And more, someplace reliable where they could load and unload cargo.

The dock had been built, as far as Ryan could tell, out of rubble from fallen buildings and planks most likely salvaged from the river itself.

"It's bigger than I expected," Mildred remarked as they escorted Emerald from the whaleboat. Her arms remained tied behind her back. She was hobbled by a rope tied between her ankles that allowed no more than two feet of play, against a last-second break. And as they stood on the warped planking they tethered her wrists by a twelve-foot length of rope to Ryan's waist. They were taking no chances on their prize using her demonstrated ingenuity to thwart them.

"They need to move some pretty substantial cargoes in and out of here," Krysty said. She was helping unload the remaining backpacks. Ryan had shouldered his before cinching Emerald to him.

When Doc tried to place Ryan's coat around the naked girl's shoulders, she haughtily shrugged it off.

"I don't want anything you bastards own touching me," she said. "Let the people of Soulardville look all they want. I have nothing to hide, and nothing to be ashamed of."

Once on the dock with packs on their backs the others looked at Ryan. "Let's do it."

"You sure you want to do this?" Mildred asked.

"I'm triple-sure I don't," Ryan said. "I'm also triple-sure this is the one and only shot we got for getting out of here with the Armorer and mebbe even all our parts."

"I must admit, my dear Ryan," Doc said, shaking his head, "that I fail to see any possible pathway that leads to such a salubrious resolution."

Ryan grinned and clapped him on the shoulder. "Then let's hope the nuke-suckers in the ville won't, either."

They marched up the well-trod slope from the water to 7th Street. When the wide path swung left around an intact cinder-block building, they saw the main Soulardville gate scarcely a hundred yards away.

As they approached, the gate began to creak open to reveal Brother Joseph. Flanking him stood Garrison and the little wizened Booker. When he saw their prize, Booker did a little dance in place in monkey glee.

"Here's your girl," Ryan said.

At a fractional nod from Garrison, black-jerseyed sec men stepped in briskly to detach the rope from Ryan's waist and secure the prisoner themselves. She didn't deign to glance at them. She flung one last glare of emerald hate at Ryan, then stood with her head elevated and those deep green eyes staring at a point above the horizon.

"We brought what you asked for," Ryan said. "Now it's time we got paid."

Bro Joe's smile broadened. It was like the sun coming out from behind thunderclouds.

"Bend over, here it comes again," Mildred muttered under her breath.

"Hush now," Ryan said softly back.

"And you shall indeed receive what you have coming to you," Brother Joseph said. "There is one unfortunate complication. I'm afraid that in your absence our beloved Baron Savij has died. You must, of course, be arrested and tried for daring to lay hands on the sacred person of his daughter, our new ruler."

"So you finally found the balls to finish him off," Emerald said. She spoke without heat or contempt or even sorrow. It was as if something she had long since known had happened had simply been confirmed.

Brother Joseph only smiled at her. Ryan noted the way his pale amber eyes seemed to caress every curve of her body.

The preacher looked at Ryan. "What? No protestations or complaints?"

"Why? Reckoned you'd backstab us."

Brother Joseph frowned in what seemed genuine puzzlement. "Then why return at all?"

"We made a deal," Ryan said simply. "Plus there's the little matter of our pal, J.B."

"Ah, yes. Well, you'll soon be sharing his company. It appears he's served his function."

"No point delaying the inevitable," Garrison said, as calm as always. "Haul it."

His sec men marched their captives up the main street through growing dawnlight. Already there were a lot of people abroad, sprinkling water drawn from the communal wells on bright flowers in pots on their front porches, or heading off to their daily occupations. Heads turned and eyes widened. Excited whispers began to spread.

At the plaza the companions were steered left down the half block to their house of earlier confinement. Emerald, still haughty and unwilling to acknowledge the very existence of her captors, was led on to the palace, which was now, technically, hers.

The stains on the hateful tilted slab in the plaza's center, he noted, were once again covered by its canvas shroud.

Inside the house it was already hot and still. Relieved as expected of their gear and weapons, the companions immediately went about opening all the windows to get the air circulating. As before, neither Doc's sword stick nor Jak's concealed knives were taken.

As before, it didn't look as if it would make much difference.

As Ryan was pushing open a window in a top-floor bedroom, he heard a rattling from the front door. Since he was at the back of the house he couldn't see who it was. He emerged and went down the stairs as Krysty opened the inner front door.

"J.B.!" she cried.

Ryan rushed down the last few steps to stand beside her. There indeed sat the Armorer himself in a wheelchair pushed by none other than Strode, more grim-faced even than usual. Though J.B. wore his trademark fedora tipped to a rakish angle, his head hung. His eyes were half-closed and his jaws slack. His facial skin was gray and seemed to hang loose on the underlying framework of jaw and cheek and brow. He looked like Death rolling. But it was him, and alive.

"You try to take the healer hostage," said the sec man who'd unlocked the door, "you're dead."

"Young man, don't be more of an idiot than you absolutely have to!" Strode snapped. "They won't harm me. Their overactive senses of self-preservation assure that if nothing else."

Glaring back at both the sec-men quartet and her own pair of anxious assistants, Strode muscled the wheelchair and its burden inside by herself. Ryan and Krysty obligingly stepped back. Neither offered to help. For a fact, the ville healer had forearms and shoulders like a dock worker from moving her patients over the years.

"You can shut the door, now," she said with a fierce glare at Ryan. He obeyed.

J.B. shook his head, opened his eyes wide and grinned.

"How'd you like my death's-door act? Had you going as well as those sec stupes, didn't I?"

A dark missile flew across the well-scuffed hardwood floor. "J.B.!" Mildred yelled, enfolding him in her arms as she stood.

"Careful there, young woman! He's still in need of substantial recuperation!"

"Keep your hammer lifted, healer," Ryan said. "She knows what she's doing. And believe me, you don't care a spent casing more about the patient than she does."

Strode glared like an angry buffalo bull about to charge for a couple heartbeats longer. Then the tension went out of her powerful neck and shoulders, which wasn't the same as saying she relaxed.

"Very well," she said. "Although it's difficult for me to imagine any of you really caring about anything but yourselves!"

"Don't mind her," J.B. called. "She's not as mean as she lets on. Though, granted, she is as tough as hundred-year-old jerky."

"If you don't believe I'm as mean as I let on, young man," Strode said, "I clearly didn't give you enough enemas."

"Sit down!" Mildred exclaimed when they broke their clinch and J.B. tried to step forward to greet his other comrades. "Sure, you're better. But no way are you well!"

"Your friend is a tough customer himself," the healer said. "And as with most people these days, a wound that doesn't kill or cripple a person, a wound that can heal, usually does so fairly fast. Only the hardy survived the megacull top pass on their genes. For better or worse."

"How do you feel, man?" Ryan asked, gripping J.B.'s forearm to forearm.

"The truth?" J.B. asked with a grin. "Like nuke death rollin'. Every breath is like somebody driving a railway spike through both lungs. But I'm fit to travel and fit to fight."

"He exaggerates," Strode said. "A typical masculine failing. Still, his determination to get back on his feet as soon as possible did aid the healing process, as any form of positive frame of mind will tend to. But as is often the case, it also rendered him less than ideally cooperative."

"He's a terrible patient," Mildred agreed as Krysty came forward to give the Armorer a hug. The physician stood behind J.B.'s chair and massaged his left shoulder with her strong right hand, as if she couldn't bear to break contact for even a moment.

Doc approached, his face wreathed in smiles. "Welcome back, our boon companion."

Jak sort of sidled up to touch hands with J.B. "Good you back."

"So you two seem to have cooked yourselves up a little conspiracy," Ryan said.

"Let's say we came to a meeting of the minds," Strode said. "Your friend has a devious turn of thought."

"Wouldn't reckon a healer to have one," Ryan said.

Strode's laugh was so hearty it startled him. "You haven't thought much about the art of healing then. Every good healer's at least half mountebank. The best tend to be even more."

Her face darkened. "Brother Joseph could be the best, if he cared about anything but power."

"We reckoned there was no point letting that rad-sucker know I was healing fast," J.B. said. "Now that you're back, I think he calculates I'll be a drag on you, so I ought go back to being your problem."

"But his possession of you was what brought us back with the princess in the first place!" Krysty said. "Why would he relinquish that?"

"Because he hates to waste resources, as he says," Strode said. "He has the princess back. You can care for him now."

She studied each of them in turn. "You seriously expect me to believe that was your motivation in returning that poor child to such a horrible fate? Concern for Mr. Dix rather than reward?"

Krysty laughed as Ryan waved at their surroundings. "Here's our reward, Healer."

Mildred put both hands on J.B.'s shoulders. "And *here's* our reward. We're whole again." The Armorer reached up to pat her hand.

His own hand was still gray and a bit on the skeletal side, Ryan noted. But coming back from a wound like that was never easy. He knew himself.

Strode shook her head. "I admit, I don't know what to make of you people. You know that in your absence, Savij was murdered?"

"No," Ryan said, drawing out the syllable, "but I reckon none of us're much surprised."

"How did it happen?" Krysty asked.

"Horribly. Apparently that…creature, Booker, came up with some raw plutonium."

"How come *he*'s not thrashing and shitting himself to death?" Ryan asked in amazement.

"It was only a tiny amount. A single shaving, perhaps. The baron was fed it in his stew."

"Wouldn't it take an awful lot for rad sickness to act that fast?" Mildred asked.

"Not rad sickness at all," Strode said. "From what I read in an old battered science book, plutonium is violently toxic. Once it gets inside you it eats its way right through you by sheer chemical action. It's like being burned alive from your guts outward. I'd have given him poison to finish him quickly when he started shrieking and bleeding from the mouth and rectum. Or broken his neck. But Garrison's goons held me back."

She was in full-on glare mode at the companions again. "How can you be so stupe? Or are you just evil? Brother Joseph will—"

The door opened. The angry word stream shut off as if a floodgate had slammed shut. A mellow baritone laugh rolled into the hot and humid living room like liquid honey.

"Perhaps our visitors aren't the only ones with impaired mental capacity," he said, "since your passion apparently caused you to overlook the dangers of loudly spewing sedition before an open window."

She turned to him. "Fine. You caught me. Go ahead and strap me to that sadistic lunatic altar of yours and sacrifice me in front of the whole ville. See how the people love you then!"

He laughed again. "No need," he said. "I, like everyone in this ville, am under your care. I repose perfect confidence in your total adherence to that predark saying of yours—first, do no harm. I have nothing to fear from you."

Her big shoulders rose as she drew in a deep breath, then she let it out in a sigh.

"Don't feel bad, Healer," Krysty said. "Your spiritual leader is a man with a gift for knowing where to grab people to get a hold on their souls."

"Why, yes, I am, Ms. Wroth," he said. "Most astute of you to notice."

"It wasn't a compliment."

"Ah, but I took it that way. Have you never heard the phrase, 'the meaning of a communication is the message received'? Another ancient truth from the days before the cold and darkness that is widely overlooked today."

He looked around at the rest. "You will join us for dinner tonight," he said.

"What if we fail to find ourselves in a social mood?" Doc asked.

Brother Joseph laughed that maddening happy laugh of his. "Why, Doc, whatever led you to believe that was an invitation?"

Chapter Twenty-Four

"Eat up, Jak," Ryan said. Around them conversation gurgled and chucked like water underneath an old wharf, and utensils clattered on dishes as if there was nothing unusual about having dinner with a group of people in chains. Emerald, similarly chained, sat wearing a simple shift at the table head beside Brother Joseph.

"How eat?" the albino youth asked, fixing Ryan with hot ruby eyes.

"Hungry," Ryan said, taking another bite from his roast chicken drumstick.

"I can't believe they bull-rushed us," Mildred said. Just around sunset the front and rear doors had burst open simultaneously and a dozen sec men armed with truncheons had charged the companions, who were sleeping soundly on their pallets after their sleepless, frantic night. Ryan hadn't even known the back security door opened.

"It was a hell of a way to get invited to dinner," Ryan agreed. "No reason not to eat hearty, though."

Mildred looked as if she were about to pursue the matter, then her face went studiedly blank. Ryan suspected J.B., who was sitting slumped in his wheelchair at her side as if semiconscious, had given her a quick thigh-squeeze with his hand under the table.

They'd need their strength to jump when the opportunity presented itself, he thought. And if it never came, why die hungry?

Anyway, the food was plentiful and good. No denying that. Even if Emerald, the guest of honor, didn't seem to have much appetite.

Doc was chattering away about nothing consequential. The plump little shopkeeper sitting next to Doc was hunched all into himself as if hoping his flab would serve as a turtle shell, to protect him from the strange wrinklie who wouldn't shut up. Jak was sulking, and Krysty sat right across from Ryan eating with her usual good appetite, without an apparent care in the world.

The meal ended. Nervous young servers plucked the plates and utensils away from the captives under the stony gaze of the same twelve sec men, six to a side of the table, who'd fetched the companions here to the baronial palace. Ryan was amused. They hadn't even been allowed butter knives or even forks, evidently for fear they'd try to take a hostage or maybe fork their way to freedom.

It was strike they were all used to eating with their hands. Even Doc in full-on Victorian gentleman mode seemed to think nothing of chatting away, casually waving around a half-eaten pork chop. The ville people around them looked scandalized, which didn't exactly hurt Ryan's feelings.

An annoying ringing sound came from the head of the table. Booker had stood up beside the guru and was beating on a big gold-colored metal goblet with a ladle for attention. He persisted until everybody shut up and dutifully looked toward the self-proclaimed holy man, who sat there with eyes half-lidded, smiling as if he were listening to God telling him what an ace job he was doing.

"Thank you," Brother Joseph said when he had full silence and attention. He rose.

"Sisters and brothers of Soulardville, on the heels of the worst of news, I bring the best—our beloved princess, daughter of our lost lamented leader Baron Savij, has been returned to us, safe and sound! And of course, a greater obligation has superseded Princess Emerald's earlier duty. She is now called upon to step forward and assume her beloved father's mantle as Baron Savij of Soulardville."

The applause started out tentative, then swelled to thunder. People cheered.

Then they began to falter and look confused. If Emerald was the new baron, why was she being treated as a captive in what was after all her own palace?

Brother Joseph, beaming, spread his hands and smoothed them all to silence.

"It is my privilege and pleasure to announce my betrothal to the Princess Emerald," he said. "In three days, in the best interests of Soulardville and our beloved people, we shall be wed."

The girl jumped up. "You'll have to rape me, you fake!" she shouted. "I'd rather give myself to the screamwings than you!"

Into the shocked silence Brother Joseph shook his head sadly and said, "The poor child still suffers nervous exhaustion engendered by her terrible struggles and privations. She is clearly not herself. She will be removed to my chambers, where she may be cared for properly."

Burly young male acolytes in the guru's signature tie-dyed T-shirts stepped forward and grabbed Emerald's bound arms to hustle her off.

When the new Baron Savij had been hauled kicking and screaming up the stairs to her father's former quarters, a boil of excited conversation was bubbling off the dark-stained rafters. Booker banged furiously on his improvised gong.

"Shut it, motherfuckers!" he screeched. "Your spiritual

leader is gonna speak! Shut your holes or win the lottery for free!"

That silenced the house. Brother Joseph would never suggest his so-called compact and the lottery that fulfilled it so bloodily, month after month, were pure tools of terror and social control. Oh, no, he was much too benign and holy for that. But what else was a toady for?

"We see, for the second time, strangers in our midst," Brother Joseph said, nodding toward Ryan and his friends. His face looked less kindly now. "When first they came among us we made them welcome guests, did we not?"

"Yeah!" shouted someone enthusiastically. It was one of the bully boys in the gaudy shirts, Ryan noted without surprise.

"And now," Brother Joseph said, "we see how they repay our hospitality. Charged with safely returning the precious princess to us, they did accomplish that task. But they also misused her in a most indecent and unacceptable way."

"What!" Mildred exclaimed in outrage.

"Relax," Krysty told her lightly. "They're going to play their little game."

"Yes, these men especially laid their profane hands upon her naked flesh," Brother Joseph intoned. "Our princess. Daughter of our lost, exalted leader. They have profaned the very flesh and blood of our righteous Baron Savij, profaned our new baron. What price shall we exact, with sorrow in our hearts, for such an outrage?"

"Death!" shouted one of the acolytes.

"Death! Death!" shouted more.

It took a while, but the acolytes were young. They had leather lungs and boundless energy. They kept chanting, "Death! Death! Death!" until, one by one, the whole crowd joined in. Even the fat-rabbit pot maker sitting next to Doc was red-faced and pounding on the table.

By the end, Ryan figured, the crowd probably thought it was all their own idea.

AN HOUR after the spectacular conclusion to the evening's banquet, Strode appeared at the door of their prison house.

The companions were nursing black eyes and bruises, and Jak had got another split in his scalp to join the first one. As one they had decided not to go peacefully. Except for J.B., of course, who was still playing possum. He'd been griping the entire hour since about how he didn't get to take part in all the fun as Mildred and Krysty tended the group's hurts as best they could with no equipment but water and some rags.

Strode bustled in without ceremony, lugging a huge pack on her broad pack. This she dumped in the center of the floor and began to root around in, taking out rag bandages and jars of alcohol.

"You show up so Bro Joe'll have us in good shape to face his chillers?" Ryan asked.

"Don't be stupe," the healer said. "You, boy—"

She pointed a finger at Jak, then at the floor before her. "Sit," she commanded.

"Uh-uh," he said.

"You took at least two severe blows to the head," she said. "You need care so your brains don't start coming out your ears. And don't even think about what'll happen if those scalp wounds get infected through lack of attention."

Jak growled.

"Jak," Krysty said, "do what she says."

Pouting, the albino youth got up from his pallet, padded

to stand before the wide healer and knelt. The hair at the back of his head was pinkish, now, from Krysty doing her best to wash it with their limited supply of water. Strode, examining his wounds, called for her attendants outside to hurry up and replenish the water.

"Why are you helping us, then?" Ryan asked.

"You're in my ville," she said. "You need healing."

"Ow!" Jak yipped, as she began to swab his wound with a clean rag dipped in alcohol. "Stings!"

"Don't whine or I'll show you the real meaning of sting," she said. "And quit wriggling. Or I'll have to clean this cut out all over again. I *won't* be gentle!"

When Strode had finished her cleaning and patching as best she could and was repacking her gear, Ryan, who sat on a pallet next to Krysty, said, "We need you to take a message to Tully."

"Tully?" she asked, continuing to pack without glancing at him. "He likes you less than I do. He's a big defender of Emerald's, if you didn't notice. And there's the little matter that you killed his buddy Lonny."

She stowed the last item, sealed her bag and turned to face Ryan with hands on hips.

"Lonny was a pig," she said, "but did you have to actually kill him?"

"Yeah. Now listen. Please. This is for Emerald and the ville as much as us. Tell Tully we can help him if he'll help us."

"What is it you want him to do?"

"Break us out."

Strode laughed in Ryan's face. "Why would he do that? He hates you like poison."

"You know McCoy, a little black kid?"

"I delivered him," Strode said. "Like every other Soulardite born in the last twenty-three years."

"Tell Tully to send him outside the perimeter. He knows ways through."

"He does?"

"Trust me," Ryan said. "Or, nuke that. Ask Tully. He knows. Tell the kid to poke around some outside the ville. Especially down by the river."

"You want me to send a child into an area infested with stickies?"

"If he didn't know how to keep out of the stickies' suckers, Healer," Krysty said, "do you think he'd still be alive? He can obviously go through the fence whenever he likes."

"He'll find a crew of scavvies led by a dude named Dan E. Kind of a heavyset guy, white, thirties, brown hair, brown eyes. Got a goatee. Totes a SIG handblaster at his hip. Or this Dan E.'ll find him, more like."

"What then?"

"If Tully can get Dan E.'s bunch inside, they can help him. Twenty-thirty scavvies, armed to the teeth and hard as rail iron. Together with Tully's allies here in the ville they ought to be able to spring Emerald. Shift the balance of power, like."

"It'll take time for all this to happen," Strode warned. "Tully may not go for it. A thousand things could go wrong."

"So?" Ryan said. "What do we have to lose? What do *you* got to lose? Or do you want to go on delivering kids so Brother Joseph can have his screamwing pals rip them to bloody rags?"

She stared blue hate at them, then she shook her silver-haired head. "No," she said. "I'm not going to hate you for telling me truth to my face. Mebbe for other things, but not for that."

"Will you do it?"

"Yes," the healer said without hesitation. She was a person who picked a direction quick and just put her head down and went that way. Ryan admired that.

"I can't lie to you and tell you I see any realistic chance of your plan working," Strode said, "but it's the best shot I can see. For you or for us."

NEXT DAY they were awakened at dawn to have a big bowl of oatmeal and some spoons thrust through the slot to them. They got fresh water and towels, too.

The companions mostly passed the day sleeping. J.B. was still healing; he had plenty of that left to do, for all that he claimed to be mobile and fully functional. The others were exhausted by their quest for the fugitive princess and their thumping of the night before.

It was too rad-blasted muggy to talk or even think. Sleep was the only sanctuary.

The sun was spilling light over the peaked gray roof of the house behind them through the back door security bars when hammering on the front door's steel frame roused them.

It was the hard fist of Garrison himself raising the racket. He had a dozen of his men to back him.

"Get yourselves straightened up," he said.

"Why exactly should we?" Mildred asked, sitting up from the sleeping pad she shared with J.B.

Garrison showed yellowish teeth in a brief grin. "Because Brother Joseph would prefer you turn out to the plaza without being all beat to shit," he said. "If you would, too, get hustling."

Chapter Twenty-Five

The late-afternoon air, enriched by the yellow slanting sunlight, seemed to crackle above the heads of the crowd with electricity. The glow turned Brother Joseph's face and beard the color of gold.

"People of Soulard!" he cried, holding high his staff. "I have prayed and meditated upon the vexing problem of how to handle these strangers who have abused our hospitality and our virgin princess!"

"Wonder if still virgin after last night," Jak muttered. Then he sagged at the knees as the sec man behind him gave him a savage baton jab to the kidneys. Mildred and Krysty caught him by the elbows and saved him from banging his knees on the pavement.

"Likely she wasn't when she left here," Ryan said. He glanced over his shoulder at the sec men behind him. "Any of you boys want to feel what's like having one of those sticks broken off in your ass, feel free to give me a poke with it, any old time."

The companions hadn't been bound when Garrison and his sec men hustled them to the plaza. The sec men guarding Ryan gave him the evil eye but decided to do nothing.

"I have consulted my most trusted advisers," Brother Joseph was saying. He waved a hand to indicate Booker and a clump of five or six local burghers, all of whom looked scared and uncomfortable. "All signs lead to one, the only possible conclusion."

He thrust out his staff at the companions, who stood facing him across the plaza, with its grisly shrouded altar.

"Death! Death is the only punishment possible. Death, moreover, in such a manner as will impress upon the enemies of Soulardville the terrible price of trespassing against us. They shall not be forgiven!"

With some blatant prompting from the acolytes the crowd began a chant of "Death, death, death!"

"Sure doesn't take them long to get into it," J.B. remarked, not bothering to keep his voice down. His companions had to strain to hear him as it was.

"The beast lies barely hidden within every human breast," Doc intoned.

Brother Joseph held high his staff. The crowd fell silent.

"We will not slaughter them all, crudely and at once," he declared. "Oh, no. We must spread out the lessons over time. Vary the teachings, so that the utmost may be learned. Today one shall meet his or her well-deserved fate. And as a reward to you, the faithful people of Soulardville, and in celebration of the safe return of our baron to us, today's execution will entail one of these evil intruders taking the place of our next lottery winner!"

The crowd cheered lustily at that. Acolytes hustled forward to yank the canvas cover from the altar and roll it at one side.

"Hum stopped, anyway," Jak said.

"Figured," Ryan said.

"And the first to suffer the just punishments for their many and hideous crimes," the preacher declaimed in his most ringing voice, "shall be the mutie boy called Jak Lauren!"

"You shitmouth old nuke-sucker," Jak screamed. "I no mutie!"

It took all the sec men on hand plus a dozen young male acolytes to beat down the companions' furious resistance. Doc laid about himself enthusiastically with the silver lion's head of his cane. Even J.B. climbed out of his wheelchair to jump on the back of a tall buzz-cut blond kid in a sunburst T-shirt, only to be dropped with a crack to the back of the head by a black-clad sec man.

Garrison sauntered across the plaza to stand and watch. Even as Ryan flung himself upright from where four sec men thought they'd had him pinned to the pavement, scattering his attackers with an angry-bear roar, he could see the sec boss gesturing for his men to lay off those already brought down.

Ryan lunged for him, but two waves of sec men crashed together in front of him. As he battered at them with his bare hands, he felt lightning blast through his own kidneys in a flash of white that filled his whole body with pain. He dropped to his knees, then a club smashed across the crown of his head and he fell on his face. The world spun and his limbs dissolved.

A sec man knelt on his back and turned his face to watch as Jak, his arms tied behind his back, was dragged to the altar. The albino twisted savagely and managed to sink his strong teeth in the cheek of a black-garbed man. The man screamed and yanked his head back, leaving a raw patch on his face and a strip of skin in Jak's jaws. The other sec men rained blows on the boy in fury, defying Brother Joseph's and Garrison's commands to stop, payback for his comrades who had injured hands when they'd grabbed Jak's jacket.

They laid off only when the sec boss, his sunburned face gone redder than usual, bellowed that the next to land a blow on Jak would take his place on the altar. The albino teen was left sprawled on his belly on the slab, his face hidden by hair dyed scarlet with his own blood. He was clearly breathing, Ryan could see, but unconscious.

There was no additional ceremony today. Clearly Brother Joseph was afraid of further outbreaks. He raised his staff toward the heavens, now streaked pink and yellow and blue with sunset, and cried the invocation to King Screamwing.

A lone black figure appeared in the sky to the north, approaching swiftly with deceptively slow beats of its long and powerful wings. If the Soulardville crowd expected another spectacle like the girl's sacrifice a few days before, they were doomed to disappointment.

The king came alone. Whether it was by some whim, or trick of screamwing biology, or because Brother Joseph had the knack of summoning the monstrous flock alpha alone, he left his retinue of crestless, seagull-size horrors behind. Only he descended, his wings beating with audible booms that sent down blasts of air so strong the spectators were bodily driven back.

He didn't deign to land, this terror-toothed monarch of the skies. He descended only far enough to sink gigantic talons into the back of Jak's jacket. The bits of glass and steel sewn there bit into his feet. The monster screeched.

But King Screamwing was made of stern stuff. He tightened his grip in the fabric, beat hard with his monstrous wings and bore Jak's limp form up and away toward the black fanglike tower that was his stronghold.

As BEFORE, Mildred tried to clean and bind their wounds as best she could with the material at hand, by the light of a pair of candle lanterns. Garrison's watchful presence had prevented any permanent damage being done to the rebellious prisoners. They suffered no concussions nor broken bones, just bloody contusions and bone-deep bruises that were already turning a sort of tainted rainbow of smudged and muted colors.

It was a quiet house as night settled into Soulardville. The evening bowl of communal gruel that had been thrust through the hatch at them sat against one wall, neglected.

Ryan sat in a corner by himself. He said nothing. He had no words to say.

"I still can't believe that monster could carry Jak," Mildred said as she cleaned a cut across Doc's forehead. "I know it managed with the girl. But still."

"Jak was a light lad," Doc said. "Undoubtedly that facilitated the monster's task in bearing him away. But truly, it staggers the mind that a creature of such prodigious size could fly itself, much less carrying such a burden."

Ryan found his voice. "Don't say 'was,' Doc."

The old man drew his head back on his stalk of neck, blinking in astonishment. "Surely you do not imagine the boy still lives?"

"Denial isn't your style, Ryan," Mildred said, rinsing her rag in a bowl of brown-stained water.

"Moreover, Ryan, are you sure you want to wish such a fate upon the lad, as still to be alive in that lair of monsters?"

"Jak isn't dead," he said. "And I reckon he isn't getting eaten, either."

Krysty stroked his shoulder. "How can that be, lover? You know how those muties are. And the little ones, I think they're the most vicious breed of screamwing we've ever encountered."

"Jak's smart," Ryan said, "and he still got his blades. When I see his body, I'll believe he's chilled."

"I'm with Ryan," J.B. said. "Don't underestimate the pale little runt."

Doc shook his head sadly. "I fear we have as much chance of seeing him alive again as of ever seeing his corpse, or whatever may remain. The former would require a miracle on his behalf, the latter, a miracle on ours."

From the door came a now-familiar pounding. They had shut the inside door, wanting to shut out the outside world and its horrors more than they wanted the extra breath of air in the still, hot evening. They couldn't see who was knocking.

For a moment nothing changed. Mildred went back to examining Doc's head. The others sat.

The pounding returned, sharper, more insistent.

"Mebbe Strode's come to tinker up our bruises," J.B. said. "Mighty conscientious, that one."

"Doesn't sound like her," Ryan said. "Then again, it doesn't sound like that stoneheart Garrison, either."

With massive effort he heaved himself to his feet and walked stiffly to the door. He opened it.

Tully stood on the porch. Beside him stood a stocky guy with brown hair, brown eyes and a goatee.

"One-Eye," the goateed man said, "you gave us one triple pain in the ass."

"Here for the payback? You're Dan E., aren't you?"

"Yeah, I'm Dan E.," the man said.

Tully unlocked the door. "Where'd you get the key?" Ryan asked.

"Off somebody who didn't need it anymore," the tall ginger-haired man said. His long face was sallow and his voice clotted with emotion.

The sec door opened. Tully and Dan E. stepped aside. A couple of men Ryan recognized from the patrol that had captured them backed in, bent over.

They dragged a pair of men in sec-squad black. The fronts of their black jerseys glistened. A shockingly bright wound gaped in each man's throat. The stink of voided bowels filled the room, crowding all else to the corners.

The newcomers dragged the chilled guards to the side of the room, leaving two broad gleaming smears of red on the floor.

"Now what?" Ryan asked.

"Done my part," Tully said. "Much as I hate to do it, I have to tell you, thanks."

"Same for me," the scavvie boss said. The pair had followed the corpses inside. "Don't have any idea why you'd want to help us after kidnapping one of my people. Especially help us get her back."

"Not sure you're going to get her back."

The brown eyes narrowed. "What do you mean by that?"

"Mebbe she'll choose not to go."

"You should probably leave now," Tully said. "We'll take it from here. You're not the most popular people here in Soulardville right now. Not even after hooking us up with Daniel, here."

"We'll shake the dust off this place," Ryan said, "and soon. But we've got some business to take care of first."

"What would that be?" Tully said.

"We've got to get our gear, and we've got to help you get Emerald free. Then we've got to settle accounts with Brother Joseph."

"That's still a pretty risky mess of doing," Daniel E. said. "Why not just walk while you can?"

"Because," Ryan said, "we owe Bro Joe a debt. And like I keep telling and telling you people, we always keep our deals, and we always pay our debts."

Chapter Twenty-Six

Earl and Verle were bored.

After a day like today, standing sentry duty flanking the door to the baronial palace was stone anticlimax.

"You see that white-haired mutie boy scream and squirm?" Verle asked his partner. Verle was the taller and blockier, and had a dark red beard wrapped around his lantern lower jaw. "Good times, bro. Good times."

"Bullshit," said Earl. He was narrow and dark-haired, with razored sideburns. He thought they went well with his sec-man black. "Wanted to see the little ones rips his guts out. That's the real show there."

"Naw. You just wanna see boobies. You get hard when the bitches are tied to the alter. Don't lie to me. I see you."

Earl moistened his lower lip with a quick stroke of his tongue. "So I like to see the bitches get theirs sometime. What's wrong with that? You know what bitches're like. Wag their little tails at you all inviting, but try to go for the goods and they push you all off like you're covered in shit. And the baron backs them. Even Garrison backs them, when they're holdin' out on sec men! 'Rule of law,' he says. What a load of glowing night shit."

"Well, we got a new man in charge now," Verle said. "Things'll change."

"Yeah." Earl licked his lips again. "I bet he tames that bitch Emerald triple-quick, now. She's a handful, though.

Mebbe he'll need help. Mebbe he'll, like, send somebody down here to say—"

"Evening, boys."

Earl felt his eyes stand out from his skull as if they were being pulled by magnets. It was a redhead, tall and unbelievably lush bodied, with a face from a wet dream and green eyes that glowed like jewels in the lights of the lanterns hung above the door guards. Her red hair stirred restlessly about her shoulders though there wasn't even a hint of breeze. And the front of her white shirt was pushed way, way out by what hung beneath. As Earl's pulse quickened so hard he felt it beating like fists in his temples.

"What're you doin' out?" Verle demanded hoarsely. "You're one of them outland kidnappers, aren't you? You should be locked down."

"You sec boys should know a woman has her ways," she said, her voice throaty and low. "She also has her needs. And two strong sec studs are just what I need to help me with mine."

"Now, wait," Verle said, "this ain't right—"

"Verle, don't be a droolie! Look at what's offered!"

"I dunno. I think we need to call for backup."

"How're these for backup," the redhead said, pulling open the front of her shirt, which apparently she'd been holding shut with her hands rather than having buttoned.

Two large pale-skinned breasts plopped out as if eager for the open air. The pink firm nipples looked at Earl like wide eyes.

They were the last sight his own eyes saw. All-consuming blackness smashed into the back of his skull. He felt his world break apart as redness filled his vision. Then white.

Then nothing.

THE TALL BEARDED sec man's eyes stood out from his face as his partner dropped forward onto his hatchet face. Mildred stood behind him with an ax, its blade dripping gore and brains and wisps of hair.

"And that's my rule for bastards like you," the physician declared in a fierce whisper. "Do harm *first*."

The remaining sec man's hand scrabbled for the blaster at his hip, but a hand clamped on his bearded lower jaw and yanked his head back hard. Then the edge of a panga was drawn across his exposed throat with such fury that it cut through arteries and windpipe and tendons.

As she stepped daintily aside to avoid the sudden arterial gush of blood, Krysty heard steel grate on neck bones. She buttoned her white shirt quickly.

"Good to see you still got it," J.B. said. He had his hat tipped back on his head and was toting his big scattergun. He moved like an old man, but it thrilled Krysty's heart to see him back in action again. And where he belonged: with them.

"Dang," said one of the mixed crew of Dan E.'s scavvies and Tully's men, coming out of the shadows into the plaza behind the companions.

Next stop would be the former baron's bedroom.

The palace's front door wasn't locked. Mildred turned the handle and opened it quietly. Doc was first inside. He had his cane stuck through his belt, his LeMat handblaster in one big knobby-knuckled hand, his sword in the other. Mildred came next, holding the bloody ax across her chest. Hastily finishing up the front of her shirt, Krysty drew her S&W 640 and went in after. Ryan had knelt briefly to wipe his blade clean on the seat of the fallen door guard's trousers. Now he brought up the rear, panga sheathed, SIG in hand.

Doc stopped to sweep the darkened entry room and

dining hall with his handblaster. J.B. checked the other direction. Mildred took up station at the bottom of the stairs. A curious rhythmic sound came down, similar to the noise the strange night creatures made in the trees of the shattered metropolis.

Without a word Ryan blew in like the wind and up the stairs, followed by Krysty.

All this happened with no talk and little noise. Bro Joe might not think it necessary to lock his front door, but he had a couple of guards on his bedchamber. These sat in chairs with their heads nodded to their chests, snoring. That accounted for the cicada sounds.

"Huh?" said the one on Krysty's right. His eyes blinked once, then his head snapped up. He reached for his handblaster.

Krysty shot him in the gaping mouth, and his head snapped aback against the wall. Blood blossomed around it on the brick.

Ryan backhanded the other out of his chair. As the guard scrambled to clear his sleep-addled wits and rise, Krysty heard Mildred's Czech-made ZKR 551 handblaster bark twice from the stairs, filling the upper landing with yellow pulses of light. The man rolled to the wall, streaming blood.

Ryan yanked open the door. A blast of humid, rank-smelling air hit Krysty in the face. It was weighed down and shot through with the smells of incense, some cloying sweet, some astringent. But they couldn't mask what they were clearly intended to: the smell of unwashed bodies, prolonged sickness and nasty death.

Brother Joseph sat bolt upright in the middle of the canopied bed. His mouth gaped and his eyes blinked in the light of hundreds of candles placed all over the room. He couldn't seem to assimilate what he was seeing.

Krysty was surprised to see he was alone. She didn't know whether to be pleased or disappointed.

One way or another the task of liberating Princess Emerald would fall to others. Well, those others were ready, willing and able. She'd have just been in the companions' way. Their business lay elsewhere.

Following close behind Ryan, Krysty swung right and dropped to a knee to cover that way. J.B. was next in. He stepped left to clear the door and covered his side of the room with his shotgun.

Ryan marched to the bed, reached through the half-open silk curtain, grabbed Brother Joseph by the front of the pair of baronial purple silk pajamas he was wearing and, turning hard, hurled him onto an ornate rug.

The guru landed hard and slid on his side on the rug almost to the feet of Mildred, who stood in the doorway while Doc guarded the landing.

Brother Joseph pushed himself up on one arm. "What is the meaning of this?" he demanded, spittle flying from his mouth.

"Is that the best you've got to say?" Mildred demanded. She brandished her ax with her left hand. "If you go on and say we'll never get away with this, I'll chop parts off your piece of shit phony Jeffrey Dahmer ass."

One thing Krysty had to say for the fraudulent spiritual leader: he recovered his composure quickly. He rolled to a sitting position and blinked around at them, as mild as a lamb.

"But what will you say to my parishioners?" he asked. "What of the compact?"

"I got your compact right here," Ryan said, emerging from behind the diaphanous curtain. He had clambered across the big bed on all fours and now was coming back. "Literally."

He thrust out a hand. It held a strange boxy assemblage of what looked like green plastic with random bits stuck to it. In the light of the many candles it took Krysty several beats of her hard-driving heart to recognize the object.

"That's the head of Brother Joseph's staff!" Mildred exclaimed.

Doc snapped his long spidery fingers. "Of course! That is the very device that our false prophet both summons and dispels the screamwings. Most ingenious, I must say."

"Yeah," Ryan said, climbing off the bed. "Remember how Jak kept hearing weird sounds none of the rest of us could? A kind of deep hum, and a real high buzz, like mosquitoes?"

"Yes!" Mildred said. "He heard the hum stop and the high-pitched whine begin right before the screamwings appeared to take their sacrifices! Subsonics must repel them, and supersonic frequencies attract them."

"Absurd!" Bro Joe cried. "I have no idea what you're talking abou— Ow!"

He clutched the side of his head where Mildred had clipped him with a one-handed blow of the back of her ax.

"Lie better," she commanded sternly. "Better yet, keep it shut."

He glared at her with undisguised hatred.

"Where's our gear?" Krysty asked.

"Stored in a back room," Brother Joseph said.

"I'll get it," J.B. said.

"No, you won't," Ryan said. "You'll sit on the bed and help me guard our friend here, while Doc scares up something to tie and tether him with. Krysty, why don't you and Mildred go check out and see if our stuff's there like the man says, which for his sake it best be."

"Sure, Ryan," Krysty said.

"And, Mildred, you can leave the ax."

She clutched it protectively. "No way. May need it to open the door."

"Just as long as you remember that's what it's for," Ryan said.

"QUIET NIGHT," J.B. remarked as they emerged into the street. Looking from the windows of the baron's room they had seen no activity in the plaza or any sign of movement. But Ryan and Krysty had still gone out first to make sure things were safe before giving their friends the all-clear.

"No crickets, no birds," the Armorer said. He was moving like an old man, Ryan saw, but he kept his usual nonchalant grin and banty-cock attitude. *He'll be all right,* he thought. *He's a tough little bastard.*

Two pops sounded somewhere off to the south. "Blasters," J.B. said. "Reckon that's why the bugs and birds aren't talkin'."

"Power struggle playing out," Ryan said.

"Doesn't seem to involve Brother Joseph," Krysty said.

The self-proclaimed holy man emerged from the palace now. He wore a long tie-dyed T-shirt and loose linen trousers over sandals. He held his head high despite the fact his arms were tied before him and his legs hobbled by long, strong, brightly colored silk scarves from a chest of drawers in the baron's rooms. Mildred held a rope tied to his bound hands in one hand and her blocky revolver in the other. She had been persuaded to leave the ax behind.

"Reckon everybody counts him out of the equation now," Ryan said.

"Our young friend Emerald is probably consolidating her power base at this moment, if I might hazard a guess," Doc said. Like the rest he carried his full pack on his back.

"She and her friends'll have their hands full with Garrison's bunch," Ryan said. "Oh, well. As long as none of it gets on us. Step it up, holy man."

"You discount my loyal acolytes?" Brother Joseph asked haughtily. "You err grievously there."

"No, we don't count them out," Ryan said. "Matter of fact we're about to address that little issue right now. Let's pay a visit to your temple."

Brother Joseph frowned at him. Ryan smiled blandly back.

"Go," Mildred said.

The guru went, like a lion crossing its territory he strode across the plaza, right past the altar. It had been covered again after the evening's entertainment. Ryan frowned at sight of it.

"Faster," he said.

They reached the door to the temple. "I'd be happy to admit you, if you'd but untie me," Brother Joseph said.

"Nice try," Krysty replied. She produced a key ring she had taken from the table beside the late baron's bed. The third key turned the lock.

She looked back at Ryan with her hand on the knob. He nodded at Brother Joseph.

"Him first."

A frown flitted across the spiritual leader's face. "Very well," he said. "If you can bring yourself to walk into a house of God with your souls in such disarray, I shall happily lead you. Perhaps you will find enlightenment."

"Can it," Mildred said in a dangerous tone. Ryan relieved her of the other end of Brother Joseph's leash.

Krysty pushed the door open and stood clear. Ryan

prodded the guru forward with the muzzle of his SIG-Sauer P-226. He followed the holy man inside.

It was dark but for the moonlight spilling in from outside and a furtive yellow gleam beneath a door down a hall that led into the building to the right.

Ahead of them another door was a black oblong of darkness. From it suddenly emerged a small, hunched-over shape.

"Die, unbelievers!" Booker screeched. The muzzle-flash of the Uzi he was carrying filled the room with jittering light and shattering noise.

Chapter Twenty-Seven

Brother Joseph's head snapped back. Grunting, he sagged against the door frame, then fell left into the room out of the doorway.

Ryan hit the floor. Salvaged vinyl tiles had been laid long ago and long ago begun to dry, shrink and crack. They still provided a little buffer between him and the hard concrete floor.

Screaming like a man afire, Booker held the weapon in front of him with both hands and ripped another long, fiery burst from left to right.

Despite the Uzi's weight, the twisted little man couldn't keep the stubby weapon from climbing with its own recoil. Plywood sheets nailed over the big windows boomed as 9 mm slugs punched through them. Concrete dust began to shower from cinder blocks in the wall above as the bullet-stream tore into them.

Ryan stuck his handblaster out one-handed. His eyes were dazzled by the machine pistol's muzzle flare, as big as a land wag in the darkened room. He pointed the SIG in its general direction and started cranking shots.

Booker screamed. He held down the trigger, the Uzi's bullets sawing into the ceiling.

With a noise shatteringly loud even next to the Uzi's blare, a huge chunk of the wooden sheet covering the right-hand window blew in. The weapon's flame died.

Booker was down on one knee. He screamed continuously, as if he didn't have to draw breath. Ryan couldn't tell if he'd hit the man. He was blinking at big purple blobs of afterimage, although faint light filtering through the hole in the plywood let him see Booker as a darker shadow against shadows. He tried to line his sights up on the little man.

At last pausing to inhale, Booker turned his weapon to the gap in the window-covering and yanked the trigger.

The Uzi's stub muzzle dipped, then rose as Booker's finger pressure slacked. Then it did a little up-and-down dance as the toady yanked at it furiously, as if somehow that would make it go bang.

But nothing would. Ryan could see the charging handle locked dead back. Booker had blazed away a full mag.

Fire roared through the hole. By its garish yellow light Ryan saw the whole right side of Booker's head, shades and all, turn to cloud as the buckshot charge hit.

The little man continued to crouch. He seemed to be staring through the remaining lens of his dark glasses. His finger kept tugging on the Uzi's trigger, mechanically and futilely.

Another shotgun blast blew what was left of his head to pieces. Booker fell, flopping like a decapitated chicken. The final spasms of his heart sprayed the bases of the walls with blood ink-black in the gloom.

"Clear!" Ryan called. Krysty stepped in the door over Brother Joseph's legs. She shifted right. Mildred came in next and went left. Each had her .38 blaster gripped in both hands, ready to engage.

"Oh, my," Doc said, stepping over Brother Joseph like a fastidious stork. "Our sky pilot appears to be hoist with his own minion's petard, so to speak."

J.B. strolled in, feeding fresh shells into his scattergun's tube magazine.

"Check the preacher, Mildred," Ryan said, picking himself up. He was feeling the beatings he'd gotten, both the previous night and earlier that evening.

Mildred balked. "I want him patched," Ryan said, "unless he's too nuked to keep up. He's gonna help us get Jak back."

"But—"

"Look, just fix him. If he's fixable. We need him."

"Give me a light at least."

J.B. flicked a match alive with a thumbnail. Mildred bent over Brother Joseph to examine him. Krysty brought a candleholder from a study table. The Armorer lit the candles, then straightened to help Ryan and Doc stand guard.

"He's alive," Mildred said. "Worse luck." She helped him to a sitting position and propped him against the wall. A thin blood trail ran down the right side of his face.

"What's behind the door, there, Bro Joe?" Ryan asked, nodding down the darkened hallway.

Joseph gave him a thin, taut smile. "Look for yourself."

"Fine. J.B.?"

"Right with you, Ryan."

With the Armorer and his scattergun backing him he went to the door where the light showed along the bottom. They took up position either side of the door. Ryan, on the right, knocked with the back of his knuckles.

Nothing. He nodded to J.B., who stood on the side of the frame by the knob. Gently and with a deft touch the Armorer tested the knob. He nodded to Ryan to be ready: unlocked.

J.B. turned the knob and gave the door a push to start it. Ryan came around with a kick that snapped it wide. He followed with his SIG at the two-handed ready.

Ceiling-high racks holding consoles and instruments lined three walls of the room, their dark faces alive with amber and green lights. An electric trouble lamp clamped to one of the racks accounted for the shine beneath the door. A folding table had been turned on its side in the middle of the room, with its legs pointed away from the door. Two upset chairs, a game board, cards and plastic pieces lay strewn on thin sour-smelling carpet around it. Two men crouched behind it, peering at the door with big eyes. When they saw Ryan, they ducked back down.

"What do you want?" one demanded in a shrill voice. "Who're you? Go away!"

"Come out," Ryan said. "Or do you really think that stupe table's going to stop bullets?"

Reluctantly the two rose. One was tall and skinny and round-headed, with dark lank bangs falling across his forehead. As he stood up, he pushed a pair of eyeglasses up his forehead. Their bridge had been repaired with tape. His partner was fat, with a buzz haircut and heavy-rimmed glasses. Both looked to be no more than kids.

"Where's the big screamwing repeller?" Ryan said.

The skinny kid folded his arms across his tie-dyed acolyte shirt. "Uh-uh," he said. "You won't get anything from me."

"Okay," Ryan said. He shot him through the tape-wrapped bridge of his glasses. The kid fell straight down as if his bones had melted.

The other jumped straight up. "You killed Mark!" he cried in a shrill voice.

"You in a mood to answer questions?"

"Oh, yes. Please don't hurt me. I'll tell you anything you want to know!"

"Sit down," Ryan directed. "Your quivering makes me nervous."

The boy sat down so suddenly his folding chair threatened to give way beneath him. "Sorry, sir. Please, what did you want to know again? I'm sorry, seeing Mark get shot like that just totally drove it out of my head, please, I'll answer—"

"Where's the big screamwing-repelling thingie? Some kind of generator keeps those nuke-suckers away from the ville. I want to know where it is."

"The big what? No! Wait! Don't shoot! I— There isn't one. I mean, there are several of them! Six. Six of them. They're sited around the ville. They run off solar-powered batteries we bought off the scavvies, with alcohol-fueled generators for when the charge gets low. Just like this place. It—they don't draw much power. They—"

"Enough. Sit tight. You shouldn't open the door for the next half hour. Bad things could happen."

The fat kid stared at him with his moist-lipped mouth slackened and his eyes wide. "You're gonna leave me in here with *him?*" he asked plaintively, indicating the late Mark.

"You rather join him?"

"No! No, please."

"Then sit tight."

J.B. backed out of the room first, covering with his shotgun. Then Ryan left, closing the door behind him.

"Interesting," J.B. said. "Love to get my hands on one of those repellers. Pull it apart, see what makes it go."

"Yeah," Ryan said. "Well, however things shake out tonight, J.B., I don't give good odds we're going to be welcome back here for a protracted stay anytime soon."

"Sad but true, Ryan. Sad but true."

They returned to the worship area at the front of the church. Mildred was just straightening. She looked disgusted.

"What's the damage?" Ryan asked.

"Nothing much. The bullet just clipped the side of his head. Gouged him a little eensy bit. I cleaned it up and put on a pressure bandage."

Indeed she had, Ryan noted. In fact she'd wrapped what looked like a whole five yards of the lightweight cotton cloth they used for bandages hereabouts around his head. Bro Joe looked as if his religion had suddenly decided what it really needed was turbans.

"It bled most copiously," said the preacher, stung by the obvious contempt in her voice. "Plus it was quite extraordinarily painful."

The companions laughed.

"Pray you never learn the true meaning of pain," Doc told him.

"If you don't want to get a quick tutorial," Ryan said, "tell us where we can find the fuel for your genny, double-quick."

"It's out in back," the preacher said in disgust. "In a small shed next to the one that houses the generator. You'll find the door unlocked. Soulard is an honest ville."

"Or a triple-stupe one," J.B. said. "You leave fuel unlocked?"

"Thieves automatically win that month's lottery," Brother Joseph said.

"Well, I guess there's one point in favor of the system," J.B. said.

"Don't get carried away, J.B.," Ryan said. "It's the only one. Now, on your feet, holy man. We got a ways to go before you get to rest."

"Where we headed?" Krysty asked.

"First off, to tell Strode where to find the generators and electronics. Bet she can come up with some use for them. Mebbe for that techie acolyte you got back there, too. He'll probably be right eager to help."

"Acolyte? There are supposed to be two on duty—oh." He realized the implication of the gunshot he'd heard after the door into the control room was kicked open. "You're quite inhuman, you know."

"Aren't you a fine one to talk," Mildred said, "feeding people to your pterodactyls."

"What do you intend after you reveal my secrets to the people of the ville?" Brother Joseph asked. "Are you going to leave me to their putative vengeance?"

"Hard to say, since I don't know what 'putative' means. But no. Not to any kind of their vengeance, *putas* or not. You're coming with us."

"Where?"

"To rescue Jak."

"You fools! He's dead. The screamwings ate him. You saw how rapacious they are!"

Stubbornly Ryan shook his head. "I haven't seen his body nor any identifiable loose parts. Until I do, he may still be alive, as far as I'm concerned."

"You're mad!"

Krysty came to stand beside her man. "Yes, he is," she said. "With a most magnificent madness. But don't delude yourself. Ryan Cawdor usually gets what he wants, and always what he sets his mind to!"

BLASTER SHOTS PEPPERED the night in several directions as they emerged from the healer's clinic. Strode had seemed nonplussed by the turn of events. Her eyes had gotten wide when she saw the yards of bandage wound around Brother Joseph's head, but she hadn't made any comment.

"What now?" Mildred asked. She wrinkled her nose

at the smell of burned lubricants and propellant that had tainted the warm night air.

They had unloaded the contents of their packs in Strode's back room, trusting her bemused promise to keep it safe against their return. If they didn't come back in three days, Ryan told her, it was all hers. In turn they had stuffed their packs with jars and pots of fuel meant to power Bro Joe's secret scavenged generators, and fish oil used in lamps, all sealed with wax.

"We leave," Ryan said, "unless anybody just can't bear to part with this place. Excluding Brother Joseph, of course."

"How do you propose that we do that, friend Ryan?" Doc asked. "Simply stroll up to the gate and ask nicely to be allowed egress?"

Ryan grinned. "Exactly. If 'egress' means what I think it does."

"Won't the sec have a word or two to say about that?" J.B. asked.

"Not if they care about Bro Joe."

"How d'you mean?"

"I mean, specifically, not if they care whether you blow his head off with the big old scattergun you're going to be poking in his earhole."

J.B. grinned. "Must have lost a step, staying in bed a whole week. Or I'd have been there ahead of you!"

He turned to the preacher. "On your way there, Brother."

"Aren't you supposed to be poking the shotgun in my earhole?"

"Plenty of time for that when we get there," J.B. said. "Never rush a craftsman at his work."

RYAN LED THE WAY down the street with SIG in hand. J.B. followed with his shotgun's muzzle a handspan from Brother Joseph's back. Then came Doc and Mildred.

Krysty bought up the rear. Both women held their double-action .38 handblasters ready for action.

But nobody was quite prepared when Garrison himself strolled into the light of the lanterns burning on either side of the gate from the guardhouse.

"Going somewhere, folks?" he asked casually.

J.B. grabbed a handful of Bro Joe's T-shirt, which fortunately stretched enough to actually allow him to stick the shotgun's muzzle into the guru's ear.

"Don't try to stop us, Garrison," Ryan said. "We got your holy Joe."

"Kill them!" Brother Joseph shouted. "Kill them! I know you've got enough men at the gate to gun them all down before they can hurt me."

"Nothing could be further from my intention than stopping you, Ryan," Garrison said in a conversational tone. "And he isn't my holy Joe."

"But I'm the spiritual leader of this commune!" Brother Joseph said. "I'm to marry the baron! And what about the compact? What will you do without me to intercede on your behalf with King Screamwing? How will the people react when they find you've exposed them to risk of hideous death every time they venture outside?"

Garrison shrugged. "Don't think they'll react much when I tell them what a crock of shit the whole 'sacred compact' thing was," he said. "How it was all you keeping the hoodoos away with that funny little dingus on your staff, and calling them the same way. Which I don't notice you carrying, by the way."

"Blasphemy!" Brother Joseph screeched. "How dare you?"

"Oh, cool your pipes. I figured it out years ago, but the baron went along with your game. He seemed to think it promoted social order, so I didn't see fit to piss on your prayer meetings. Not on me to make policy."

"People of Soulardville!" Brother Joseph shouted in his brassiest voice. "Hear me! Traitors and blasphemers are trying to abduct your prophet! They would leave you defenseless before the wrath of King Screamwing! Defenseless, I say."

"If you wanted to reverse that scattergun and lay the butt upside his head to shut him up," Garrison told J.B., "nobody here'd be much upset over the fact."

He turned a scowl on the self-proclaimed prophet. "If you cost people around here any more sleep, Brother Joseph, they're likely to get pretty cross with you. They gotta get up and go to work in the morning. Not like you'd know anything about that."

"But you're supposed to serve me!"

"I serve the power in the ville."

"But I am the power! I'm the regent, with the baron dead."

Garrison shook his head. "The rightful baron is back," he said. "And it appears she has the support she needs to make her claim to the ville stick. So I'm her man."

"What about the shooting we heard?" Krysty asked. "Your men weren't involved?"

Garrison shrugged. "Mostly Emerald's loyalists mopping up Brother Joseph's diehards, I reckon."

"Shouldn't you have been defending me, as power in the ville?" Brother Joseph demanded, outrage momentarily overpowering his common sense.

"I had no dog in this hunt. Now the power seems to have been effectively transferred, doesn't it?"

"But this is ridiculous! I command you—"

"Looks to me like you don't even command the direction of your own footsteps," Garrison said. "A Savij rules

Soulardville. That's how it's supposed to be. Not much need to keep you around anymore, now, is there?"

"You're just going to let us walk out of here?" Ryan asked, thunderstruck.

Garrison turned away. "Open the gate," he ordered.

Sec men raced out to obey. The metal wheels squealed in the metal track as they forced the heavy-weighted wag attached to the gate out of the way.

"Got no orders from Baron Savij to hold you," the sec boss said. He turned to the companions. "Gentlemen, ladies. Have yourselves a fine evening. And if you really intend to take this prick along with you, you might want to do something to quiet him down. That kinda racket draws stickies."

Chapter Twenty-Eight

"Do we have to walk right down the middle of the street?" Brother Joseph asked plaintively as they marched at a double-fast pace north along the street that led in front of Soulardville. He carried himself with immense dignity despite the fact that his wrists were still tied and he still had an outsized bandage wound around his head. The companions had cut away the rope that hobbled him.

The moon was mounting up the eastern sky. It cast eerie blocky shadows of the mostly flooded buildings to the right, and the stands of trees and dense brush that had sprung up between.

"Yep," J.B. said. "Need to move fast if we're going to have any chance of saving Jak. So speed'll have to be our best defense. This gives us the clearest road. Also it means the bad things have a ways to go to get at us any way they try it from."

The five companions were spread out in a diamond pattern: Ryan leading, J.B. winged out right, Doc on the left, Krysty bringing up the rear and Mildred in the center, guarding their captive and holding his lead. Except for Mildred, who kept her attention fixed on Brother Joseph, the companions constantly swiveled their heads, looking for signs of ambush.

The night was hot and thick and full of sounds. None of them were out of place for the gutted-out St. Lou, so far as Ryan's keen ears could tell. Then again, some of those were pretty alarming.

"Why do you need me, anyway?" the guru asked.

"You're going to help set right what you did wrong," Ryan said. "I told you—help us get Jak back."

Brother Joseph shook his head, laughing in disbelief. "You know he's meat, now, don't you?"

"Mebbe," Ryan said grimly. "Then we'll find his remains and make sure. We don't break a deal, and we don't leave anybody behind."

He nodded at J.B. "For good, anyway."

Brother Joseph shook his head. "Admirable in a way. But folly."

"You're not going to talk us out of it that way," Mildred said.

"Very well," the preacher said. "You say you take deals seriously. Your behavior tends to back that up, I must admit. So I propose a deal to you—I help you recover your friend. I do not attempt to escape, or to hinder or harm you in any way. And at the end, when we find the young man, you let me go."

"Why would we ever trust you?" Mildred demanded.

"That's problematic, I admit."

"How's this," Ryan said. "You try to screw us around, we shoot you in the leg and leave you bleeding for the stickies and cannies to fight over?"

"Not especially appealing."

"We could do that now, save us the hassle and him the suspense," Mildred pointed out.

"You're pretty bloodthirsty for a healer," Joseph said aggrievedly.

"You're pretty sneaky, sociopathic and sadistic for a holy man," she said. "It evens out."

"You've definitely gotten on Mildred's bad side," Krysty said. It didn't sound as if she was much fonder of him.

"Believe me," Ryan said, "no matter how hot and heavy we get caught in it, you try something, one of us'll see. So realize that making the deal and then breaking it is going to be your worst-case scenario."

"Are you quite sure you want to do this, Ryan?" Doc asked.

"Yeah. I am. Bro Joe here has an eye for the main chance. He knows I mean what I say, from one end to the other. He knows we'll carry out everything we told him we would. So he'll go along with us because that's the path of least resistance. Plus, he may be a survivor, but even if he could get away from us, he's not going to be in love with his chances wandering around outside the wire at night alone. He's way safer sticking tight to us. And way safer if we all stay alive to buffer him from all the nocturnal nasties."

"This is true," Brother Joseph said.

"What do we get out of it, Ryan?" Mildred asked.

"Another set of eyes turned outward, where the triple-bad things are," Ryan said. "You don't have to hang on to the rope like you're walking a dog in the middle of a well-run ville."

"I think we might as well go along with this, Mildred," Krysty said. "Also the walking's going to start getting tough when we hit the fallen-in underpasses, and then the serious rubble downtown. We don't want to be dragging him then."

"Well…what do you think, Doc?"

"I think that brillig were the slithy toves," Doc said cheerily, "to say nothing of the mome raths."

"'Jabberwocky'?" Mildred said. "Jesus, you barmy old fart."

"Focus for us, Doc," J.B. suggested.

"What? Oh, to be sure, John Barrymore. To be sure. I—I shall most certainly go along with what the majority decide."

"Sorry I asked. J.B.?"

"Believe me," Brother Joseph interjected, "if you're foolish enough to chase after your friend after he was carried away by a giant carnivorous flying mutant to its nest of ravening lesser horrors several hours ago, I truly and sincerely believe you're…of a frame of mind to honor your word to let me go should we all survive this madman's errand. And I assure you I have no desire to test my survival skills on either cannibals or mutants with adhesive fingers and an unseemly love of fire. So you've nothing to lose."

Ignoring him, the Armorer looked to Mildred and shrugged. "Might as well. He isn't liable to slip anything by us."

"Plus you want to be free to keep a double-close eye on J.B., don't you, Mildred?" Krysty asked softly.

Her shoulders slumped. "All right," she said. "You win. It's your funeral."

Krysty snicked open her lockback folding knife. Stretching her long legs a little longer, she caught up to the guru from behind. With a quick twist she severed the rope that had replaced the silk scarf binding his wrists. Mildred looked down at the other end of the rope, then threw it on the road.

"Damn!" She snorted a laugh. "I still feel bad for littering."

"What's that?" Krysty asked.

"Irrelevant. Don't worry about it."

"You don't get any weapons," Ryan said.

"I want none," Brother Joseph said grandly, massaging one wrist. "I am a man of peace."

THEY PASSED the garden area that marked the northeast corner of the Soulardville perimeter. Instantly everyone went to an even higher alert level. Even Brother Joseph, Ryan noticed, taking a quick check over his shoulder.

He was already beginning to wonder if he'd made a stupe mistake allowing the man to be cut free. He found that whenever his back was turned on the murderous man of faith he got a tingling sensation between his shoulder blades, as if they expected to have a knife planted between them. It was distracting.

But he put it from his mind and drove on. Blood wouldn't go back into a body.

Before they'd gone two blocks past the Soulardville boundary, bright light flashed to Ryan's left and he heard the distinctive hollow boom of Doc's black-powder blaster. He looked back to see a dark figure lurching at them.

Mildred had stopped and extended her right arm, Olympic target-shooting style. She fired twice. The figure, still shadowy and indistinct, spun and fell down to disappear in knee-high weeds.

"Okay, ace," Ryan said. "Keep it moving, now."

"Right, Ryan," Mildred called. She turned and began to trot along. As she did, he was pleased to see, she broke open her revolver to eject the two empty casings and reload the chamber with fresh rounds.

When the street ducked beneath a still-intact section of highway, Ryan had them sprint through, blasters at the ready. Nothing jumped at them in the darkness, but he wouldn't slack the pace for half a block.

"Have mercy," Brother Joseph puffed when they slowed

to a rapid walk. "I'm not as used to high-speed hiking as you are."

"Mercy?" Mildred asked. "Like you showed Jak?"

She sighed. "Still, Ryan, he's got a point. We're not doing ourselves any good if we push so hard our muscles knot up or we just keel over from exhaustion. Nor Jak."

What she really meant, Ryan thought, was that she was worried about pushing J.B. this hard with his half-healed thoracic wound. She just didn't want to shame her man's spiky pride by singling him out in weakness. On the other hand, she did make a valid point. They *were* beat to shit, and no mistake.

He made himself slow his pace. Not much, but perceptibly.

"Thank you, Ryan," he heard Krysty say.

After they picked their way over the debris of the collapsed bridge, Ryan had them climb up onto the highway, which Mildred said she thought she remembered was Interstate 55.

"Did not Tully tell us these thoroughfares were dangerous?" Doc asked, when they had made it to the wide and largely intact roadway.

By unspoken but unanimous assent they had paused for a breather. Ryan knew it was risky up there in an exposed position. Then again, they'd see anything that came at them far in advance. Taking a quick but close survey of his companions, Ryan noticed that their unwilling guest seemed a little tenser than he had been. He also got the impression Brother Joseph wasn't quite as winded as he made himself out to be.

Fair enough, he thought. The phony preacher didn't owe them the whole truth, any more than they owed it to him.

"What's going on over there in that big triple-squat sucker of a building?" J.B. asked, pointing northwest.

"That's Busch Stadium," Mildred said. "It's just a night ga— Oh."

"Yeah," Ryan said. An orange glow wavered in the thick air above the stadium. He could see little glows through the sides, too, as well as flickering little lights that were probably torches, moving around the ramp that wound its way up the sides of the structure.

"You know, it almost sounds as if there *is* a game going on," Mildred said.

Even though they were a good third of a mile away Ryan could hear a roar from the stadium, as though of a cheering crowd.

"Must be a couple hundred in there to raise that kind of noise," J.B. said, coming up to stand at his friend's side. It felt comfortable having him there again.

"Who might it be in such a multitude?" Doc asked.

"Nobody good," Krysty said.

"Still feel so confident about risking the downtown ruins by night?" Brother Joseph asked.

"Never felt confident at all," Ryan said. "Confidence's got nothing to do with what's got to be done."

"An admirably simple philosophy," Joseph said, "if perhaps unrealistic."

Ryan frowned at him.

"Who's in that stadium, Brother Joseph?" Krysty asked quickly.

"Why would I know?"

"Don't piss down our legs and say it's raining, Bro Joe," J.B. said. "You were Baron Savij's main man. You must have had access to all the info about what was going on in the area. And don't even try to tell us a man like Garrison wouldn't have spies out. Listening to the scavvies in the market, that kind of thing."

"Plus we know Soulardville patrols the downtown area," Krysty added.

Brother Joseph shrugged. "Please believe me when I tell you our best information was limited. Our patrols seldom venture past the stadium. They tend not to come back. The same for any scouts and spies dispatched by Garrison. The bulk of the information we receive about what goes on comes from gossip by scavvies come to trade, both in Soulard and Breweryville."

"So you got spies inside B-ville?" Ryan said.

"Yes. And they have spies in Soulard. Neither side makes much effort to root them out. We're at peace. And anyway, if we eliminated each other's spies that we knew about, each side would just send more who'd hide better."

"Talk on the move," Ryan said. "Not triple-healthy here in the open. Plus we got a clock."

"There were rumors," Brother Joseph said as they pressed north along the broad highway. It was as if the rubblescape to either side of them was a different world, somehow. Ryan felt disconnected from it all.

He knew that was an illusion, a potentially deadly one.

"The scavvies spoke of some kind of strange cult among the cannies, certain less scrupulous scavvie gangs, other survivors eking out a living in the ruins. Because of the nuke, the earthquakes and the floods, St. Lou is still rich and largely unexploited in terms of salvage. And as you've seen in the villes, if you can protect crops from the occasional acid downpour, you can grow food quite readily here. So there are all manner of folk crawling through the ruins of the city and suburbs."

"What manner of cult are you speaking of, Brother Joseph?" Doc asked.

"One so terrible our informants would do no more than

hint about it," the preacher said. "Hints of blood rituals and human sacrifice on a terrible scale."

"And that's speaking as a man who ran his own human sacrifice cult?" Mildred demanded.

"As I indicated, the cult is said to go in for sacrifice on a much larger scale. And I saved more lives from the screamwings than I ever fed to them."

"After you started calling the screamwings down on Soulard in the first place," Krysty said.

"Well, some things are needful in the name of establishing and maintaining social order. A spirit of sacrifice strengthens community, which in turn is necessary for a ville to survive, much less prosper and grow."

"Seems Soulardville prospered just fine for a century or so before you started helping them out by calling down screamwings to eat them," J.B. said.

"Don't judge me. You don't know the whole situation."

"Our judging you," Ryan said, "is the last thing you have to worry about. Now shut it. If you have the wind to yap, you got the wind to go double-fast!"

Conversation died down as they picked up the pace again. The roadbed was intact as far as Ryan could clearly see by the moon and starlight. But he quickly came to wonder if perhaps canning the small talk was such a good idea, once the first protracted, blood-freezing howl of unendurable agony rose from the stadium as they approached what had been the beginning of another great bridge.

Another voice joined the chorus of pain. Then another.

They moved among the tracery of shadows cast by the remains of what had once been a complex overpass system. Roads soared to nowhere, ending in air. Railway tracks were twisted. A diesel engine with three cars behind it, long-gutted by looters, lay on its side to the west of them like the corpse of a colossal mutant worm.

The highway remained clear. Ryan guessed some enterprising souls—or harsh slave masters, depending—had cleared away the rubble that had fallen onto it over the years. There were, he realized, a million stories in the dead city.

Not that he gave a baron's promise for any of them.

They passed through the skein of ruined roads and pressed on. As they drew abreast the firelit stadium Ryan held up his hand.

"Hold up," he called softly. The shouting and cheering and screaming from the bowl of firelight to the west seemed loud enough to drown out any noise they might make, up to and including setting off grens, if they had any, which sadly they didn't. But he really and truly didn't want to take any chances of drawing the attention of whoever all those fusies in there were.

"What is it, my dear Ryan?" Doc asked.

"Something to the north," Ryan said. "Other side of the road."

"Rider," said Krysty. With Jak gone she had the sharpest eyes of the group. "Coming south fast."

Ryan could see it now. More by chance than anything else they followed the eastern, once the northbound, half of the divided highway. As if following the same long-dead traffic rules, the dark rider came down the southbound side. Mebbe the trade caravans coming through just followed the old rules to avoid conflict.

"Defensive positions, everybody!" he shouted. "Go to ground and get ready to fight."

Chapter Twenty-Nine

With the unspoken harmony of long practice the companions went prone to form a defensive star with Brother Joseph in the middle.

"Aren't you even going to ascertain their intentions first?" the guru asked.

"We aren't going to shoot at them unless they make a move toward us," J.B. said. "Now get your triple-stupe ass down!"

But the horseman showed no sign of noticing them. They heard the distinct clip-clop of the hooves as it approached. The horse was huge. If it wasn't midnight-black, it was dark enough to make no difference. Despite the heat, humidity thick and clinging as a wet wool blanket, the rider wore a hooded cloak that obscured his features. Or hers, Ryan supposed. Or *its*. The cloak billowed out behind its black-clad form.

Without a sideways glance at the group it galloped on past to the south. It quickly became one with the twining shadows of the devastated flyovers.

"What in the name of the days of the smoke clouds was *that*?" J.B. demanded.

"You're the local, Bro," Ryan said, cautiously picking himself up.

Brother Joseph shook his head. "I have no idea," he said. "But I must admit, seeing it caused me to feel a chill. Quite inexplicably."

"Much as I hate to agree with him," Mildred said, "I felt the same way."

"Yeah," Ryan said. "Me, too. But whatever kind of horror that thing was, it's somebody else's horror now. We got enough ahead of us.

"Start hauling it, people. Time's blood!"

Gradually they left the old stadium behind. Ryan felt relief. This road wouldn't take them to their goal, which he could see clearly, a spike of greater darkness against the night, hiding stars. But it would get them to within a few blocks.

Granted, those blocks were sheer lethal obstacle courses of rubble, infested with enemies. But nobody said this would be easy.

Then he spotted lights bobbing on the roadway a couple hundred yards ahead of them. As he watched, more seemed to join, appearing from the half swamp, half flooded area to the right of the road, by the nearer, big-angled leg of what Mildred claimed had once been a golden arch taller than the skyscraper that was King Screamwing's lair.

"What's that?" Brother Joseph asked sharply.

"Stickies, likely," J.B. said. "They do love them some fire."

"It doesn't matter much who they are, does it?" Mildred asked.

"Not a spent round's worth," Ryan said. "Whoever it is, we don't want to meet them."

They hurriedly headed left, across the divider between the halves of the road. The torchbearers, whoever or whatever they were, spilled over both halves of the old interstate. So the companions kept moving west, toward where a skeletal dome rising from a colonnaded rubble pile loomed above a strip of dense forest.

Ryan began to breathe easier when they slipped through

the outer screen of brush in among the trees. Stickies didn't generally care much for woods.

"Mebbe I should take point," J.B. said. "I've got the scattergun. If something busts loose here, it'll bust loose at hand-shaking range."

Ryan nodded. "Take it. I'll flank right."

"Ryan," Mildred said, coming up alongside him, "are you sure—?"

"Everybody keeps asking me that," he said. "He needs to do it. No matter how much his chest hurts. He's got to show he can carry his weight, on the trail or in a fight."

She shook her head. "Testosterone poisoning," she muttered. But she made no more protest.

Drums abruptly boomed from the stadium.

"I wonder where they got drums that big?" Krysty said.

"I don't," Ryan said.

They followed trails that led through the brush. It enabled them to move faster as well as more quietly. For all Ryan knew they might be game trails. Deer could live in these woods, he knew from experience. If old St. Lou had boasted a zoo, and given its size it probably had, there could even be descendants of exotic escapees roaming the ruins. A stand of woods like this would draw them like flies to a fresh chill.

"Eyes and ears wide open, people," he said quietly. "All we need is to run into a tiger in here."

J.B. led them deeper into the woods. A wordless chant rose from the stadium, joining the drums. Whatever the evening's entertainment was in there, it appeared to be reaching a climax.

From somewhere ahead, Ryan heard a branch swish against another.

He froze. Turning his eyes left, he saw that J.B., caught

in midstep, was slowly lowering his left boot to the ground. Convalescing from his chest wound hadn't messed up his balance, fortunately.

Something swooshed from the brush ahead. In the moonlight Ryan saw J.B. twist his body clockwise. Whatever it was swept past him, a pale blur in the moonlight. As it passed between Brother Joseph and Ryan, Ryan reflexively grabbed at it, afraid it would hit Krysty behind him.

Almost to his surprise he caught it. He found himself holding a slender pole, actually a not terribly straight branch devoid of twigs. In a cleft in its end a wicked narrow wedge of flattened can was bound with what looked liked sinew.

J.B.'s shotgun roared answer to the sudden spear. The brush ahead began to thrash furiously, to the tone of frenzied catlike yowling.

A shower of rocks and crude spears erupted from the woods ahead of the small party. J.B.'s M-4000 boomed again. Then an earsplitting rattle of blasterfire erupted from his four companions' handblasters.

"North!" Ryan shouted. "We can't just bust caps blind!"

But he did, firing twice more toward where he thought he'd seen missiles fly.

He was glad to see J.B. turn right and run, pumping out blasts from the hip that shredded foliage and lit up the woods as he ran. He glanced back to see Brother Joseph stumble forward, propelled by a hand in the back from Mildred. Then came Doc, high-stepping, holding his sword stick and his smoking blaster.

"Krysty!" he shouted.

A figure burst from the undergrowth not a dozen feet in front of him. The cannie was buck-naked and brandishing a nail-studded branch as a club. Ryan aimed for the center of the pallid mass and fired a double-tap. His attacker went down with a gut-shot wail.

Something grabbed Ryan's right arm and pulled with surprising strength. "I'm right here!" Krysty shouted. "Time to go!"

He couldn't argue with that. He went.

A dozen desperate heart-pounding lung-tearing paces took them out of the woods and into the street. The building directly across from the woods was a sprawling heap of dark rubble a good forty feet tall. No refuge there.

J.B. knelt, shooting into the woods they'd just left and stuffing in single shells after each shot. He'd shot his tubular mag dry. Running quite well, all things considered, Doc led the pack toward the northbound street west of the huge dark mass. Ryan and Krysty followed, bringing up the rear.

"C'mon, J.B.!" Ryan shouted to the Armorer as they sprinted past. To his relief the little man jumped up as if he were in the best shape of his life. He ran right after them, holding his shotgun in one hand and clamping his fedora to his head in the other.

From the mouth of the street Doc and Mildred laid down covering fire. A spear arced over Ryan's right shoulder and scraped off the pavement in front of him. The cannies hadn't given up yet.

As he and Krysty sprinted between the mound of wreckage and the building across from it, Ryan noticed that a spill of rubble lay across the street a hundred feet down. It looked like an extension of the huge pile of debris to their right. This side of the tall building on their left was largely intact. The front part of that structure, an extension maybe three stories tall, had apparently had only windows for walls. These had been blown out long ago, leaving the structure consisting mostly of framed black spaces.

Brother Joseph sat on the ground between the two, rubbing his knee. Mildred looked up at Ryan as he slowed down.

"He didn't seem to want to stop," she said, "so I tripped him."

Bro Joe muttered something about madmen and women.

J.B. stopped and turned back, his shotgun on his shoulder. His breathing was labored. "Looks as if they quit chasing us," he said.

Doc had his head tipped to one side and his eyebrows knotted. "Do you hear something?"

Ryan listened. "Huh? No."

"Precisely. It's what the dog didn't do in the night, my friends!"

"Doc," Ryan said urgently, "you got to be here and now for us."

"He means the rad-blasted stadium, Ryan!" J.B. exclaimed. "You hear the noise from there?"

"No. I— Oh, holy shit!"

They looked back. To the south, across the trees, they could see lights flooding the ramp that wound down from the upper levels of the stadium, as if people carrying torches were swarming out of the seats and down toward the ground.

"They heard us shooting," Krysty said. "Now they want to play, too."

"Could things possibly be worse?" Brother Joseph moaned.

And something brushed the hair atop Ryan's head.

He reached automatically up to brush at it, thinking it was a bat. Then he heard a solid thunk of something striking rubble right behind him. He wheeled around to see a head-size chunk of masonry bouncing down the side of the vast mound.

He spun back. Obviously the missile had come from the skeletal structure on the west side of the street. He aimed his SIG that way. He didn't see movement there now.

Krysty stood facing him. He saw her eyes go wide in the moonlight.

"Ryan," she said in a choked voice, "up there!"

He turned back to the great mound of ruined building yet again. Pale shapes were rising from it like maggots from the bloated corpse of a dog.

"Cannies!" he shouted.

"They're in the other building, too!" Mildred cried.

Pales figures danced against the sky atop the low structure, waving arms against the stars. Others moved along the upper floor.

"By the Three Kennedys!" Doc exclaimed. "The devils are behind us as well!"

A rock grazed Ryan's cheek from the mound. More missiles slanted down from the building across from it. And then he saw figures rise up on the low arm of debris that blocked the street to the north—blocked their path to the great dark tower. And Jak.

"Well, we're surrounded," Brother Joseph remarked in disgust. He moved his head aside as a half brick flew past his ear. "Are you happy now?"

"Krysty, grab one of the Molotovs we made in the ville out of my pack. Light it and throw it at that barricade!"

"But we need them—"

"Now!" He shot upward at the figures, hurling broken bits of concrete and brick from the mound. "We need it now!"

The others had opened fire again. Ryan felt Krysty yank at the flap of the pack on his back. He knew she was working efficiently despite the adrenaline that had to be sizzling in her veins, but it felt like an eternity as he sighted and fired at the dancing, chanting cannibals.

"Ark! Ark! Ark!"

Ryan ducked his upper torso right to avoid a brick thrown at his blind side, which he caught from the corner of his good eye at the last possible instant. He felt a flash of fear: what if he made Krysty drop the lethal concoction?

"Got it!" she cried triumphantly. He heard the rasp and crackle of one of the spring-powered flint-strikers J.B. had cobbled together for them out of bits of salvage. Then a blazing blue meteor arced toward the low wall of rubble blocking their passage.

Before leaving Soulardville they had each hurriedly made up two improvised Molotovs—ceramic jars and vases filled with a mixture of Bro Joe's fuel alcohol and the fish oil the ville used to fire a lot of its lamps, a bad-smelling but effective expedient, and apparently a useful byproduct of the river-fishing industry thereabouts. When it shattered on a masonry chunk the Molotov didn't make as vigorous an explosion as a gasoline bomb would, nor as bright and hot a rush of flame. But it made plenty, and it was what they had.

Ryan rushed toward the sudden blaze of blue fire. A figure was spinning in circles atop the low wall, shrieking, waving arms like wings of flame. Apparently cannies had lost the ancient lore of stop, drop and roll.

The one-eyed man ran to the left of the burning cannibal, firing his SIG. He hoped nobody—meaning Mildred—would chill the suffering cannie out of a mis-guided sense of mercy. Nothing like having one of their buddies on fire to get enemies' minds right, no matter who they were.

He hit the rubble wall running as the cannie—his

whole upper body now ablaze—fell over the far side. Ryan reached the top of the six-foot-high slope on all fours. A cannie stood to bar his way at the top, and he backhanded the creature across the face with his SIG. Bones crunched. The cannie's head snapped to the side and it fell.

Gaining the top, Ryan ripped his panga from its sheath left-handed, chopped down one cannie, shot another in the chest and belly as it rose up to his right.

"Come on!" he shouted back at his companions. "Speed's all we got!"

"Forgive me, madam," Doc cried before he cracked a cannie woman wielding a big knife across the face with his sword stick. J.B.'s shotgun roared. He butt-stroked a cannie who wasn't quick enough getting out of his way.

Here came Brother Joseph, looking unusually pale, with Krysty and Mildred howling at his heels like furies. The fact they were shooting past him to either side couldn't have been a comfort to the man.

Even as he turned a club blow with his panga and slashed its wielder across the mouth with the return stroke, Ryan grinned.

Then his friends were across the barrier and running up the street. The way lay clear—at least as far as their next intersection. A left turn there would bring them one more block closer to their destination.

The cannies who could still move seemed to have cleared out. A glancing impact on the back of Ryan's right shoulder told him their friends on the big rubble mound were still in the game. On the west side of the street the building shot up ten or more stories. The cannies didn't seem to be going there. He ran on, clutching a weapon in either hand.

Just before the corner, which Doc had turned at a run, followed by the two women herding Joseph, Ryan caught up with J.B. The Armorer was visibly limping, and his breath sounded like a man ripping a sheet to strips. But he was busily reloading his shotgun magazine, pretending nothing was wrong.

"That bonfire'll bring the stonehearts from the stadium right here," he said as Ryan slowed beside him.

Ryan turned to walk backward alongside his friend. The rubble mound rose higher at this end of the block. The cannies either couldn't climb it or didn't care to at the moment. No more missiles came their way. But he thought he could see movement at the far end of the block, over the top of the wall of broken concrete. The Molotov fuel still burned cheery blue.

"I was counting on it," Ryan said with a grin.

"And it'll draw every stickie for miles around."

"That, too."

J.B. looked at him, blinking through his wire-rimmed glasses. Then he smiled.

"Here I thought I was the tricky one!"

"We all do what we can, old friend."

From somewhere to the south came a rattle of blaster-fire, quick and vicious. Screams of pain and fury answered it.

"Somebody just found something better to do than chase after us," Ryan said. "We best catch up before the others hog all the fun."

Chapter Thirty

"In my youth," Brother Joseph said, puffing as he pulled himself onward and up by the metal handrail, "I liked to tinker with salvaged electronics."

His words echoed slightly in the narrow vertical cavern on the stairwell.

Holding a fish-oil burning lantern in front of him, Ryan trudged in the lead up the endless concrete stairs. It was stiflingly hot in here, as if the whole heat of the river-valley day had accumulated and concentrated right here. Though the smell was largely must and dry concrete, the impression given by the narrow twisting passageway, illuminated vaguely by his lantern and the one Doc carried in the party's rear, was of climbing up the intestine of a colossal concrete monster.

"That was, of course," Brother Joseph continued, "before I discovered it was even easier, and far more gratifying, to tinker with the minds and hearts of men. And then a decade or so ago a chance discovery in simple frequency modulation put the perfect tool for social engineering into my hands."

"Your subsonic-supersonic screamwing control mechanism," Mildred said. She was climbing right behind the fallen spiritual leader. Since she seemed to have the most active dislike of the man, she seemed a good candidate to keep his sandaled feet to the straight and narrow, as it were. As if he had much opportunity to stray in here.

They came to a landing. It was marked 20.

"A trifling twenty-two floors left to go," Doc said.

"One more," Ryan said, making himself pick up one foot and put it in front of another. Slick cloying sweat encased him inside his clothes.

They hadn't had the kind of day that really prepared them triple-well for climbing as near as maybe to six hundred feet inside an airless, brutally hot stairway. He couldn't readily imagine what sort of day that would have been, actually. But he was sure it was about the opposite of this one.

While J.B. covered with his scattergun and Doc stood by with his lantern, Krysty pushed open the door to the twentieth floor. Ryan made himself continue as she vanished from sight to the other side. After an interval she reappeared.

"Got it propped," she called.

"Okay," Ryan called.

He reached the next landing and stopped. He continued to walk in place for a spell to keep his legs from knotting up. The others did likewise as they arrived.

He set down the lantern so its light played on the door. "Somebody cover me," he said. "I got this one."

His P-226 in hand, he stepped through. As always, the door led onto a little service area. Beyond it, he knew, waited the metal doors of the elevator bank. Beyond that the shells of whatever businesses had occupied this floor of the great tower.

A breath of breeze blew past him from the outside. From exploring several of the lower floors, they knew that while the monster skyscraper seemed to have survived the thermonuclear airburst with structural integrity mostly intact, all the windows were gone on all four sides. Meaning quakes had probably settled for those left behind by the blast wave.

By the yellow lantern glow Ryan saw a mop in a rolling wringer bucket standing out in the open. He pulled over the bucket and used it to wedge the door to the stairs open. Then with a metal-on-metal clangor he pulled out the mop. Its head had fossilized into a weird squashed wavy pattern.

It would save them time they could ill afford, and possibly risk, next time they had trouble finding something to hold open the door.

Doc was squatting just outside the door fanning himself with his hand when Ryan returned to the landing. He had set his lantern down beside him.

"It seems almost as if I can feel a breath of air stirring," he said.

"Object of the exercise, Doc."

He reached for his lantern. Krysty's white hand closed over the handle first. "No. Mildred and I'll carry the lights for a while. Won't do us any good when we get to the top if your arm's too tired to fight with."

"Hadn't thought of that."

They climbed on. Krysty took lead, while Ryan followed close, as watchful as a prairie falcon. Next came Brother Joseph, with J.B. on his tail. Then Doc, and finally Mildred with the other lantern.

"So you set out to invent a screamwing controller?" J.B. asked Brother Joseph. A passionate tinker as well as master armorer and gunsmith, he was fascinated by gadgetry of any sort.

"Of course not. It happened by accident when I was... employed by a baron in a ville far to the west of here. I was experimenting with generating tones of various frequencies when a flock of screamwings attacked my shop. It was really quite alarming, and most exciting until the sec men drove the horrid creatures off. In fact, the things kept coming, kept attacking, until acting on a hunch I switched the machine off. Then they simply seemed to lose interest and turn away.

"None of the sec men was able to hear the tone. Nor was I, nor my assistant. I later chanced to discover that certain children were able to hear it. Your friend Jak must enjoy an acute range of auditory response if he can hear both the high and the low tones at all, much less so deep into adolescence."

"Your employer must have lost patience with you rapidly, if your experiments continued to attract the unwanted attentions of screamwings," Doc said.

"Oh, he lost patience with me soon enough. For reasons having nothing to do with those particular experiments, the short-sighted fool. All my life I've been tormented by lack of vision among my patrons. I suppose if given a chance I'll work up quite a virulent hatred toward you people. After all, I no sooner contrived the optimal environment for myself than you showed up and spoiled it all."

"Hear that, Brother?" Mildred said. She held up her thumb and index fingers, rubbing the pads together. "It's the sound of the world's smallest violin, playing 'Tea and Sympathy.'"

"Well. Yes. I should know better than to expect sensitivity, under the circumstances. No, I was quite circumspect while I fine-tuned my discovery. Not to mention alert to any sign of the approach of screamwings, so that I could shut the tone generator down without attracting a swarm of winged Judases to my lab.

"It came to me to seek a tone to repel the mutants. Likely far more marketable than attracting the frightful things—and one which, frankly, made the initial discovery much more potentially useful as well."

"So this wasn't the first time you've run this particular protection scam?" Mildred asked.

"Oh, but it was. I wandered for years until I found the proper petri dish to culture my final and finest social experiment. A prosperous ville, a weak-minded baron—and, of course, a convenient colony of screamwings. Which serendipitously happened to be ruled over by that prodigy of twisted nature that I so aptly christened King Screamwing."

"Even better for us," Mildred said, "because guess who's waiting for us upstairs."

"I suppose I would only incur your ire if I pointed out the screamwings are likely to be in torpid state, having recently gorged themselves?"

"That seems like a good guess," Ryan said.

"Then instead I shall simply point out that the screamwings are seldom active at night. While I can't confirm from firsthand observation that they sleep, it would seem a logical surmise."

He climbed a while in silence. His step had gotten labored, Ryan noticed. But the fallen spiritual leader was canny enough to know better than to slow down his captors. Or even gripe.

At least not directly. "You really should be grateful to me," Brother Joseph said. "It was I, of course, who summoned the screamwings whose so-timely intervention helped save you when you were caught between two fires in the Millennium Hotel ruins."

"Don't start us figuring up any balance sheets," Ryan said. "Don't reckon you'll like the sum we come up with."

They passed the next landing. Ryan let the others climb

ahead, then while Mildred covered with her ZKR 551 he took the lantern and opened the door.

A skeleton lay just inside. Whatever clothes it had once worn had long vanished, rotted to dust or devoured by rats, insects and microbes, just like the skin, flesh, organs and cartilage, as well as the sinews that had held the mottled yellow bones together.

"Thighbone'll work just fine," Ryan said. "We don't have to use our mop."

He jammed the nearer thighbone under the door. It held. He frowned a moment at the skeleton, then collected the other thighbone, and such other large bones as he could find, and stuck them through his belt. Then he recovered the thighbone he'd used to hold the door open and substituted the mop with the ossified head. It was turning out to be a major pain in the ass to tote up the stairs.

"What the hell!" Mildred exclaimed when Ryan emerged back to the stairwell with ribs and leg and arm bones stuck through his belt like a sort of armor corset.

"Door stops," he said, picking up the lantern and handing it to her.

"I *hate* this century."

THEY WERE ALL dragging like the living dead when they finally reached the top floor, the level right beneath King Screamwing's rooftop domain. But a sense of urgency animated them like an unholy remnant of life.

They recced the level. As elsewhere, there wasn't much smell up here, except for the odors of sun-heated rubble and masonry and late-spring green growth that blew in from outside. There was a hint of old mouse droppings; that was about it.

By this time a perceptible breeze came in the door, propped open by somebody's rib.

Most of the floor seemed to have been a restaurant at the time of the big nuke. Coming out the open, eastern end of the elevator banks, the companions found themselves in a spacious dining room with a high ceiling. It was neatly arrayed with tables and chairs, some with settings still in place.

In fact some came complete with skeletal diners, apparently held together by their garments.

Exploring, they found a number of smaller rooms, apparently storage areas and lesser dining rooms. The floor's northern half was mainly occupied by a kitchen, with big stainless-steel sinks, counters and ovens hardly tarnished by time. Or at least as far as they could tell by lantern light.

A corridor winding around the outside of the kitchen took them past more little rooms, then to a cracked glass-brick partition with a door in it. The door seemed solid, also solidly stuck in its frame. J.B. rapped it hard with his steel-shod shotgun butt. Glass powdered and fell away, leaving a hole.

"Knock, knock," Mildred said. She helped the others take out the glass-brick the rest of the way down with well-placed boots.

"Musta been microfractures in that glass-brick from the dynamic overpressure," J.B. muttered.

"I beg your pardon?" said Brother Joseph, who accompanied them looking half contemptuous and half amused. One way or another they always managed to keep at least one set of eyes on him.

"Blast wave from the nuke," J.B. said. "Musta weakened those bricks pretty bad for them to powder so easy. Usually they're triple-tough, even after all these years."

"What's that smell?" Mildred asked.

Nobody knew. It was acrid. There was a certain nose-wrinkling familiarity to Ryan's nostrils, but he couldn't place it.

They pushed on. An office complex took up the level's southwest quadrant. Office chairs lay strewed across the floor, along with desks and toppled and charred or half-melted partitions. Papers had accreted in drifts in the angles of the interior walls, turned into papier-mâché by generations of rain and hail and snow blowing in unimpeded.

And of course, the skeletons. As elsewhere on this floor, some were bare, others fully clothed, some in between. "Wonder what the story is here?" J.B. asked.

"I would hazard a guess," Doc said, "that the various scavenging organisms found some varieties of fabric more toothsome than others."

"Synthetics," Mildred said.

"Or they were having themselves a triple-fine orgy," Krysty said, with her lantern picking out a mischievous glint in her emerald eyes.

She laughed at Doc's sudden flush and stammer. She enjoyed teasing him. He still harbored a lot of what Mildred termed Victorian notions of propriety, which he always countered by pointing out he'd lived during the reign of Queen Victoria. Doc reckoned that entitled him to be Victorian if anything did.

"What's this crap all over everything?" Mildred demanded. She held her lantern over a desk. Its top was splotched with white splattered deposits. In places they seemed to have accumulated to nearly an inch thick. They realized the stuff was splashed all over most of the horizontal surfaces. Some of what they initially took to be paper was the same substance, that looked like lumpy plaster.

Leaning down, Mildred said, "It *is* crap!"

"What would be defecating in here, I wonder?" Doc asked. "Pigeons?"

"Now we know why the smell, anyway," J.B. said.

"Not pigeons," Ryan said. He'd been bending down to examine the stuff. Now he turned and slowly straightened, staring out the window. And *up*.

"They wouldn't come around here, would they?" he asked.

"Why not?" Mildred asked. Then her eyes followed his. "Oh, dear God. The screamwings."

In the sudden stillness they became aware of a sinister muted chittering sound from above. It raised the hair at Ryan's nape.

"Jak," Krysty whispered.

"Well," Ryan said, "they say guano burns pretty good."

He shrugged out of his backpack and dropped it to the floor. Opening it, he began to remove the jars and jugs of fuel alk and fish oil, carefully sealed with wax, that they'd carried from Soulardville.

It felt as if he'd just set down an ox he'd been carrying on his back.

"Let's get busy," he said.

Chapter Thirty-One

"There they are," Ryan said, pressing his eye to the small glass window set in the very last door at the top of the endless stairs. The screamwings roosted or sat everywhere: on the girders, atop structures, on the floor, hundreds of them, as if the tower's roof was hell's chicken coop.

He stepped back to let the others peer out, despite almost exploding with impatience to get out and learn Jak's fate for sure, even though at his core he knew Brother Joseph had to be right.

"That's one ugly bastard," Mildred said, peering up at the immense creature that sat amid a great tangle. It could only be a nest, built upon a tracery of girders a good twenty feet above the housing that held the heads of elevators and stairwell, and perhaps thirty below what remained of the high peaked roof of the gable.

"Indeed it is," Doc said, leaning in sideways to peek. "And— My word, that nest! Is it built of bones?"

"Looks like," Mildred said grimly, stepping back. "Human bones, some of them. Like that big huge pile below."

"Plus some brush and branches to hold it together, it looks like," Krysty said, stepping up to take her turn.

She looked back over her shoulder. "Wait, if it's got a nest, should we mebbe be calling it Queen Screamwing?"

Everybody looked at Bro Joe, who stood back watching with ill-concealed amusement on his bearded face. While the others took their turns looking at the screamwing eyrie, Ryan had kept his eye on their captive.

The guru shrugged. "The late Baron Savij was, like his illustrious predecessors, a great believer in the patriarchal principle. He was far more willing to accept a screamwing king. As for the beast's actual sex, I'm as much in the dark as you."

"What's that other stuff, everywhere?" J.B. asked. "I mean, aside from the big pile of bones and skulls in the middle of the floor."

Ryan glanced back through. "More shit."

It was true. Whatever the floor inside the gable roof had once consisted of, it was now carpeted inches deep in the same stuff they'd seen spattered all over the office below. There was more splashed across the top of the housing to the north, down its side, down the sides of the other small structures Ryan could see, whose function he could only guess at. And couldn't be bothered to.

Even through the door the ammoniacal stink made Ryan's nose burn. "The little guys don't seem to mind sitting in the crap of ages," Mildred said.

"All right," Ryan said. "Showtime. Doc, guard the door. Brother Joseph, how do you work this gizmo of yours? How do I set it to 'repel' and turn it on?"

Brother Joseph reached over Ryan's shoulder and turned what appeared to be a sunburst medallion counterclockwise to the left. "There," he said. "Shall I turn it on for you as well?"

"Not yet," Ryan said. "We'll use when we need it. Right now these bastards seem to be asleep. No need fixin' what isn't broken."

He favored the fallen holy man with a one-eyed squint. "You know that no matter what goes down, you try shit, we *will* drop you."

"No need to belabor the painfully obvious, Ryan," Joseph said bitterly. "I take your martial competence for granted. And that notwithstanding, please believe me when say I fear the screamwings far more than I do you. I still don't see why I have to come along on this stage of this fool's errand."

"Because you need to help make right what you did wrong," Mildred said in a voice that didn't invite debate.

"Ready?" Ryan asked. The others murmured assent. He turned the knob, pushed open the door and stepped through.

If he thought it stank up here before, he realized at once he'd had no idea. The reek hit him in the face like a club. His eyes watered, and his nose and throat threatened to pinch shut in rebellion. It wasn't nauseating as much as a lot like getting a shot of tear gas.

He persevered, holding his SIG-Sauer P-226 in his right hand and the preacher's magic jim-jam in his left. Like the rest, he'd left his backpack on the level below. He carried his slung Steyr, though, both because he was loath to leave it unguarded and because a person just never knew.

To his surprised relief the turd carpet was neither slippery nor ankle-deep ooze. It was mostly dry, forming a spongy mat. He could see occasional wet gleams in the light of the moon that now shone in the huge gap above.

"Watch your footing," he said quietly. "Step in a wet patch, you're triple-screwed."

The pitched gable roof had been blasted or melted back from the west side for a good quarter of its length. Bare support beams made a shadow network over the nearer part; the end was simply gone. Likewise the window that had formed its western end: it was a *U* of starry blackness.

Aside from the great gable, the roof level was sur-

rounded on three sides by inward-slanting metal-clad
sheets that suggested solidity from below, but in fact left
most of the building's summit open to the sky. Whatever
had made up the gable's vertical walls had collapsed at
floor level, leaving upright structural beams. The outer
roof's northwest corner, though surviving the nuke's thermal pulse, had been buckled inward by the blast so that
some of it actually was molded over the tall oblong concrete structure that occupied much of the north section.

The dried-shit flooring muffled sound. Ryan's flesh
crawled at being surrounded by hundreds and hundreds of
the seagull-size, flesh-craving mutants, not to mention the
monster in its house-size nest looming over everything,
with its crested head tucked under one wing.

Ryan glanced back. J.B. backed him tight, shotgun
ready. His hat was tipped up, and his head and his face
looked pinched and pallid beneath a gloss of sweat. Next
came Krysty, her normally full lips almost vanished in a
resolute line. She carried her Smith & Wesson 640 in her
right hand and a cleaver from her backpack in her left.
Behind walked the unarmed Brother Joseph, trying to look
nonchalant, and as ever, close after him stalked Mildred.

Ryan wasn't really sure where they were going. He
steered left, around the house-high pile of bones beneath
the monster's macabre nest. Something about the shadows
of that crumpled-in roof corner drew his eye.

From the left came a peculiar chirp. "Ryan," J.B.
muttered through clenched teeth, "I think we've been
noticed."

Ryan looked left. A small screamwing sitting on the
guano mat just eight or nine feet away had taken its head
out from under its wing. It shook it, triple-fast, like a wet
dog. Then as if accidentally it turned to look up at Ryan.

Its eyes, half-lidded with sleep, shot wide. It opened its beak and squawked.

Ryan hit the on switch of Brother Joseph's device.

"Damn!" Mildred whispered. "Bro Joe just broke away! He ran right around the elevator bank to the south side before I could stop him. Freaking screamwings distracted me. Sorry."

And hundreds and hundreds of screamwings raised their sleepy heads, turned and stared at the intruders. Then with a booming of many wings they took flight. Almost directly overhead, the king—Ryan still thought of the monster that way; how the hell did he know what sex it really was?—unfurled its own wings with a sound like a cannon going off.

The lesser screamwings flew up about ten feet in the air and began swooping toward the companions. They seemed chiefly curious as to what these strange intruders were. What they didn't seem was repelled at all.

From the black shadow pocket beneath the crumpled-down roof corner a figure emerged, with ghost-white face and hair and wearing a camo jacket and ragged jeans.

"Ryan, no!" Jak yelled, waving his arms. "That brings 'em!"

But Ryan had already switched the sunburst counter-clockwise until it hit a detent.

The diving seagull-size screamwings braked as if they hit an invisible wall. The device, which had been vibrating so fast in Ryan's hand it stung his skin, now rumbled at a low frequency that rattled in his bones.

With a skull-shattering shriek, King Screamwing took off straight up, fleeing the hated low tone. The downblast of his wings almost battered Ryan to his knees.

"Jak!" Krysty shouted through the diminishing thunder

of the giant flyer's wings as it flapped away from its lair. "You're alive!"

Instead of answering he dived back into the shelter of the shoved-in roof. A whole cloud of lesser screamwings hit it like a sudden hailstorm. Ryan heard multiple thumps as a number of them bounced off the roof.

The muties raised a terrific screeching clamor. Ryan saw a wild churning of wings and toothed beaks, and a flash of steel in moonlight. A screamwing fell, its finger-wing sheered through. Others swarmed over its thrashing body. Its cries rose higher as its fellows devoured it alive.

Jak's fighting knife slashed patterns of dazzle in the air right outside his shelter. Blood and body parts flew. Some of the screamwings settled down to cannibalistic feasts. Others retreated in squawking haste.

One bold mutie ventured close, managing somehow to evade the fast-moving blade. A white hand grabbed it by its skinny throat. It vanished into shadow. A beat later it was flung out again. It was limp, and its head dangled loose at the end of a wrung neck.

"Stick tight!" Ryan shouted. He sprinted toward Jak, holding the screamwing repeller high. He had no idea if it helped; he did it anyway.

"What about Brother Joseph?" Krysty yelled. He didn't look back. By her voice he could tell she was right behind him, which was all he needed to know.

"Nuke him!"

The screamwings had started circling like a noisy living dust devil in front of Jak's shelter. Now they broke apart and shot off in all directions, like drops of water from a big rock hitting a pond. They triple-hated that low-freq hum.

The companions reached Jak's shelter. "Come on," Ryan

shouted. "We don't know how long this noisemaker'll hold them off. We're in their damn house!"

Jak popped out like a prairie dog, his knife and knife hand dripping blood. His face was streaked with gore the color of the eyes that glared wildly from it.

"Why *all* come?" he demanded. "All gone droolie suddenly?"

Knowing how risky it was to hug the albino teen with his shard-encrusted jacket, Krysty squeezed his upper arm.

"Strength in numbers," Ryan said. "You walk?"

"Can run!"

"Don't," Mildred said. "Footing's pretty slippery in places. You go down in this shit, you won't get up before these things're all over you."

Ryan gestured with the repeller and his P-226, herding his crew back toward the stairs. They started back past the big rectangular concrete structure that formed one wall of Jak's hideout.

A cry loud as an air horn made them look up. The giant screamwing settled onto the girders next to its nest, waving its enormous wings in agitation. Another echoing call, and the cloud of little screamwings, which had begun orbiting above the gable roof, arrowed back down through the open west end.

Right toward the companions.

Most of them sheered off again, screeching dismay at the subsonic hum. But one blasted right through. It struck Ryan's left shoulder, flapping its furry left wing in his face. Its toothed beak sliced into his cheek below the eye patch. He shouted, in angry surprise far more than pain.

A flash. A wash of heat. Ryan heard nothing, merely felt an impact like a huge hand slapping the left side of his face, hard enough to sting.

The screamwing exploded into blood and bone shrapnel.

"Glowing night shit!" Ryan yelled. He could only hear in his right ear. The whole left side of his head felt numb. "What the fuck happened?"

"Sorry, Ryan!" He barely heard J.B. He realized he wasn't hearing triple-good with his right ear, either, at the moment. He also realized the Armorer had stuck the muzzle of his shotgun close to the furry little horror and blasted it at near contact range, which meant he'd lit off the 12-gauge blaster right next to Ryan's left ear.

By reflex Ryan clapped a hand to that ear. There was no blood on his palm when he took it away. *Mebbe I didn't lose the drum,* he thought.

In screaming fury Mildred stamped a fallen screamwing with her combat boots. Krysty slashed another's furry belly open. It fluttered brokenly a few paces and fell thrashing to the floor, kicking at its own spilled guts.

The companions had halted when the first screamwing broke through their repeller tone. The giant screamwing tipped its crest back and vented another sky-ripping screech. A squadron of the lesser horrors dived on them again. As before, they turned away as they got close to the source of the painful vibration.

Most of them. Ryan whacked one out of midair with his SIG. Another descended claws-first toward his face. He slashed at it with the repeller. The mutie backed air and he shot it with a 9 mm slug. The muzzle-flash set its fur smoldering as it fell flapping in frantic agony.

"Run!" Ryan shouted, stomping the fallen flier with his bootheel and breaking its back.

"But the king!" Krysty shouted, slashing the furred wing membrane of another that had broken into the repeller field.

To get back to the stairs they'd have to pass directly above the crested monster. The giant also seemed to be egging its juniors on to the attack, whether by design or accident literally blowing them toward the intruders with beats of its huge wings when they held back. It didn't seem to like the repeller tone any better than the little ones did. But between their overlord's urging and their fury to defend their nest, the lesser screamwings by ones and twos overcame their distaste of the throbbing hum to attack the invaders.

Sooner or later they'd get in close enough to do real damage. His friends' faces already bled from cuts and nips. They were losing this game fast.

Ryan pointed his blaster at the king and emptied the magazine into it.

The monster's blood rained down on them. As the SIG's slide locked back, the king took off again, screeching its titan fury. Ryan doubted he'd done it any real damage—he wasn't that lucky. But like anything the creature didn't like getting shot.

"Haul ass!" he yelled. The companions lit out for the stairwell at as brisk a pace as the yielding floor would allow.

J.B. put a foot into a patch of poorly dried guano and sank. He stumbled and began to pitch forward onto his face.

Once down, he'd never rise before the little monsters swarmed him.

Chapter Thirty-Two

Mildred and Jak caught J.B. under the arms before he could fall. With frantic strength they yanked him out of the deep muck that had tripped him. He got boots beneath him on more solid footing and staggered onward, coughing as though his lungs would burst.

Ryan feared they might do just that. But he had no attention to waste on that. The giant screamwing hovered directly above the opening in the gable roof, screaming. The sound was driving the lesser screamwings to suicidal fury. They dived in again and again. Each time a few got close enough to slash at the interloping humans with needle-toothed beaks.

Ryan stuck his P-226, its slide still locked back over an empty mag, back in its holster and drew his panga. The big blade whistled a figure eight of death in the air before him. J.B. blasted his M-4000 empty, then reversed the weapon and, holding it by a barrel that had to be scorching fingers and palms, swatted and broke furry bodies that dared wing too close.

Krysty and Mildred had put away their empty blasters, too. Handblasters weren't ideal for dealing with the fast-moving, swarming monstrosities. Instead they used knives and bare hands, grabbing and snapping fragile wing bones or crushing throats, slashing at eyes and bellies.

At least these muties weren't as tough to chill as some breeds of screamwings they'd encountered. But what they

lacked in hardiness they more than made up in numbers—
and ferocity.

Despite the giant screamwing's shrieking rage, the
friends all reached the door alive. Doc's short-barreled
shotgun slung beneath the primary barrel of his LeMat
blew apart a last diving screamwing. Ryan turned and
again held the thrumming device up before him like a
talisman as the others dived to safety inside.

Apparently the little monsters weren't as proprietary
about the area around the concrete blockhouse that en-
closed the stairwell. Or maybe, despite their monarch's
rage, they were getting wary. Scores of torn and broken
bodies littered the guano-mat floor, some thrashing and
squalling, others moving and croaking feebly, and most
just lying there cooling. The last pursuers turned away as
Ryan thrust the repeller at them. They flew across the roof
near Jak's former hideout and, landing, began to tear at the
fallen bodies of their less fortunate brethren.

"Get inside," Doc was roaring. He gestured with the
fat-cylindered handblaster, while flourishing his black
sword stick in the reeking air to discourage any particularly plucky pursuers. None came close, though.

When everybody else was inside, Ryan shouted to Doc
to go into the stairwell, too.

A great shadow descended. King Screamwing had at
last decided to join the fray.

Ryan jumped backward. His boot soles were slick with
gelatinous screamwing shit—he slid out of control. Mildred
caught him, kept him from going down the stairs or tumbling over the rail to plunge almost six hundred feet to make
a wide stain on the concrete floor. Krysty slammed the door
shut.

A darkness blocked the window. For a moment the right
eye of the giant screamwing glared yellow hate at them.

Then the great crested head went away. Ryan felt the boom of the sky monarch's wings even through the steel door.

"He's perched up on the girder again," Krysty reported. "He's preening. The others have lost interest in us completely."

Ryan and the others had collapsed onto the floor of the landing. The concrete felt wonderfully cool to Ryan's spent and battered body. After two beatings in twenty-four hours the companions had been near the ragged edge of exhaustion before ever setting out from Soulardville. Now, without the immediate threat of being ripped to pieces to keep them going at any cost, fatigue landed on all of them like an asteroid from space.

Vaguely Ryan was aware of Jak, squatting and panting like a wolf, describing breathlessly how he survived. "Possumed when big fucker lifted me up. Didn't want fall. Then came here. Took hider knife, stabbed fucker triple-good in leg. Dropped me. Saw hidey-hole, got in before little screamers got me. Then held off till sun went down, monsters got sleepy."

Ryan shook his head and struggled to his feet. "All right," he said. "A few more steps and we're done." It was metaphor rather than truth. But it seemed to get them all moving, however painfully.

A violent pounding came from the door. Heads snapped that way.

Brother Joseph stared in the little window at them. His eyes showed white all around.

"For the love of mercy!" the preacher shouted, "Please, let me in!"

"After that dirty trick you played with the screamwing device, Brother Joseph?" Mildred asked.

"Ryan would've done the same! All's fair in love and war!"

"Mebbe," Ryan said.

"You can't leave me for these monsters!"

"Watch me," Jak said.

"We had a deal!" the fallen spiritual leader screamed. "I bring you here, and you'd let me go when you got your friend back. Well, you've got him. And he's even alive! A miracle! You talk a lot about keeping bargains, Ryan. Keep the deal you made with me."

"Sure," Ryan said. He turned the sunburst on the device all the way clockwise.

"What did you do?" Brother Joseph shrieked immediately. "They're looking at me! Oh, sweet mother of mercy, no!"

Ryan pushed past the others and yanked the door open.

Brother Joseph stood staring with round eyes. Behind him the lesser screamwings had taken flight and were circling once more in obvious agitation. King Screamwing slowly extended his mighty wings and looked down toward the source of the most intriguing noise.

"Oh, thank you, Ryan, thank you, I'll—"

Whatever else Brother Joseph was going to babble came out in a wordless whoosh of air as Ryan brought up his knee and thrust-kicked the man in the gut with the shit-coated sole of his right boot. Brother Joseph reeled back five steps before doing a comic pratfall. Guano squelched beneath him.

"What are you doing?" he howled. "We had a deal!"

"Yeah," Ryan said. "And I just kept it. You're free to go, Bro Joe. Anywhere you please."

The literally fallen spiritual leader and man-who-would-be baron gathered himself to leap for the sweet tempting shelter offered by the open door. Ryan brought his hand down and back and lobbed the fast-vibrating device in a low arc above Brother Joseph's head. It landed with a soft plop fifteen feet behind him, bouncing to rest against the base of the pyramid of discarded bones beneath the king's wicker-and-bone nest.

"Right now I'd try to go switch that thing to repel, if I were you," Ryan said. "Glad I'm not."

Brother Joseph turned and scrabbled on all fours after the device. Though his hands sank into shit to the elbow and came out dripping white custardy foul ooze, he drove himself forward by sheer will until he was almost in reach of the device, sending out its siren song, inaudible to all but Jak. Several hundred screamwings who were taking an ever more lively interest orbited closer and closer like a flapping, chittering tornado.

But in its nest, high above a great city's rubble, there was only one screamwing that mattered.

As he stretched a clawing desperate hand for the mutie attractor a moon shadow fell across Brother Joseph's face. He looked up.

And screamed at the point of King Screamwing's beak, poised a handspan from his face.

The huge crested head darted down. Like a spear the monster's beak struck between Brother Joseph's shoulder blades, pinning him facedown to the mat of pliant, fermenting shit.

Then a new color overwhelmed the sunburst pattern tie-dyed on the back of Brother Joseph's T-shirt: solid scarlet, gleaming and fast-spreading.

Ryan backed into the housing and shut the door on his screams.

"Okay, I'll hold here. You all go do what needs to be done. When you're clear, give a shout and I'll follow. But don't wait for me. Get out of this hellhole as fast as you can. Hear me?"

"No," Jak said.

Ryan stared at him. In his current state he literally had trouble conjuring what the single emphatic syllable even meant.

"Now, hold on just a—"

"Said no. Meant no. I faster best times. Fastest. You all beat. Had better day, me."

"Well," Doc said, "it's true the lad didn't have to walk here, Ryan. And he got one fewer thrashing."

Krysty laid a hand on Ryan's arm. "Surely you don't think you have to prove anything, Ryan? He's right, you know," she added.

Ryan slumped. Krysty tightened her grip on his forearm. It was enough. He forced himself to stand upright.

It took about the same effort it had to climb forty-three flights of steam bath stairs.

"You got it, then, Jak," he said. "But when we give the word, you throw open that door and move like hell's on your tail.

"'Cause it sure as shit will be!"

WHEN EVERYBODY but Jak, keeping guard above, had cleared out of the forty-second floor and down to the landing below, Ryan cocked back and hurled the makeshift Molotov.

It struck the upper edge of a stainless-steel counter and shattered. Instantly blue flames, stinking of fish, spread out.

Then the mixture of fuel and fish oil they'd splashed so liberally around the kitchen before climbing up to the roof took fire with a giant *whomp*. The fires they had already set, out of sight at north and south ends of the level, burned with a deep crackling roar, devouring fuel-soaked furniture, paper and deep drifts of mostly dried screamwing guano.

Ryan thought he was prepared for the result. He wasn't. A blue wave of flame rushed at him. He turned and rolled down the stairs, coming to rest one flight down with his eyebrows crisped.

Fire jetted out the door. The others were already hollering at the tops of their lungs for Jak to jump.

A human shape dropped through the howling, billowing flame. For a moment fire wreathed the slight figure. As he fell clear, Jak unfolded the arms he'd had crossed to protect his face. His sleeves smoked. His strong white hands caught the top steel railing at the forty-first floor landing. He even got a foot up in time to save himself from falling face-first into a lower rail.

Then the others were hauling him up over the rail, laughing, clapping him on the back.

As Ryan picked himself up from his graceless huddle at the foot of the flight of stairs, Jak gave him a twisted grin.

"Lessee you do *that*, Ryan!"

Slowly Ryan shook his head. "Not if I've got anything to say about it."

"WELL, WHAT HAVE we here?" Ryan asked as they emerged to the street. They were sweat-soaked and staggering from their trip down the giant tower, even though the fire at the very top was sucking air up from the ground into a very respectable breeze blowing up into their faces the whole time.

What they had was Tully and twenty men of the ville, armed to the eyeballs with the usual Soulardville assortment of crossbows and black-powder blasters. Garish orange flame-light from above cast sharp shadows on pavement and mounded brown rubble behind them.

"You just cause immense amounts of shit wherever you go, don't you, Ryan?" the ginger-haired patrol leader said.

"Heard it said," the one-eyed man said, "once or twice. What happened to the cannies? That big old mound of shit there seems to be their own special little ville."

"It is," Tully said. "Got burrows all through it like rad-blasted ants. But they had a disagreement with a bunch of jolt-fused scavvies *and* who knows how many stickies. By the time we got here, everybody'd just about decided they had a bellyful and it was time to head home."

He showed teeth. "We shot a few, just to make sure they kept heading in the right direction. Cannies went right to ground in their ant heap here. After the first two heads that got poked up came back within a crossbow quarrel through 'em, they haven't seemed much inclined to curiosity anymore."

"So are we prisoners again?" Krysty asked wearily. She sat on the curb.

"I'd say you're guests of Baron Emerald."

"But not guests who are at liberty to decline the good baron's hospitality, I presume?" Doc asked.

"You presume right, old man."

Disgustedly Mildred shook her head, her beaded plaits making faint tinkling sounds.

"I hope you don't mind carrying us," she said. "We had a hell of a night. I don't think any of us is in anything near shape to hike back to the ville. Except maybe Jak. He flew here."

Some of the patrol members goggled at the albino youth, who showed them a feral grin.

"All you got to do is hoof it back to 55," Tully said.

"We've got a horse-drawn wag you can ride the rest of the way."

"Thought you folks were afraid of the highway?" Ryan said.

"We got safety in numbers tonight," Tully said. "Now we'd best move on before you people keel over."

Wearily, the party hoisted themselves to their feet. J.B. shrugged off Mildred's assistance to rise, but she had to catch him to keep him from going right over again.

As they began hiking east down the wide, mostly clear avenue between the great rubble mound and the woods, a great cawing shriek made everybody stop and turn to stare upward.

King Screamwing rose from the pyre of his domain. In his claws wriggled a frantic human shape.

Both were aflame. The king made three mighty beats of his vast pinions, spewing sparks. Then he and his final prey crashed back into the inferno that crowned the dark tower.

Orange flames rose up like an eruption to mark their fall.

For a moment nobody spoke or moved.

"You know, Ryan, I was wrong," Mildred said. "Bringing Brother Joseph along was totally worth it."

Chapter Thirty-Three

The stern-mounted paddlewheel splashed rhythmically through the brownish-green water. The thud-thud-thud of the *Daisy Belle*'s steam engine vibrated up through the wooden deck and the soles of Ryan's boots, as well as his bare forearms where he leaned on the wooden rail, which was heated near stinging hot by the midmorning sun.

It was fine with him. He was glad the wind was out of the west, so that it blew the black smoke plume from the single stack away toward the wooded bluffs, and away from him.

He felt a familiar presence at his side. An arm slipped around his waist.

"Cartridge for your thoughts, lover," Krysty said.

"I'm thinking how glad I am to be shaking the dust of this whole damn shithole off my boots," he said, "and us all more or less intact."

He shook his head. "Still have a hard time believing it."

She tipped her red head against his shoulder. "This was tough. We could've bought it."

He sighed. "Well, everybody pulled together. We're an ace crew. The best."

"WHAT HAVE YOU to say for yourself, Ryan?" Baron Emerald demanded from her throne of sorts.

Ryan blinked his eye. *This shit's getting old,* he thought.

Although the morning sun had barely started climbing up the sky behind them, the glare that splashed off the pavement of the Soulardville main plaza and the big tilted concrete slab with the dark stains on it was painful anyway.

"You got all the blasters, Baron," he said, "so you hold all the cards."

True to his word, Tully had brought along a wag drawn by a pair of sturdy horses. Ryan wasn't sure about his friends, but he knew he had slept like the dead on the ride back to Soulardville.

Their captors were remarkably considerate, considering. The wag had clip-clopped and creaked through the front gate and right up to the door of that same familiar gray-brick house with the black iron on the windows and doors. They'd been given water and some kind of vegetable stew, with rough brown bread, which they'd wolfed down. Then it had been all they could do to reach their pallets before passing out again.

Unfortunately they hadn't gotten but more than four hours of sleep before Garrison's ham hand rousted them out again, hammering yet again on the front-door frame. And here they were. They weren't shackled or bound in any way, but they were disarmed, and a crowd of both ville patrol men and sec men surrounded them. And beyond them a throng of Soulardites, who, Ryan knew, had a definite taste for a little blood sacrifice.

Emerald smiled. She was wearing a loose purple kaftan and sitting on a big heavy chair carved out of dark-stained oak. It had been set out in the plaza just west of the sacrificial slab, with a huge green parasol with yellow tassel fringe set up to shade it.

"No excuses?" she asked.

"Nope."

"Pleas for mercy?"

Ryan shrugged.

"With all respect, Baron," Krysty said, "we've seen and heard plenty of pleas for mercy in our time. What we haven't seen is them do a spent round's worth of good."

The girl sat and studied them. For all her youth she looked every inch a baron, Ryan had to admit.

He was halfway sorry he wouldn't be here to watch what happened to anybody who calculated to take advantage of her based on the fact she was a young woman with a pretty face and a body worth killing for.

"I notice you got your former holy Joe's altar uncovered today," he said.

"I'm thinking of having Brother Joseph's surviving acolytes break it apart with sledgehammers," Emerald said. "Then…mebbe have them beat each other to death with those sledgehammers and decapitate the last one. What do you think, Ryan?"

"Well, that's harsh but…harsh."

"No," she said. "Harsh would be making them suffer a similar amount to what the people they helped sacrifice suffered. Something along the lines of skinning alive. Over days."

"Remind me never to get on your bad side, Baron."

"Too late," the girl said. "I'm having a hard time forgetting you kidnapped me from my friends and dragged me here to suffer that very same fate."

The goateed man who stood next to her throne said, "Emerald…Baron—"

She waved a hand at him. "I know, Dan. We've been all around that warehouse. You wouldn't expect the man whose hospitality you violated to speak up on your behalf, would you, Ryan?"

She grinned. "I think he respects you because you got the better of him. Not many can say that."

"Didn't think of it as getting the better of anybody," Ryan said. "We had a job to do. That was all."

"Yes. And you did your job. And then you did your employer a pretty nasty turn."

"He ripped us off on payment," Mildred said, "not to mention sentenced us to death, and gave Jak up to that devil-bird of his. I'd say any contract he had with us, he broke."

Slowly Emerald nodded. "I agree," she said. "My only regret is that I wasn't there to see what happened to him at the end. You people don't do things by half nukin' measures, do you?"

That got a chuckle from Tully and the patrol members who had witnessed Brother Joseph's fiery end.

"That's just Ryan," J.B. said. "He's got him a certain style, y'know?"

"I see," the baron said. "When you were bringing me back you talked a lot about keeping deals, Ryan. Whatever it cost you—or anybody else."

"That's the law I came up to live by," he said.

"And you did keep your deals. Plus there's the little matter that by bringing me back to Brother Joseph, and then when you were shut of that obligation, managing to get me set free to reclaim my rightful throne here as baron of Soulardville, you did me a pretty major service. Even if— Never mind."

Ryan suspected that what she wanted them never to mind was whatever she had gone through at Brother Joseph's hands her first night back in his clutches. He doubted she'd much enjoyed it.

"So. You were promised payment for bringing me back, then Brother Joseph stiffed you when you delivered. Well, if a bunch of outlanders straggling in out of the waste-lands can keep their contracts no matter what, the ville of Soulard can do no less."

Emerald gestured. Their refilled backpacks and weapons were brought and laid at their feet.

"For let's call 'em additional services rendered, I've doubled what Brother Joseph promised you in food, ammo and meds."

Ryan's eyebrows rose. "You're letting us go?"

The girl laughed. "I'm insisting on it."

She stood and stepped into the sunlight. It glanced blindingly off the huge pendant she wore, which bore the letter *S* in a circle.

"Ryan, Krysty, J.B., Mildred, Doc and Jak, I thank you all. Your service has earned you the gratitude of the people and baron of Soulardville.

"Now take your shit and go. You have until sunset to get out of St. Lou. And if we ever catch you this side of the river again, I'll feed you to the stickies myself!"

THE STUBBY LITTLE riverboat was just abreast of the northern perimeter of Soulardville, well out in the deep channel and making good progress with the current's help. As far as Ryan could tell, it had been built since the big nuke, cobbled together out of salvaged parts. He hoped the boiler didn't blow and cook them all.

"What kind of baron do you think she'll make?" Krysty asked.

"Better than most," he said. "Which isn't to say I'm all broke up about not having the option of staying and being one of her subjects. I don't think she's the sort to go in for having little kids beat to death to show the people how much she loves them. But I don't think she'd be an easy boss, somehow."

"No," Krysty said. "Probably not."

Dan E. and his crew had given them a lift back across the Sippi to Eastleville in their boat. Not only were there no hard feelings, the scavvie boss and his crew seemed full of admiration for Ryan's bunch and their audacious exploit in hooking the princess right out from under their noses. Dan had even invited the companions to sign up. Plenty of good salvage left, in the deserted suburbs east of the river, he said.

The friends had declined as vigorously as they could and stay on the friendly side of polite. It wasn't, as J.B. said later, when they were settling down for the night in the Platinum Club's best room-to-let, that it was a bad offer.

"We've had worse invites," the Armorer said. "Most of them, truth be told. But I'd wake up every morning wondering if Princess Emerald had decided we were still too close to Soulardville for comfort, and reckoned mebbe we needed to meet some stickies up close and personal."

That had been on the others' minds, too, the two days it took to wangle passage south on the *Daisy Belle*.

So Ryan and the goateed scavvie chieftain had gripped each other arm-to-arm in farewell. Then the crew hit the trail back north to their abandoned-factory fortress.

The boat came abreast of the Soulardville front gate, up on its bluff above the wide river. A work crew moved around the makeshift rivermen's dock down at the waterside. At Baron Emerald's decree they were surveying how best to expand it to a full-blown trading port.

A figure turned and, spotting them, waved. Ryan thought he recognized Tully's narrow head and ginger hair.

Krysty waved back enthusiastically. When she elbowed Ryan in the side, he raised his hand, too.

"Don't brood, lover," Krysty said. "We'll find a place for us all, someday. Find a safe haven that's real."

"Yeah," he said. "Sure we will."

The paddlewheel steamer chugged down the mighty river, and they stood together at the rail until Soulardville and the ruins of St. Lou disappeared behind them.

TAKE 'EM FREE

2 action-packed novels plus a mystery bonus

NO RISK

NO OBLIGATION TO BUY

GEI1